THE GHOSTS OF BLACKTHORNE ISLAND

PROLOGUE

She saw it then. The strange shadow just at the corner of her eye. The strange shadow that was darker than the others and oddly shaped. A shiver shot through her and not for the first time. She had felt...seen things at night, but this was the first time they had come in daylight.

"Matilda!" she shouted as she struggled to her feet with a grimace of pain and headed out the parlor door. "Attend to me at once!"

"Comin' as quick as I can," was the answering shout from down the hall as a short, dark haired woman emerged from one of the rooms at the far end and scurried her way.

"I'm headed up to my room for a lie down," she told her hiding her fear as best she could. "Fetch me something hot to drink. Tea will do. Tea with cakes and bring Bart up to me. Now hurry along."

Matilda frowned thoughtfully as she watched her employer head down the hall towards the stairs thumping her gold-headed cane with each step. She had been white as a sheet. Had she seen what she'd been seeing? What found her at night when she lay in her attic room...nudging her awake...touching her? She smiled as hope stirred. Perhaps she believed her now. That she was not weaving some "fanciful tale" or "relating a nightmare from too many sweets". That other beings…creatures...ghosts...lurked within the walls of the ancient house that had hunkered above the hungry sea for centuries.

She sighed as she headed to the kitchen at a run. It was probably only wishful thinking that whatever haunted the house had frightened the Mistress of Blackthorne Island. She was incapable of feeling something as human as fear. "She'll never leave here no matter how bad things get. Not till she's dead and carted out feet first," she muttered under her breath then added, "Anything could happen to her in a place like this. Most anything at all, and no one the wiser 'cept me who'll have a tale to tell no one will believe."

Meanwhile, Florence Blackthorne had reached her room. Still out of breath from the climb up the stairs, she headed to the window that looked out across the wide expanse of gray, restless water that met the equally dark sky in a barely perceptible line. It would storm later, she thought. The fierce kind that rattled the windows of the old family mansion where she had chosen to end her days. The last of the Blackthornes come home to roost. She had heard tales of the island growing up in Portsmouth. Tales of the mansion clinging to the cliffs that had been built by royalty then abandoned by the family till they reclaimed it in the late 19th century. It had been abandoned a second time when they had grown tired of the isolation, the cold, the damp, and the endless upkeep of a place poised dangerously close to the crumbling cliff with a two hundred foot drop into the sea. She wasn't entirely sure what made her want to reopen it. To

3

sink enough money into it to make it habitable for the short term. There was no doubt in her mind the sea would claim it some day, but not before she was gone. At 91, there weren't that many years left to her...especially if the nonsense her physician was spouting had a grain of truth in it. She snorted derisively and shook her head. She'd live to be a hundred just to spite the old vulture.

Tired now, she headed to her canopied bed piled high with pillows and settled in amongst them. She was increasingly tired of late. Perhaps because she wasn't sleeping well despite the pill she took with a glass of warm milk that Matilda brought to her each night at precisely 9 p.m. A good girl for the most part and loyal, which was something she valued above her sadly lacking cooking and cleaning skills. Truth be told, there was too much to do for one person. She had hoped to have sufficient staff, but no one who had replied to her advertisement wanted to work on the island. Most claimed it was haunted. Not that she had believed them at first. Nor had she believed Matilda's nonsense, but time had changed that. Now she knew that other entities...ghosts shared her home. Beings that were now manifesting themselves in broad daylight instead of confining themselves to the dark of night.

At one time, she would have chided herself for being a senile old fool. She smiled wryly then sighed. Perhaps she was all of that, but what she saw was real as impossible as that sounded even to her. It was past time to deal with the matter. Time to rid the place of those who still lingered here, so she could enjoy her last years in peace.

A knock on the door interrupted her reverie. "Enter!" she called imperiously.

Matilda pushed her way through the door. "Brought what you wanted, Ma'am, but couldn't manage both Bart and the tray. Will need to bring him up on a second trip," she told her as she headed towards the bed and placed the tray across her lap. "You want me to pour?"

"I'll handle it, Matilda. Isn't the supply boat do in today?"

"In an hour or so, Ma'am. Joe will be on it. He's comin' to do a few repairs this week."

"Much needed repairs. You can bring Bart later. When you come back, I'll have a letter ready to send. Make sure it goes with the boat. Now off you go. I have much to think on."

She watched the door close softly behind her and thought about what she was about to do. Her old friend Lyndon would know who could help her rid the house of its specters. He had taught classes at the university dealing with the paranormal and would surely have some idea whom she could contact since he was far too old to come himself. She smiled then poured her tea.

CHAPTER ONE

Traffic had thinned, and darkness had claimed the city as Bella the beagle and I sat on the steps enjoying the breeze off the water before going inside. Simon had left her in my care while he disappeared on a mysterious errand telling me that he would return as soon as he could with what he hoped would be a welcome surprise.

"I've never been all that fond of surprises," I told Bella who was leaning against me and nearly asleep after her long walk.

I looked up at the star strewn heavens, and let my mind wander through my final memories of Greystone. Memories of Allison and Cinda. Memories of Millie Grey. I had met Simon there, and my life had never been the same. I had left to sort things out. To see if the feelings we had for each other were real and ours alone. We had both gone in different directions except for the time we had shared during Henry's last days. Some time later, he turned up on my doorstep with Bella in tow. He had wanted to stay, and I had been so happy to see him that I let it happen.

Being with him had been a tiny slice of heaven until the third day when we quarreled over something as ridiculous as how I stacked the dishwasher. I don't remember much of what was said on both sides, but it was enough to send him out the door that I held open. I had plenty of time to wonder since then if I had deliberately sabotaged the relationship because I cared too much. That I was too happy and believed it couldn't last. During our short time together, all my past insecurities had resurfaced with a vengeance, and maybe I had made him leave before he left me. He had told me I would come to my senses some day and realize we were meant for each other. For that to happen, I had to trust him. Believe what he said. Believe that whatever tie linked us wouldn't break no matter what happened on the road ahead. All of which came hard for me. At one time, I would have said it was impossible.

I sighed. We were still friends who spent a lot of time together when he was in town. He wanted us to team up and go 'ghost releasing' as he called it, but there was no way I would go through that horror again. He kept trying to change my mind, and I kept saying "no".

My cell phone rang interrupting my thoughts. Pulling it from my pocket, I checked the caller ID but didn't recognize it.

My "Hello" was hesitant. I was surprised to find Simon on the other end.

"Hello back! Finished up and headed your way, Jodie. You should be tucked up in bed by now with those cat print PJs you hid in while I was there."

"Bella had other ideas. We just finished our last walk of the night and are sitting on the back steps looking out over the harbor. At least, I am. She's almost asleep. Where are you?"

"That would ruin the surprise. I want you to meet me at the restaurant you like down at the south end marina for lunch tomorrow. You can bring Bella. They have pet friendly outside seating as you no doubt remember?"

"Why there? What's going on?"

"No questions allowed. Just be there. I missed you."

I sighed. I had really, really missed him, too, but found myself saying, "Bella has been listening and watching for you every single day."

I could hear his own sigh on the other end and then, "Look. It's late. Go to bed and dream of me. See you tomorrow."

Rising to my feet, I slipped the phone in my pocket and headed for the door with Bella leading the way. Punching in the security code, we pushed through the door and made our way to the elevator that ground its way slowly to my third floor loft where Bella checked out her food bowl...lapped up some water then jumped on my bed. She would be asleep again in moments while I would lie awake for hours, I thought with a grimace as I headed to the hot shower I should have made cold.

A short time later, I joined her there. I remembered those few nights I had shared with Simon. An adorably rumpled Simon who soon realized my innocence and took his time with me. I had never in my wildest dreams believed it could feel like that. Fierce and heated then tender as I nestled against his shoulder until we both fell asleep. We woke several times during the night, and each time he ......

I groaned and punched my pillow again and again. The last thing I needed was to remember all that. Not now though 'some day' wasn't off the table. Tomorrow was a mystery. Things could change. Maybe I would risk a life that could be happy, exciting, or heartbreaking if my worst fears were realized. I had come to know with Simon anything was possible.

***

Bella was still snuggled next to me when I woke the next morning. For a sleep fogged second, I believed it was Cinda then remembered she was gone. I had thought about adopting another cat from the animal shelter, but each time I went there I couldn't get past the door. It was too soon. The pain of her loss too raw even though I knew we would find each other again.

Before I could even think about breakfast...or even coffee for that matter... I threw on some clothes and took Bella out for her first walk. We headed towards the harbor down the steep, brick paved street sandwiched between re-purposed warehouses and factories like the one I lived in. Most were occupied to full capacity by those who could afford the sticker price. I wouldn't have been one of them without my inheritance from Allison and, every time I looked out the window to the water below, I thanked her for that and so many other things. She had rescued me, and now I was here and missing her every day.

I had set up a foundation in her name to help fund women starting new businesses. It was still in its infancy, but things looked hopeful on several fronts. Women of all ages were now presenting their business proposals to me and sorting through them took a lot of my time. I had thought about getting an assistant and had already interviewed several candidates with that in mind. One met all my qualifications. A call would get it handled, but I still hesitated to let go of the reins. I needed to stay busy especially now that my latest novel had stalled due to a bout of writer's block. The first one had sold well because of Allison's contacts in the publishing world. Every penny earned had gone into the foundation, which made me proud I was doing my share.

9

I sighed and sat down on a bench with Bella at my feet. Simon wanted me to meet him at the Flying Bridge restaurant down at the south end, which gave me just enough time for a quick shower, coffee, and then a 'make do' breakfast while I shuffled through paperwork for the rest of the morning. Perhaps I would make that call I kept putting off...perhaps I wouldn't. My mixed thoughts were interrupted by an impatient Bella who pawed at my knee until I continued our walk down to the pier where we watched the boats for awhile then returned home.

Completely absorbed in what I was doing, time passed quickly...too quickly. I was running late when I changed into a flowered sundress and strap sandals, which were a far cry from my usual summer attire of tank tops and shorts. I had to wonder why I was going so 'girly'...taking so much time with my thick, coppery hair that always frizzed as soon as it hit the outside humidity. Was I trying to revive what I'd squelched when I sent him out the door? Maybe missing him had made me a bit crazy. The thought made me smile. Simon had told me more than once that he liked me in my favorite 'grubbies' as I called them, so all my efforts were quite probably a waste of time.

It was nearly noon when I packed my roomy shoulder bag with Bella's water bottle and dish, snapped on her leash, and headed out the door to my SUV in the lot behind the building. The streets were jammed with tourists and too many minutes ticked by before I pulled into the parking lot of the Flying Bridge. I was quite late by the time we reached the outside seating area and looked around. He had been sitting on a bench off to the side and rose to his considerable height when he spotted me.

I was more than surprised to see him in cutoff jeans, a t-shirt, and baseball cap instead of the impeccable way he usually dressed. His dark hair was longish, his glasses held together with safety pin, and he was tanned, which meant he had spent his mysterious four weeks out in the sun instead of behind a desk.

Bella ran to greet him pulling me with her. Simon was the first to speak as he bent down and gathered Bella in his arms. "Been waiting for a while. Ordered lunch to go. Wasn't hard since you always order the same thing whenever we come here. Like the dress. You look like a flower garden. Come on. Let's find a place to eat farther down the marina."

Bella led the way to the pier that jutted out into the water. The likelihood of finding a place to sit among the coiled ropes, fishing gear, hoses and drying nets seemed remote to non-existent. Mostly, I was busy trying not to trip over something in my heels when he pulled me to a stop in front of a sailboat.

"She's an old C & C which stands for Cuthbertson and Cassian the Canadian design team. See her beautiful lines? She's 30 years old and 36 feet long. Beam is twelve feet or thereabouts. None like her on the water in this man's opinion. She was named Edith's Wish, which was why Grandpa had to buy her as soon as he saw her some twenty years ago. She's the one I told you about that I used to sail whenever I visited. He left her to me, and I went back to get her. She was in sad shape. Needed to be dry docked and the bottom scraped then painted followed by a lot of refitting, and diesel repairs. Every inch of teak on her from the deck to the handrails had to be sanded and re-varnished. I lived on board and did most of the work. Grandpa taught me. Said 'If you are going to sail her, you need to know how she works from the keel on up...be able to make repairs if you're out at sea'. So...what do you think of my surprise?"

"She's gorgeous! Can't wait to see inside, but what about Bella?"

Simon grinned. "Bella often went sailing with me. Started when she was a pup, and I was just out of high school. The boat has all the necessary safety rigging she needed when out to sea. Even a patch of dunkable astro turf to take care of that end. I'll go first and help you board in those shoes."

He dropped lightly down on the deck with Bella close behind. I took the hand he offered and stepped on board not at all liking the way the boat rocked when I landed, but I managed a smile. "I've never been on a sailboat before, so I'll let you give me the grand tour."

He smiled back then pointed to the blue canvas covering above us. "It's called a bimini and keeps you dry and out of the sun. Folds down if there's a storm. Follow me down the companionway and hang on to the railing. You might want to kick off those shoes. Not exactly the thing on a boat this size."

He disappeared down the four steps that led below with both Bella and me right on his heels. As my eyes adjusted to the dim light, I looked around in surprise. It was bigger inside than I had thought with enough headroom even for Simon. The walls and ceiling were paneled in what might be mahogany with four portholes on each side.

A small kitchen was on the right and Simon told me, "It's called the galley. The stove and fridge run on both propane and electricity when there's shore power available. Those padded benches you see over there provide storage, seating, and extra bunks when needed. There's a fold out table in between them. Take a peek in there," he told me pointing to a wedge shaped space in the back of the boat that proved to be a built-in bunk piled high with boxes, cases, and empty canvas bags. "Sail bags and extra stuff that could come in handy. I'll show you the head and the v-berth next then we'll have our lunch that is rapidly getting cold."

To my surprise, the tiny bathroom or 'head' was also the shower. Simon explained how it worked though I knew a second lesson would be needed if we ever went sailing. The tousled 'aft v-berth', as he called it, was wedged into the prow of the boat and could easily sleep four people with some wiggle room. A hatch overhead let in a warm breeze and blue-sky view.

Bella had followed us there and stretched out with familiar ease. "Looks like she remembers this place, Simon," I told him with a smile.

"First time she came here she was bouncing all over the place. Likes the water, which is not at all characteristic of beagles. Come on. Let her nap and dream while we eat."

13

I followed him back to the middle section that he called the 'salon' where he opened the table and spread out the bags he'd brought. "Sit. I'll get us something cold to drink."

He returned a moment later with two bottles of green tea. "There's more I haven't shown you that took a long time and a lot of work which included rebuilding the engine. Long story short, it's in great shape now. I guess you could say the trip here was her shakedown cruise, and she performed flawlessly. Eat up. Day's still young, and I want to take you for a short sail."

To be perfectly honest, I was both excited at the prospect and nervous, so I had to ask, "What's between us and a whole lot of water?"

He laughed. "Sounds like you want to chicken out? The woman who loved the sea? The Mermaid of Courage Cove? Tell me I'm wrong."

"You never answered my question."

"Let me just say that these old boat hulls were way overbuilt compared to what's on the water these days."

"Why is that not at all reassuring?"

"Come on. It's only a short time on the water. If you really hate it, I'll bring you right back."

I really did want to go sailing. Had always watched sailboats skimming the water and envied those onboard. It was a sunny, calm day, and Simon was an experienced sailor, so I smiled brightly and told him, "Let's do it then. What can I do to help?"

"I'll handle everything. You just need to grab a life jacket, sit up in the cockpit with me, and enjoy the day."

He showed me where he wanted me then started the motor and let it idle while he climbed up on the dock. After casting off both the bow and stern lines as he called them, he took his place behind the wheel.

We backed slowly out of the slip...turned and threaded our way past other boats anchored out in deeper water. "They have a full, deep keel which makes them handle better when blue water sailing," Simon explained over his shoulder, "but they can't get too close to the dock due to their draft."

I settled back and watched the marina and shoreline dwindle with distance until we passed through the harbor entrance. Out in open water, the wind picked up. My calm day was no longer all that calm, but there was no way I could chicken out now.

"Now comes the interesting part. I'm putting her on autopilot while I hoist the sails. I'll be keeping an eye on the water. We don't want to run into anything. Under other circumstances, I'd let you handle the wheel and not worry about it."

Which sounded like a bad idea to me no matter what the circumstances. "So I just sit here, right?" I confirmed.

"Yep. Everything's under control." He grinned boyishly then climbed up on top and shouted down to me. "This big one is the main. I'm going to hoist it first and then the smaller jib."

He moved with a brisk efficiency I had to admire. Soon, the wind filled the fluttering sails, and the boat leaned over slightly. "It's only about a ten knotter, so we're not going to heel over too far," he reassured me. "You looked scared to death. "

"Hardly that," I lied as I clutched the rail next to me. "Just concerned about Bella."

"She's handled much worse," he replied as he dropped back down next to me. "Checked on her through the hatch when I was raising the jib. Still asleep. I'm cutting the engine, and we're now officially sailing. Relax a bit. You'll love it."

I soon found I sort of did though relaxing was out of the question. Land had dwindled to a speck and all around us was a vast teal blue emptiness that stretched as far as the eye could see. "It's been fun, Simon," I shouted to be heard above the sound of the wind and waves. "But I think it's time to turn around and head back to port."

"Look under your seat cushion," he shouted back. "I left a note there for you."

My heart seemed to stop as I lifted the edge and pulled out an envelope with my name on it. I opened it slowly then began to read:

Jodie,

It seems like whenever I try to tell you something it never comes out right, or you overreact. Well, let's just say there's been a lot of unsaid things between us. I meant what I said. I need you in my life. I know I can be a royal pain in the ass at times, but that's mostly because I'm feeling uncertain and maybe even a bit scared. I never 'needed' anyone before and then you literally fell into my arms and that was that.

16

I tried the long weekend on your turf and it didn't end well. Out here, there's no escape for either of us. We need to sort things out because deep down I know...I hope...you return my feelings. I'm just as afraid of this thing between us as you are. Who knows. Maybe more. I am sailing to a place called Blackthorne Island to investigate a haunting there as a favor to an old friend. I know you told me 'no' when I asked you to team up with me, but I could really use your help. Judging from what happened at Greystone, you seem to attract spirits although, in one case, it was more like piss her off. Anyway...consider yourself kidnapped.

To say I was shocked would be a colossal understatement. Horrified described it better. My face reflected my thoughts, and he told me, "Look. We aren't going back...at least for a while. You're on my turf now. You can't run away. Can't make me leave. You'll come to your senses and see this is the only way."

I had to admit...if only to myself...he was right. Out here in the middle of the vast blue, I couldn't run away from my feelings. Open a door and show him out. Granted, I could shove him overboard, but then what? I'd die at sea and take poor Bella with me. Not to mention I'd miss him far more than I was willing to admit at the moment. But none of that kept me from hoping I could change his mind.

I took a deep steadying breath before I shouted, "You are even crazier than I thought...which would be saying a lot...if you think I am going to go along with this. Turn this boat around...Now! I want to go home."

17

"Not going to happen, kidnappee. There are clothes and proper shoes down below in the stern cabin I showed you. Had to guess at your size though the salesgirl helped in the unmentionable department. Just the kind of stuff you usually wear that you can hand wash and hang over the rail. I'm going to need help with the boat where we are headed, and you are going to learn what's needed. I haven't had much sleep the past three days. Kept offshore and sailed clear of the shipping lanes to avoid most of the traffic, but still had to watch the radar screen for boats that came too close at night. We'll take three hour shifts."

"And if I refuse?"

"Think of Bella. In addition to boats out here, we could run into a lost sea container or other debris. You'd be surprised how much stuff is floating around in these waters. Not that you're too likely to spot it unless it's pretty big before it punches a hole in the hull. Just sayin. Don't want to scare the crap out of you, but it happens."

"Sure you do or you wouldn't have said it, and why are we out here if it's so dangerous? Head for shore...now...at once!"

"Nope. I am the captain, and what I say goes."

"Even if you've kidnapped me like some pirate?"

He grinned. "Yep. Now go below and fix us some dinner, wench. Don't use the head till I give you full instructions. If you don't shut the valve, you could flood and sink us."

"Lovely," I muttered under my breath as I climbed down to the galley and looked around. I knew Simon. He wasn't about to

18

change his mind. I was his prisoner, but I'd make him regret it starting with the supper I'd been ordered to fix.

***

Over the next three days at sea, I learned quite a bit about sailing. Knew how to handle the wheel and follow his course...trim the sails...read the all important radar screen... even tie a bowline knot. He and Bella shared the aft v-berth, when he wasn't on watch, while I had the one in the stern once I had dumped off enough stuff to find what passed for a mattress. Tank tops, shorts, and sneakers were my wardrobe along with plenty of sunscreen. Each day gave me more and more confidence, and soon I was enjoying myself...though I took great pains not to show it. During my night watches, I wore a life jacket and never left the cockpit where I kept an eye on the radar, watched my surroundings, and tried to stay awake any way I could. I often had to wake Simon via the walkie-talkies when the wind shifted, I heard something strange on board, or saw lights on the horizon. He had told me that sometimes the big ships ran on autopilot while the officer on duty just watched the radar and didn't make a visual check for the running lights on small boats like ours. Not a comforting thought.

We continued on. When the wind failed, the engine took over. We didn't talk about our destination until the fourth day when he spread a chart out on the table and showed me where we were headed. Blackthorne Island was a mere speck in the north Atlantic about thirty miles offshore.

19

"From what I learned on the Internet, the island is ringed by two hundred foot cliffs except for a hidden harbor on its south side. A Florence Blackthorne lives there now with her maid. She contacted my old professor asking for help with the entities haunting the place. He contacted me and here we are."

"The reluctant team."

He grimaced wryly then tweaked my ponytail. "It's not been all bad. I think you like sailing more than you care to admit."

I slapped his hand away. "Says the kidnapper to the kidnappee. Look. Say I help you with this. After we finish whatever we're there to do, will you take me to the closest port and drop me off, so I can find another way home?"

He was quiet for a long moment as he looked deep into my eyes, "If that's what you really, truly want when this is over, so be it. It's a deal."

I smiled. "Good. Let's get this done and dusted. I have work and a life to get back to."

He sighed then told me, "Might mention, a storm's brewing according to NOAA weather radio. I'm going to hoist all sails and try to outrun it. Head to a port called Banning and put in till it passes. Will take us a bit off course, but it's a chance to refuel, stock up on supplies and get some necessary shopping done."

The hours passed, and the sky darkened as the waves and swells steadily increased in size. We were watching the sooty gray clouds sweep overhead driven by a strong northeast wind when Simon reported, "It's fast moving and getting pretty intense. Go below and make sure everything's secured down there. Doesn't look like I can outrun this bitch, so we have to make ready. I'll keep the sails up as long as I can, but time is running out. We'll need to snap on our lifelines if we're up top and things get much worse."

The minutes ticked past. The temperature had dropped still lower, and the wind now whipped the sea into a fury as Simon dropped the sails and lashed them down while I held on to the wheel and prayed we'd survive. By the time Simon rejoined me and sent me below, I was both seasick and beyond terrified. Cuddling an equally scared Bella, I clutched a saucepan tightly and hoped I wouldn't need it as we rocked and rose and sank then rose again as the boat climbed each swell. Through the portholes, I watched the fierce black sky, listened to the clang of the halyards against the mast, the shriek of the wind through the rigging, and felt the slam of the enormous waves that Simon was 'quartering', so they wouldn't catch us broadside and knock us over.

The worst blew by quickly though the sea remained churned up and furious. Clutching the railing, I took my wobbly legs and queasy stomach up the companionway to check on Simon.

He looked rather the worst for wear but managed a grin. "Got your first storm at sea out of the way. Could have been worse."

"I don't see how. I thought we would all be dead by now."

"How's Bella?"

"Shaken up, but okay just like I am for the most part. Please tell me that's really land up ahead and not just an hallucination conjured up out of desperation?"

21

He laughed. "Yep. Must be Banning according to the GPS. Sea should be calmer in the harbor once we pass that headland over there."

As it turned out, he was right. A short time later, we motored into the marina and tied up at an empty spot along the long dock that jutted out into the water.

"I'll download Bella, and you can walk her," he told me. "I'm going to talk to the guy in charge. Need to pay for this slip and find out where we refuel. Looks like there's a cafe over there. If you're feeling better, maybe we can grab some breakfast afterwards."

I think Bella was as grateful as I was to be on land again. We walked through the parking lot to some trees along the back then returned to the dock where Simon rejoined us a short time later. After leaving Bella on the boat, we headed to the cafe. He ate a hearty breakfast while I drank coffee and wolfed down several doughnuts, which was a sure indication I had made a full recovery when I hadn't thought that even remotely possible.

It was Simon who asked the tall, freckle faced waitress what she knew about Blackthorne Island. She shrugged and replied, "Not much. Too far out for most. Best person to ask is old Captain Greenley. He runs supplies out to all the outlying islands no one else wants to go to. Blackthorne being one of them."

"Where would we find him at this hour?" I asked with a smile.

"Saw his boat docked when I came in for my shift. Might catch him there or at the office. Tall guy. Kind of scruffy with a patch over one eye and a beard. Looks like a pirate. Might even be one or a smuggler from what some say."

I made sure she was out of earshot when I whispered, "Why does that sound not so promising?"

Simon grinned. "Another fun element added to the mix. Let's go find him.

We found him leaning against the side of the marina office, smoking a pipe and humming some tune I didn't know. Simon made the introductions then asked, "We're headed to Blackthorne Island and wondered what you could tell us about it if you have a few minutes?"

He eyed us both up and down slowly, took a long draw on his pipe then said, "Might. What's your business over there? She don't like no one droppin in out of the blue."

"We were invited," Simon told him. "Why don't I buy you a cup of coffee over at the cafe, and you can fill us in on what you know."

He knocked his pipe against the wall...stomped on the embers...then pocketed it. "Might do. If you plan on coming on my next run, it won't be till Friday."

"We have our own sailboat," Simon replied. "Came in a short time ago."

"The C &C. Saw it. A real beauty. Must have seen some weather."

"A bit. Come on. Let's grab that coffee.

We headed back to the cafe...took a booth...and flagged down the waitress. The captain waited till the coffee was served then told us, "Back a few centuries ago, there were a British royal. A Duke of somethin' or other. Had this son who ran into trouble with the law back home. Suspected of rapin' and killin' young women. They might have hung him if his pa didn't get him broke out of prison then out of the country. Bought the island and had his old mansion disassembled and rebuilt there. A ramblin' monstrosity of a thing the likes of which no one in this neck of the woods had ever imagined. Money weren't a problem. Had most of the available men in these parts camped out and working on it for mor'en twenty years. While all that were goin' on, they stayed in some old wreck of a shack that he had 'em fix up to make do till the house was finished enough to move in. Kept his son prisoner there. No one knows what happened to either one of 'em. Must have just died in that place though there are some who believe they still walk the island if you get my meanin'. There's more stories about that place I could share. Ones that include pirates. A bit of lunch might jar me memory."

Over lunch, we learned that pirates had once used the island as homeport until the Colonial Navy put a stop to it. We also learned that the area around it was peppered with ships driven up on the rocks and wrecked during the fierce storms that rolled in from the northeast and west.

"A ghost ship or two have been seen by them fishin' near there," the Captain told us with a glint in his one eye. "Some real old. Clipper ships and the like that ain't been seen in these waters for centuries."

"And have you seen any?" Simon asked as we watched him wolf down his second burger.

"Might of. It was a foggy morning and somethin' was out there. No mistake. Looked like an old ship with all sails up and full even though the wind was calm. No sign of a crew. She was there one minute and gone the next."

Despite Simon's efforts to learn more, the Captain said little else as he finished his lunch...muttered "see you 'round" and headed out the door.

"Well, I am beginning to wonder just how many ghosts haunt that island," Simon murmured to me.

"Good chance there's a lot more than just the Duke and his son. What's next for us?"

"I'm holding you to your promise to stick with me till this is finished, so you'll be on your own for a time. You can shop for clothes or whatever while I handle the rest. Meet you back at the boat in say...an hour?"

We went our separate ways a short time after that. I looked back over my shoulder as I climbed the steep street that led to the town. Down below, Simon was talking to a fisherman and laughing about something. I felt a twinge of regret at what I was about to do. It meant breaking my word, but there was no way I would go through what was shaping up to be another horrific experience like we'd had at Greystone. Spend another day at sea after what had just

25

happened. I would find an airport... if they had one...or rent a car, but first I needed to grab a few things off the boat and leave Simon a note. He deserved both an explanation and an apology.

I pretended to walk on then ducked into a nearby shop. From behind the window display, I watched Simon head back towards the marina office. Taking advantage of any available cover, I sprinted back to the sailboat and climbed on board. I knew he had locked the companionway doors, but there was a chance...a slim one...he had forgotten to secure the hatch cover above the v-berth. To my immense relief, it popped open, and I dropped down inside waking Bella who greeted me with a soft "woof".

"Sorry, girl. I'd love to spend some time with you, but I am in a major hurry," I told her as I scratched behind her floppy ears.

She followed me about as I threw a few things into my shoulder bag then grabbed a scrap of paper and left a hurried note for Simon that read:

Sorry about this, but I don't want to do this ghost releasing thing, and I don't think you should do it on your own. Not that pig headed you would ever listen to me. I broke my promise, which is a big deal to both of us, but there it is. Please be safe. Remember Bella will be in danger, too, and perhaps the best reason for you to reconsider this whole thing. Anyway...have to get going. Hopefully, I will see you later if you've managed to forgive me.

I left it propped up on the sink and hurried back to the v-berth. Standing on my tiptoes, I had just started to lift the hatch cover, when I felt the boat rock. Someone had boarded her. It had to be

Simon. My best shot was to hide where I was and wait him out. Hopefully, he had no reason to come back here. When I didn't return at the designated time, he would look for me in town, and I could escape. It wasn't much of a plan, but it was all I had.

From where I crouched, I heard the companionway doors swing open followed by, "Bella! Come here, girl!"

She "woofed" twice in response but didn't move. I tried nudging her off the berth with my foot, but she still wouldn't budge.

"What's wrong, girl?" he called as he dropped his keys on the counter and headed our way. A few steps later, I was looking up at him as he smiled darkly down at me. Finally, he broke the silence, "Did you forget something you needed when you sneaked out of town?"

"It's not what it looks like," I tried telling him.

"Yeah. Like I'm going to believe that. What could have been so important that you'd risk running into me? Why didn't you just keep going when you had the chance?"

"I couldn't leave without letting you know what I was thinking."

"Which was?"

"The note is on the sink. Just let me go. Please."

To my surprise, he flopped down on the v-berth next to me...sighed...then said, "I need you. Why can't you trust me not to let anyone or anything hurt you?"

"That's not something you can control as you might well remember, since we almost died," I told him with a sigh of my own. "And I really don't want you hurt trying to protect me."

"That's why we need to do this together. The evil at Greystone was profound, but we survived as a team."

"We had lots of help."

"Maybe things will be different on the island. I promised to help out an old lady, and I value a promise unlike some people."

"Some 'people' like me."

"We had a deal."

"It was coerced, so it won't hold up in a court of law."

"How about a court of the heart. You know how I feel about you by now."

Thing was, I knew how I felt about him by now...or almost did. Doubts came and went. "Look. I have a 'trust' problem, and kidnapping me...holding me sort of against my will...doesn't help in that department. I don't want to leave you, but I don't want to stay, so what happens now?"

"I won't make you go with me you're that scared."

"I think I might be more frightened for you."

"Which means what?"

I sighed. "No point in going there if you can't figure it out."

"Okay. I'm going to get a haircut then stock up on supplies, which is why I came back early. Forgot my list. That will give you ample time to make up your mind. If you aren't here when I return, I'll know what you decided."

I followed him up to the dock and watched him walk away with a sinking feeling in my heart. Could I just leave him and Bella? Let them confront whatever was on the island without me? Could I live with myself if something happened to him...to them? The answer was an emphatic "no!". Maybe knowing he had given me the option to leave was what I needed to make me want to stay though that sounded all kinds of crazy even to me.

Needless to say, I was there when he got back. "Glad you decided to stay. Might mention that I found out before I let you out of my sight that there's no airport or car rental place in Banning. Short of stealing one or hitchhiking, you couldn't have left."

"Assuming there's a car lot, I could have bought one," I pointed out a bit smugly.

"I checked on that, too. There aren't any."

My gray eyes narrowed, but I had to smile. "I could have just stayed here indefinitely since I rather like this town."

"What about the 'life and job' you have to get back to?"

"Well, there is that. I was about to hire an assistant. Now I guess everything will have to wait till I get back which should be soon, right?"

"Hopefully, but there's no guarantee. By the way, I think you should know that we are supposed to be a married couple. This Ms. Blackthorne is a stickler for the proprieties and doesn't believe men and women should 'mingle in close proximity unless wed'."

"That's beyond outrageous! What century does she think this is?"

29

"Does it really matter? She's in her nineties and set in her ways. Just think. You will soon be Mrs. North," he told me with his infectious, boyish grin as he toyed with the end of my ponytail.

I grimaced wryly as I snatched it away. "Look. If we have to do this, there will be some ground rules."

"Such as?" he asked quirking up one dark brow.

"No hanky panky for starters."

"Please define 'hanky panky'."

"No bed sharing."

"We did share a bed for a while, and I think the results were mutually satisfying."

I could feel a blush steal over me...the curse of a redhead. "That was then. This is now. I don't exactly know where we are headed in that department, and…until I sort it out...the rule applies. Got it?"

He grinned ruefully. "Sometimes the inevitable is just that, but I'll let it go for now. Any other rules?"

"To be announced as needed."

CHAPTER TWO

I did the necessary shopping for suitably prim and proper attire while he completely his errands. Afterwards, we took Bella for a long walk along Banning's cobblestone streets. Afternoon turned into evening and we ended up at a restaurant with outside seating where we ate dinner and Simon slipped tidbits under the table. We were headed back to the boat as the lights came on in the shop windows and darkness drifted down from the star filled heavens. The plan was to spend the night docked then refuel and head out in the morning, which meant a long, uninterrupted sleep we both needed. When we reached the boat, Bella headed to the v-berth for a nap while Simon grabbed a bottle of wine from the galley and joined me in the cockpit. I found myself leaning against him...just a bit... as we watched the lights in the marina and the now rising moon. Neither of us had spoken for a while and then he told me, "Close your eyes and hold out your left hand."

I *sort of* knew what he was about to do but said nothing and did as he asked. He held my hand for a moment then slid a ring on my finger. He laughed then told me, "You can look now. It's unofficially official."

I looked down at the simple gold band then up at him. In the light that poured up the companionway, I could see his expression was far more serious than his laugh had led me to believe.

"I think I'll head down and get some sleep," I told him, keeping my tone light, as I reclaimed my hand and scrambled to my feet. "Good night. See you bright and early."

His smile was enigmatic. "You really are a chicken. Never mind. Get some rest. Tomorrow should be an easy sail."

I lay on my bunk thinking about all that happened as I twisted the wedding band around and around my finger. I'm not at all sure when sleep claimed me as I listened to the still restless water lap against the side of the boat...heard the occasional boat chugging in late...voices calling to each other from somewhere down the dock.

It was Simon's shout from the v-berth that woke me. "Hey, back there! You're awfully quiet."

I groaned then shouted back, "That's cuz I was sleeping. Something you might want to do."

"Can't. You are a very disturbing influence. Why don't you join me back here. No hanky panky. What do you say?"

"I say shut up and go to sleep."

"You get awfully cranky when woken up," he shouted back. "Something you might work on since we're going to be spending a great deal of time together."

"Only until this job is finished. After that, this *disturbing influence* returns to her normal life sans you."

He laughed then replied, "There's nothing exactly normal about you. You have all kinds of quirks which I personally find rather adorable, but that's just me, and as far as your humdrum life goes...."

"Stop now, or I will smother you with my pillow!"

"Speaking of...a little pillow talk would be nice. We shared some very special moments over your pillows back at your loft and even at Greystone as you might remember."

I sighed. Climbed out of my bunk. Snatched up one of my sneakers and stormed his way. Moonlight poured through the open hatch above him as he patted a spot alongside and offered his most beguiling smile. His dark hair was tousled...his muscled chest was bare. In short, he was looking way too sexy, so I threw my shoe at him, slammed the door shut, and left him laughing while Bella howled.

It was going to be a long night if what I had just seen haunted me as I very much feared it would.

***

I awoke to the smell of bacon and coffee...pulled my reluctant body out of bed and headed to the galley where I found Simon busily at work.

"Bout time you got up, sleepy head," he told me with a lot more pep than I could handle. "We'll be on our way as soon as we eat and clean up. You look....well, sort of a mess at the moment. Not that that is all bad. In fact, I've become quite used to seeing you in your bedraggled state first thing in the morning."

My eyes narrowed to mere slits. "One more word and I want a divorce."

"Just sayin'," he told me with a grin. "Grab a cup of coffee and go sit. Breakfast is almost ready."

"How long till we get there?"

"Well, usually under sail we average about 6.5 knots, but we have a good westerly behind us this morning. That should speed things up to about 8 knots give or take."

"And how does that answer my question?"

He smiled. "We'll be sailing at about 9.2 miles per hour. The island is offshore a bit over thirty, so do the math."

"So, some time this morning."

"We're getting a later start than I'd hoped for, but yes. If the wind holds, we'll have a beam reach all the way there, but our first stop is the refueling dock."

It was all of an hour later when we motored out to open water and hoisted the sails. The wind caught them fully and the boat heeled over in response. Something I had become used to by now...sort of. I was okay with it as long as the rail didn't touch the water at which point that changed quickly.

While he went below to make a fresh pot of coffee, I followed the course he'd plotted. I had come to love the taste of salt spray. The sound of the waves hitting the hull as we sliced through the indigo blue water. The flutter of the sails till the wind filled them, and the boat responded. Edith's Gift had connected me to the sea in a deeply personal way...the sea I had always loved at a safe distance. But I also knew after that storm we had just experienced, that the sea could quickly turn into a special kind of hell.

Time sped by. At one point, white-sided dolphins surfed the bow wave for some distance. Farther out, we spotted the stocky black bodies of three northern Right Whales breaching the surface and uttering a deep rising "whoop" as they called to each other.

"They are gentle giants," Simon told me. "Curious and intelligent. Sadly, they're named Right Whales because they were the ones chosen to be hunted and harpooned back in the day."

Sadly indeed, I thought, just as the wind shifted, and the sails began to luff.

"Looks like we need to go off our point of sail to correct it. Go farther out which will delay us a bit," he told me as he took the wheel from me and made the change.

34

"How will I know when we are getting close to the island?" I asked as the boat came about. I heard the 'snap' as the sails filled, and the boat heeled over in response.

"You might first see a bird or two then look for a cloud bank hovering just above the water. On a clear day like this, it will be easy to spot. The humidity produced by the island's vegetation creates it."

I frowned. "What if it's just a pile of rocks inhabited by Miss Prim and Proper plus the ghosts of who knows what."

He laughed. "Let's hope that's not the case. We should be there very soon."

Soon wasn't all that soon. It was just past noon, and we had eaten lunch when I spotted a seagull circling overhead. "Okay. One bird but no cloud bank," I reported.

"It's there. Just a faint line above the horizon. See!"

I squinted and then saw it. A thin rim of low lying clouds.

"We'll shift to diesel power when we get closer and follow the channel markers into the harbor. You might want to get changed. Miss Prim and Proper won't admire the shorts and tank top the way I do."

Bella followed me below deck where I picked out what I would wear. It was a conservative pair of white slacks and a top I could mix and match with the other things I had bought to stretch my wardrobe. I was busily struggling with my unruly, frizzy hair when Simon shouted down to me, "Getting closer. You need to see this."

I climbed up the companionway and looked around. Off in the distance, jagged black rocks ringed what I could see of the island. "They look like sharp teeth that could rip a boat to pieces," I murmured. "No wonder there's been so many shipwrecks in these waters."

"And dead sailors who may or may not haunt the island. According to the chart, we need to follow the coast to the south side in order to find the harbor entrance. Tide's headed out, so we have to be extra cautious though with our shallow draft we should be okay."

We found the channel a short time later. It was well marked with buoys...green on the right...red on the left. Many of the rocks we passed loomed well above the waterline, but others lurked just below the surface. Slowly, we motored on through until we came to a small open area tucked in the curve of the towering cliffs. Flocks of birds that had been nesting there flew off at our approach.

As we neared the dock, I lowered the rubber fenders over the side to protect the hull as Simon maneuvered us alongside then cut the engine and jumped off shouting, "Throw me the spring lines, and I'll tie her up."

A few moments later, Edith's Gift was securely docked, and Simon headed below to change.

"Ready to do this, Mrs. North?" he asked when he rejoined me a few minutes later looking like the impeccable Simon I'd come to know.

"Yep. A promise is a promise as long as you remember our deal."

"Just so you know, we're all going. Bella is part of the team, so she stays with us at all times. Either Ms. Blackthorne accepts that or we forget the whole thing."

He helped us both up on the dock then snapped on Bella's leash and let her lead the way up the narrow, steep path that cut between stone outcroppings. The wind caught us fully when we reached the top and looked around. An enormous stone mansion was nested in the middle of a patch of green. Turrets punctuated each corner like guard towers and banks of tall chimneys topped the slate roofs that covered the main section and its multiple wings that had attached wings of their own. The windows were small, arched and narrow...the facade grim and uninviting, and I had to wonder why the Duke of Something or Other had bothered with the trouble and expense of bringing it across the Atlantic.

"That place just looks evil, and I thought Greystone was bad after I got past the initial attraction," I told Simon as a shiver rippled through me.

I could tell he was experiencing the same thing when he told me, "It gives me the creeps, but we have a job to do. Just paste on your best smile and let's get this done. Just remember to go along with everything I have to say."

I had to laugh. "Like that's ever going to happen!"

He smiled wryly. "So soon you forget that you are my dutiful spouse who has promised to obey me."

"I believe that word is no longer included in the vows. If it was, that would require more acting talent than I could ever possess."

"As if I already didn't know that. Just try. The sooner we get this done the sooner we're out of here."

We continued on past a sprawl of stone outbuildings to the massive, weather beaten front door. It creaked open, and a tiny, dark haired woman peered through the crack. "Ms. Blackthorne don't allow no visitors. I'm to sic the dogs on you if you don't leave. They're on their way now."

Distantly, we heard a distorted howl that ended in a coughing fit. Bella was more than interested. Lunging forward, she broke Simon's hold. We were in hot pursuit when she turned up an elderly woman, dressed in unrelieved black, hiding under a table in a room just down the hall.

"A bit awkward you finding me like this," she muttered as she pulled herself to her feet and dusted off her knees. "But we are quite vulnerable here and, when we saw your boat arrive...well, we thought the worst. The only defence we have these days is what we can improvise since I don't believe in firearms. Who are you and what are you doing here?"

Simon hid his amusement. "We are the Norths and here to help with your ghost problems. I am Simon and this is my wife, Jodie. Bella is the one who found you and an important member of our investigative team."

"We weren't expecting you until the next supply boat. Certainly didn't think you'd sail in on your own. Matilda will take you to your room. I won't be seeing you again till supper, since it's past lunch and time for my nap. Now run along and take that creature with you. Can't abide dogs or cats for that matter."

Thumping her cane with each step, she swept past us as regally as a queen and headed down the hall the way we had come.

Matilda called to us over her shoulder as she headed in the opposite direction, "She won't want you to see her climbin' up them stairs a huffin' and a puffin', so we'll take the back way through the kitchen."

Simon reclaimed Bella's trailing leash, and we followed her down the dark hall past mostly closed doors on both sides. Those few that stood open offered glimpses into what might have been a parlor, a study and a formal dining room.

"Them's the rooms I keep clean. The rest be too much to handle. Some too far gone to be worth the trouble. This place is like one of them mazes with halls going every which way. A body could get lost in here, they surely could."

We pushed through a swing door into the low ceilinged, stone floored kitchen, and I looked around. Cobwebs trailed from the overhead beams. A boarded up fireplace took up much of one wall...glass fronted cupboards another. An ancient scarred table that might have been original to the house hunkered in the middle of the floor. Surprisingly, all the appliances were new.

"She spent enough money to make the place livable and that's about all. The roofs have fallen in some places, and the foundation along the west side is near to collapsin' with each storm that rolls in. She says it will last long enough to see her out and then the sea can have it all," Matilda told us as she grabbed a flashlight off a hook and headed down a back hall then up a narrow stairway that reminded me of Greystone. "Mind how you go," she cautioned when we reached the dark, upper hall. "The carpet is worn clean through in some places, and I've tripped mor'en once."

Midway down, light spilled up the stairway from the entry hall below. We stopped two doors short of reaching it, and she ushered us inside saying, "I call this the Blue Room, and you can see why. The Mistress wanted you in here 'cause it's second best to hers."

I looked around. There was another fireplace...this one in marble instead of stone...an enormous armoire and an antique canopied bed hung with heavily embroidered side curtains. The pattern was whimsical...mythical beasts...all done in shades of blue and gold.

"Might even be Tudor though I'm not exactly up on my antiques," Simon whispered.

Matilda overheard him. "The Mistress claims old King Henry VIII slept on that a time or two when the house was back in Scotland. There's a second bedroom through that door. The Red Room. I tidied it some in case you weren't into sharin' like some folks are. Had what they used for a bathroom way back when this place was built, but it's been walled up to keep the rats out. There's a heap of them in this old place. Your bathroom's third door down the hall on the left. Plumbing bangs somethin' fierce, and the hot water tank is iffy," she informed us over her shoulder as she headed to the window and yanked back the drapes to let in more light. "There's a bell pull by the door that rings in the kitchen, but you'd be better off shoutin' down them stairs or huntin' for me since I'm usually runnin' me legs off. There's no one here but me though there's a handyman comes in with the boat sometimes. He brings in the firewood and makes repairs she deems 'necessary'. Her rooms are farther down the hall near the end. Don't be knockin' on her door, or she'll throw a bloody conniption. "

She left after that and closed the door behind her. Simon and I both eyed the massive bed. It was me who said, "Let's see what your bedroom looks like."

The connecting door had a ancient slide bolt and opened on a dimly lit room which I remedied by pulling back the drapes. Its furnishings were similar to the other with its dark, heavy antiques and huge bed but in shades of black and red, which lent it a sinister appearance.

"Doesn't exactly shout 'have a great night'," Simon commented as he strode to the bed and tested what passed for a mattress. "And it doesn't have an exit door to the hall. Add that to that slide bolt we saw, and I think this must have been where the Duke kept his son."

I nodded. "Seems likely unless there's a dungeon below. Maybe he'll appear to you tonight wearing whatever they did in his day or perhaps a winding sheet."

Simon laughed. "We haven't exactly established that the Blue Room is yours quite yet."

"I have first dibs and say it's mine."

"Well, a coin toss should settle it. Any lose change in your pockets?"

"No. It was your suggestion, so you supply it."

His pockets turned up two sets of keys, a comb, and one button. "It's from a shirt I've been meaning to mend, and now I have a wife who can do it for me."

"Fat chance. Button top up, I win. Bottoms up, you lose."

He smiled wryly. "Now why does that sound like a bad arrangement?"

I had to smile back. "Okay. I call tops now just toss it!"

I lost. I tried for the best two out of three, but lost again. "Okay, I get the portal to hell with its ghost of a rapist and killer while you get the almost cozy one in there. You won our first marital skirmish in what could be a long war."

One dark brow arched up in query. "Is that a veiled threat?"

"Hardly veiled. If I can't sleep...you won't either."

After that, we headed downstairs then walked Bella. That walk took us past the building that housed the noisy generator, and another piled to the rafters with firewood. A third looked like it had once housed animals of some kind in its ancient past. Now it was roofless and the wind whistled mournfully through the broken windows.

Everywhere we went, we both experienced a shivery kind of awareness. The same kind we had when we first viewed the house. Coming to the edge of the cliffs that ringed the island, we looked out to sea where the jagged rocks jutted up from the dark blue water. A death trap for the unwary.

"I wonder how many of those who died out there haunt the island," I murmured as I moved closer to the edge and looked below where the waves crashed against the bottom flinging their spray high in the air. My approach frightened the nesting birds that rose in a white cloud of fluttering wings that sent Bella into a barking frenzy.

"You're making me all kinds of nervous doing that," Simon told me as he grabbed my arm and yanked me back. "That bit you were standing on could have broken off and taken you with it. Now let's get back to the boat and collect what we'll need for our first night. In the morning...if we decide to stay...we'll unload the equipment we need to do a thorough investigation."

It didn't take long to pack the essentials including Bella's food and dishes then head back to the house. She led the way as we took the main staircase past a row of ancient portraits that hung alongside. There were six of them in ornate gold frames...all men with a strong family resemblance. All had dark eyes...predatory noses...and a regal bearing dressed in the garb of their different times. More than one was astride a horse. Three of the paintings offered a glimpse of their ancestral home in the background.

"The Dukes of Whatever back across the pond," I murmured as we passed a spot where a seventh portrait must have hung at one time. "I wonder who that was?"

"Perhaps the black sheep son?"

"I would really like to see what he looked like."

"If he wasn't a bastard, he quite probably looked like all the others. Don't ever forget...just because he's a ghost doesn't mean he can't do you immense harm physically as well as in other ways."

"Nice thought since I'm supposed to be spending the night in his bed," I replied with a wry grimace as we reached the upper hall then headed down to the Blue Room.

Just inside the door, Simon pulled me to a stop and swung me around. "Bet or no bet, there's no way I'll let you spend the night in there. Just by coming here, we've no doubt stirred things up, and we need to stay together at all times."

"Just for the record, I had absolutely no intention of honoring our button toss. There is no way either one of us will stay in there. I'm not even at all sure about this room."

Simon smiled. "I know what you mean, but let's give it a try starting with a short nap in broad daylight while we wait to hear when supper's served. I promise to be on my best behavior."

"What could you possibly know about good behavior considering all that you've done to me?"

"I didn't say 'good'," he replied as he stretched out on the bed. "I said I would be on my 'best' which may or may not be the same thing, and...besides...aren't you having fun? You learned the

44

rudiments of sailing, and you are about to have another exciting adventure."

"I don't want to have another *terrifying* adventure. Greystone cured me of that forever."

"But you met me there."

I sighed. "How could I possibly forget?"

"And you love me. I know you do."

I sighed a second time. "I'm still sorting that out. Was actually making some progress when you abducted me and damaged my fragile trust."

"Look! If things go badly tonight, we'll spend the rest of it on the boat...make our apologies in the morning then get the hell outta here. Deal?"

"Yet another one I'll be holding you to," I replied as I climbed up next to him but kept a safe distance between us.

We talked about Bella...work...then he asked out of the blue, "Why is your thinking so screwed up? So much the opposite of mine?"

"Not always and only when you're wrong which is most of the time."

"Okay. I'm going to say a word, and you'll respond with the first word that comes to mind."

"Go for it."

"Black."

"White"

"Sailing."

"Beach."

"Marriage."

"Divorce."

"Are you beginning to see a pattern here?"

"Enough with the word association games," I told him as I plumped up my pillow and settled back with a sigh. "I think we both deserve and need that nap."

So, that's what we did.

***

A knock woke us sometime later. To my surprise, I found myself snuggled against Simon with Bella wedged in between us. Jumping out of bed, I sped to the door.

It was Matilda standing there. "Best hurry. The Mistress does not like her soup cold or her guests late. Them she has which are few to none. There will only be the three of you, so dinner will be served in the mornin' room. Less drafty."

"Three? Where and when do you eat?" I asked.

"In the kitchen where it's proper since there's company. If you weren't here, I'd be eatin' with her. That way she has someone to jabber away at when she isn't talkin' to herself or Bart. Not that I hear a word she be sayin'. Head down to the kitchen when you're ready. I'll be there and can show you the way."

I thanked her and looked back over my shoulder at a smiling Simon who was still lying in bed. "I might point out it wasn't me who crossed over the line of demarcation while we slept," he told me. "Not that I minded all that much."

"I can't be responsible for what I do when I'm sleeping. We need to get going. What do we do about Bella?"

Simon swung his long legs over the edge of the bed and searched for his deck shoes. "We'll bring her down to the kitchen and feed her there. She can wait with Matilda while we eat then we'll take her out for a walk."

"She's used to eating with us," I reminded him.

"She'll be fine with Matilda who seems a good sort. Can you imagine Ms. Blackthorne's horror if she spotted Bella lurking under the dining table?"

I had to laugh. "I'd rather like to see that. We've already broken her cardinal rule and slept in the same bed without benefit of clergy."

"Unbeknownst to her."

A few moments later, we headed down to the kitchen where we found Matilda fussing over dinner. Her smile and up tilted nose lent her an elfin quality as she told us, "Oh, you brought your dog with you. She's a lovely old thing, isn't she?"

"She is all of that. We thought we might leave her in here with you, if that's okay," I replied "Brought her dinner and dishes."

"Do you think she'd like a bit of pot roast added to it?"

"She'll love it and you," Simon told her. "She may try to follow us, so I'm tying her leash to this table leg."

"Should do nicely, but you best hurry along. The Mistress likes to make an entrance and will want you seated first. The mornin' room is through that door on the left."

A short hall, badly in need of new carpeting, took us to the morning room that had been painted a cheery yellow quite recently. The furniture was dark, heavy, and very old like the rest we'd seen, but a vase of mixed wildflowers plunked in the middle of the table offset it if only a bit. Narrow windows let in what was left of the sunlight and offered a clear view of the sea. Clouds were beginning to build up along the horizon, and I wondered if we would see another storm before morning.

My thoughts were interrupted as the door swung open, and Ms. Blackthorne swept into the room wearing an ancient, floor sweeping taffeta dress that rustled with each step. To my surprise, she had a green and orange parrot perched on her shoulder that was busily plucking at the string of amber beads she wore around her wrinkled neck.

"His name is Bartholomew...Bart for short. Found him one morning harassing the nesters along the cliff. Must have flown off a passing boat. A bit of a rascal with a vocabulary that would make a pirate blush. What is that dog doing here?"

Simon and I looked around in surprise just as Bella made a leap for the parrot nearly knocking Ms. Blackthorne over. Screeching loudly, Bart flew off and perched on a drapery rod. "Awwk! Be a good bird!" he scolded Bella who sat on her haunches and howled.

48

"I don't know what got into her!" I exclaimed as Simon hurriedly made a grab for Bella's trailing leash. "She's never seen a parrot. Perhaps she's just curious."

Ms. Blackthorne snorted loudly and snatched up her napkin to dab at the large spot of bird poop Bart had left behind when he took off. "A poor excuse indeed! Control it or keep it on the boat. I don't want Bart upset."

"I'll take her to the kitchen while we eat," Simon replied over his shoulder as he led Bella to the door. "But she stays with us at all times while we are in this house, or we all leave together. Is that clear?"

"Abundantly. If I didn't need you, young man, I'd gladly send you all packing. Since you are headed that way, tell Matilda she may serve. Don't like cold soup or bad company."

Simon disappeared and returned moments later with Matilda who was pushing a serving cart. Except for the colorful comments coming from Bart who remained perched aloft, a heavy silence hung over us. We were on the second course, when Ms. Blackthorne barked, "I am sure you have questions. Ask them!"

Simon began with, "We've heard a few things about this island...this house...but would like to know their history from you."

Her nostrils flared as her faded blue eyes swept us both. "I am a direct descendent of Joseph Blackthorne the Duke of Sutherby's younger brother. A title in the English Peerage created by George II in 1740 for unspecified services rendered. Along with the title went this manor house, which originated in the wilds of Scotland, but was reconstructed on this island centuries ago. The Duke...Richard Blackthorne... had one son named Geoffrey who got mixed up in some unsavory business and would most certainly have come to grief if his father hadn't spirited him away. They lived in a rough stone cottage once inhabited by some recluse until the house was finished. Quite a departure from their usual accommodations, but they managed with some extensive renovations that buried the original hut completely. What's left of it remains on the far side of the island should you care to look."

She paused to take a breath or two then continued, "It took more than twenty years of intensive labor to finish this place. At one time this entire island was covered in work camps...acres of tents and ships coming and going bringing materials over from Scotland. After the Duke and his son passed on...the exact circumstances unknown... the house was empty though pirates squatted here for a time. Someone called Odd Bones, or something equally colorful, kept a woman he had captured and her child prisoner here while he plagued the merchant ships that passed up and down the coast until the Colonial Navy put a stop to it. It was reported that they freed his prisoners then shipped him and his men back to Boston and hanged them on the docks."

She paused a second time to clear her throat then commenced again, "After that, the place was empty except for occasional looters who had heard about the island. In the early 1900s, my family returned here since they'd inherited it as the last of the line. Did some much needed renovations and used it largely as a summer

50

home during the decades that followed before it was abandoned once more. I must have come here as a very small child though I have no memory of it other than the sound of the sea and birds that still haunt my dreams at times. Mostly, I learned of it through photos and tales told by both my father and grandfather. It intrigued me, and when it became mine some years ago, I often thought of living here, but put it off to my regret. Time passes so quickly and never more so than when you grow quite old. I am of a solitary nature and the island...this house seemed like the ideal place to spend my last days. End of story."

"Hardly," I told her. "We heard this Geoffrey's 'unsavory business' was raping and killing young women. That this place was built as his prison. That he might still haunt here."

Her eyes narrowed and her mouth tightened like a drawstring purse. "Let's be perfectly clear, Mrs. North. All that was unproven nonsense. The verdict rendered was a colossal injustice that forced the Duke to flee with his son in order to save his life. This house served a dual purpose. It kept Geoffrey out of harm's way and became the sanctuary of a man who was also a solitaire by nature. One who had had his fill of the political nonsense...the corruption back home where such injustices were possible even for the high born. Now finish up, so we can enjoy the next course."

She rang the bell that summoned Matilda. Pushing her cart, she appeared almost too quickly, and I wondered if she'd been eavesdropping.

"When you've finished serving dessert, take a seat," Ms. Blackthorne told her sharply.

"Yes, Ma'am," she replied as she hastily complied.

"While we complete our meal," Ms. Blackthorne told us as Bart landed back on her shoulder and swept us all with his bright, beady gaze, "We will tell you what we've been seeing...hearing on the island. You may ask your questions when we've finished. Matilda was the first one aware of what was going on here. Tell them what happened, girl!"

Matilda had taken a seat at the far end of the table and looked down at her folded hands as she told her story. "All were real quiet like at first once them that was restorin' the place finally left, and we moved in. My bed was in the attic where the other staff stayed back in the day. There were shadows where none should be most every night. Come right after I turned out the light and moved about blockin' out the moon when they passed by the window. There was laughter, too. A man's. But worst of all was the touchin'. Started with just me blanket being tugged and then a hand on me leg where none but me own should be if you get my meanin'. So far, that's as far as he's gone since I've taken to sleepin' in other places where he hasn't found me yet."

"What does he look like," I asked.

"Never seen a face. Just a shadow figure, but he be taller than most. About like you, Mr. North."

Simon offered a reassuring smile then asked, "Did you notice anything else? Perhaps a smell...a scent? Did he speak to you at all."

She shuddered, and her hands fluttered nervously. "Sometime he smelled good like was wearing a scent of some kind and then there were times when he smelled like death. You know...the kind of rotten smell you get a whiff of when you pass by somethin' lyin' dead along the road."

Simon nodded. "I know what you mean. Did he speak to you?"

It was her turn to nod. "A bit. Sometimes he called me by a different name I can't rightly remember. Murmured soft like, but he shouted and cursed sometimes, too. Them were the worst times. I was more afraid then than I ever was before."

She was crying openly now, so I took the chair next to her and put my arm around her shoulders, "It's okay, Matilda. We're here, and we'll end this if we can. Why didn't you leave the island when all this was happening?"

"Where would I go? I've not got a soul in the world close enough to be of help, and who'd look after the Mistress if I left? No one else would last a day, and she's not got a bit of family left."

It was Ms. Blackthorne who told her, "Quit your blubbering, girl and go to the kitchen where you will remain till I summon you."

She scrambled to her feet and headed for the door as Bart called after her, "Fetch my shawl and slippers. Fetch my shawl and slippers, girl!"

"It's your turn, Ms. Blackthorne," Simon told her when the door had swung shut behind her. "What have you experienced?"

"Shadows and shapes where they shouldn't be. Someone touching my face and calling me 'Agatha' in the middle of the night. Thought it might have been Matilda for a moment, but it was definitely a man. The other day, someone pushed me on the stairs."

"Did you see who it was?" I asked.

"Was too busy plummeting downward to take notice," she snapped back. "Fortunately, I was unharmed beyond a few bruises. You've heard enough to get you started. What's your plan for tonight?"

Simon smiled. "Thought we would just check things out for ourselves...get a feel for the place and what's in it. Tomorrow we will set up the equipment we need for a full scale investigation."

"Then finish up here and get busy. I'm retiring to my room. If you need something, ask Matilda if you can find her. Don't be bothering me. Good night."

She rose to her quite impressive height while Bart clung on tightly shrieking, "Awwwk! Blast and be damned. Hang 'im from the mast, Matey!"

We could hear him all the way down the hall, and I had to wonder how she put up with it. "She must be deaf on that side," I concluded just as Matilda popped back in.

"Didn't quite tell it all since she were sitting there," she told us. "There's this woman weepin' and a wailin' most nights. Dressed in white, she is, and a fright to behold.

"And where is that?" Simon asked.

She hesitated for a long moment then said, "Your room...the blue one though I shouldn't be telling you that. The wailin' woman is the real reason the Mistress wanted you to stay in there. Wanted you scared good and proper like, so you would see what's goin' on here right from the get go. Did she tell you about the pirate cave?"

We shook our heads, and she continued, "This house was built over a cave though I've never found the entrance. The pirate used it to store his booty and his prisoners taken off the ships. Held them for ransom, he did. He was captured back in the 1790s. You can read about it in his journal that's in the library."

"Well, that will be helpful!" I exclaimed.

"There's more stuff in there you might find useful what's not been eaten by rats. The Mistress says they like the glue and leather bindin's."

I grimaced in distaste. "That's the second time you mentioned the rats. I'm surprised they are here on an island."

"Came from the ships...them and the feral cats. The Mistress tried to poison them, but I took the bait away before they found it. They mean no harm and there not be that many nowadays. Now I best quit me blatherin' and be on me way. Your dog has been fed fat as a sausage. She's lovely and so sweet. Wish I could have one, but the Mistress would try and poison it, too. Hates animals, but dotes on that bird what messes up all over the place. A nasty piece of work she don't have to clean up after. Got more to do around this place than one body can handle as is."

55

We helped her load up the dishes and followed her back to the kitchen where we collected Bella and headed outside. We were both surprised to see how dark it was getting. Already, an early moon had begun its trek across the sky though half hidden by a bank of fast moving dark clouds rimmed in silver light.

"Let me duck back inside and see if Matilda has a flashlight we can borrow," I suggested.

"Good idea. I'll wait here with Bella while you check."

I returned a few moments later, but there was no sign of either one of them. "Hey! Where are you?" I called as the increasing darkness gave me yet another weird shivery sensation. It felt as though I was being watched.

"Over here!" Simon called from somewhere ahead. "Next to what's left of a low wall running along an old trail of some kind. Too dark to see much else."

"Be right there!" I called back as I flashed my light in front of me and followed the sound of his voice.

"She couldn't wait and took me here," he told me when I reached him.

"You're right about the trail, Simon, though it's really overgrown. I wonder where it leads?"

"One way to find out. Might go to the place this Duke stayed while the house was being reconstructed. Let's check it out."

"Maybe in daylight but not now."

"If...and it's a big *if*...we even find it, you can wait outside. Let me have the flashlight."

"I went to get it, so I'm keeping it. Let's just get this over with if you insist on being stupid."

Overgrown with weeds and brush, the crushed shell trail was nearly invisible then it disappeared entirely. It was Bella who found it...a stone house silhouetted against the night sky and far bigger than I had expected.

"Looks like the Duke expanded the place to suit his needs," Simon murmured. "It's really quite spooky. I want to go inside. What do you say?"

"I say that's where the 'stupid' part comes in," I murmured back. "Let's get out of here."

"Oh, come on," he urged. "Don't be such a wuss. Hey, did you just see a light in there?"

I had. Briefly, a greenish glow had appeared in a second floor window. "Time to leave."

"Wait here. I'm going inside."

"What happened to the stick together at all times bit?" I asked.

"Whatever that was, it's in there. You're out here with Bella where you should be quite safe."

"And you? What about you?"

"I'm a big boy, and this isn't my first rodeo. Give me the flashlight. I'll be right back."

"You're not going in there without me, Cowboy," I snapped back just as Bella sat back on her haunches...howled.... then sped towards the house with both of us in close pursuit.

As we grew closer, the moonlight disclosed its sad state of disrepair. It was almost buried in vines and brush, and the roof had collapsed on one wing leaving the beams exposed like the rib cage of some behemoth. Bella led us to the front door...or what was left of it. There was just a gaping black hole like a waiting mouth.

We stepped over the rotted boards and followed her inside where I flashed my light around the beamed, low ceilinged interior. A soot blackened stone fireplace hugged one wall. Debris that had been blown in through the gaping door and windows littered the floor and had piled up in the corners. Nothing remained of the previous occupants except a three-legged, tall backed chair where a rat had taken refuge then fled at our approach. Bella gave chase, and I wondered if it or one of its kin had been the reason she led us here.

"Hard to imagine the Duke and his son settling down in this place though I'm sure it looked quite different back in his day. Let's see if we can find the window where we saw the light," Simon muttered as he snatched the flashlight from my hand and pointed it up the narrow wooden steps.

"Bad idea. Let's just get out of here. It's freezing in here now, and you know what that means."

"Someone is about to materialize. Hey! Look at Bella!"

Every hair along her spine bristled, and she was growling fiercely...teeth bared...as she stared up the stairs where a green light now hovered. Slowly, it began to take the transparent, indistinct shape of a very tall man. Nothing about him was clear except for his glowing red eyes that remained fixed on me as he began to descend.

58

Bella's growl became a whimper. Tail tucked between her legs, she bolted for the outside.

Grabbing my arm, Simon whispered, "Back up slowly then turn around and make a run for it. We're getting the hell outta here!"

I barely heard him, so intent was I on the approaching ghost whose eyes never left mine. "I will not let you leave again...not ever again!" he called. "Do you understand me?"

I was both strangely mesmerized and terrified...rooted to the spot until Simon swept me up in his arms and carried me outside. It was only when we were some distance away that he set me on my feet. The moon was much higher now, and I could see his face clearly as he shouted, "You scared the crap out of me! What were you thinking? He had you spellbound. In another minute, you would have gone with him to whatever hole he crawled out of."

For some idiotic reason, I didn't want him to know how badly I had been shaken. "Thank you for rescuing me even if I didn't need it. I was fine...sort of...and who was it that wanted to go upstairs when I wanted to leave?"

He grabbed my shoulders and gave me a shake. "Look! I saw what was happening back there, so don't pull that 'I didn't need it' stuff on me. Going in there was a mistake. Maybe this whole thing is a mistake."

"I couldn't agree more, but for one thing and one thing only."

"Which is?"

"Matilda. I really like her and don't want to see something like that *thing* back there hurt her."

59

"And neither do I. I'd like to stay long enough to see if something can be done though, at this point, I can't imagine how we'll make it happen. If not, we'll find a way to persuade her and Ms. Blackthorne to leave."

"Bart included."

"Yep. Might mention two things: we lost our flashlight back there, and I think you've put on some weight since the last time I lugged you around."

I slugged him in his shoulder which earned me an 'ouch!' before he added, "That could be considered spousal abuse."

"Like that even hurt!" I scoffed. "Let's find Bella. She was terrified."

We were thankful for the moon's light as we headed back whistling and calling her name. We had nearly reached the big house when she came running to us with her tail wagging and ears flapping.

We both hunkered down next to her and took turns getting our faces licked. "I almost think we should leave her on the boat tonight after that scare," Simon told me as he rose to his feet.

"I think she needs to be with us. Maybe nothing will happen and that entity confines himself to his present location."

"Sometimes they do. Maybe we'll get lucky. I really don't want him anywhere near you. Let's get back inside and settle in for the night."

***

Matilda was waiting for us when we got back. "Sorry to tell you, we dropped your flashlight when we ran into a problem," I told her with a smile I was far from feeling.

Her eyes widened as she looked at us both. "You were at the old place? The one they called the cottage?"

"Yep," Simon replied. "Let's just say it wasn't a good experience and let it go at that for now. Thanks for waiting up for us, but I think we'll be okay from here on. We'll be up early tomorrow. Lots to do."

Her eyes were still troubled as she replied, "Just be very careful...and you'll need more flashlights. The generator often gives out from time to time. Don't mind so much in the daytime, but won't go out and fiddle with it after dark. Don't be too alarmed if you see the Mistress sleepwalkin' about in the halls. Let me get them things you need, and I'll let you go on up. Already lit the fire in your room. Gets mighty cold at night. I'll be sleepin' somewhere down here I won't say out loud in case he be listening. Might mention that the old door latches were replaced back in the 1920s. You can lock your door, but many of the keys are the same."

"So another key could open it?" I asked remembering the skeleton keys at Greystone.

She nodded. "I'm 'fraid so. Let me fetch what I promised then I'll be gettin' along. The bathroom up there is six doors down on the right comin' from this direction."

A few minutes later, we headed down the back hall while Matilda disappeared through the swing door. A single bulb dangling

61

from the ceiling lit the way. Another was at the top of the narrow, well-worn stairs. We found the switch for the upper hall sconces, but only one or two responded...small islands of light in a darkness that seemed to stretch on forever. Snapping on our flashlights, we continued on past one closed door after another till we came to the bathroom Matilda had told us about. Stepping inside, I pulled the chain above the small, antiquated sink and looked around. The room had been cleaned recently...the scent of disinfectant still lingered...and a pile of fresh towels had been laid out next to the claw foot tub with its brass shower head.

Bella and Simon were waiting for me in the hall when I had finished my inspection. We had just reached our door when the lights dimmed then went out.

"That's not good," Simon murmured. "Without power, the well pump won't work which means no..."

"Much needed showers just for starters," I supplied as we entered our room lit by the fire that burned brightly in its grate. "Let's just do what we can and get to bed. Between you and the ghosts of yet to come, I doubt sleep is on the table."

"You've said that before and conked out like a blown fuse then snored like a small freight train chugging up a hill."

I sniffed loudly. "That's a ridiculous analogy. Freight trains don't snore and neither do I. You're making that up!"

He sighed. "Too bad you also suffer from memory lapses. Do you know you get a red blotch right above those amazing eyes when you're angry."

"I'm not angry! I'm irritated. There's a difference. How about we focus on the task at hand and not whatever it is you're doing. We should both stay dressed in case something happens. Since any key will open it, locking the door seems pointless."

"That's because you don't know the secret I am about to reveal. First I'll need a long strip of cloth. Got anything you don't mind me tearing up?"

"Not really. How about that shirt you're wearing? Definitely not your color."

Thankfully, I couldn't hear what he was muttering under his breath as he somehow ripped off a long strip from the bottom.. "Now watch and learn," he told me a bit smugly as he shoved it into the keyhole leaving a long piece dangling. "That's so we can get out of here when we have to, but no one else can shove a key in from the other side."

"Where did you learn that trick?"

"Thought it up myself which is why I'm the brains of this outfit."

I could have dredged up some retort, but let it go. A short time later, we crawled on top the lumpy mattress and pulled the covers over us. Bella was more than happy to snuggle between us.

"Wish we had more light in here," I murmured.

"There's plenty of wood to keep the fire going all night. Just close your eyes and drift off. If you need to, I won't mind all that much if you slide over this way."

"Like we both don't know where that could lead."

63

"Under the circumstances that would be a bit unlikely, don't you think?"

"Knowing you, probably not. Go to sleep. I'll keep first watch."

"Better make that me. I'm the experienced ghost releaser, and you are the newbie. If you need to use the bathroom again, I'll go with you. No one goes anywhere without the other."

"Fine by me...good night."

"I wish," I heard him whisper as I closed my eyes and tried to relax despite the sounds I was now hearing. The creaks and groans of an old house...the whimper of Bella in her sleep...the wind whistling through every available crack and crevice. Most of which I was all too familiar with during my long nights at Greystone. All it lacked was the mystery clock forever chiming the hour of midnight instead of the steeple clock on the mantel that had just chimed eleven times.

I was sound asleep when Simon shook me awake some time later. "Your watch, sleepyhead," he murmured as he brushed a strand of my unruly red hair back from my forehead then tweaked my nose, which was really irritating when I had thought he might kiss me. "I've added more wood to the fire, so that should last till morning. Remember to wake me if you experience any calls of nature."

I grimaced wryly. "How could I forget? Just go to sleep. I'll handle everything and only wake you if something horrific happens."

64

"Great," he replied then plumped up his pillow...turned on his other side...and was asleep in moments not minutes.

It was strange how alone I felt as I looked around the room. The flickering fire cast shadows on the ceiling that danced and moved in an eerie kind of way.

"Look, you," I told myself sternly. "They are normal, everyday, nothing to worry about shadows, and you are an idiot. You won't last the night if you keep scaring yourself silly and.............."

I gasped. Had I just seen a face at the window? I shook my head. "Impossible. It's at least thirty feet to the ground," I whispered and then there it was again...a woman's face...pale as the moon that shone above her. Her long dark hair was wet, her eyes enormous, her mouth open in a silent scream as her hands pressed against the glass. To my horror, she passed right through and glided into the room trailing her long, white gown behind her.

"Where is he?" she screamed which woke both Simon and Bella who howled mournfully.

Simon pulled me up against him then whispered close to my ear, "I don't think she even knows we're here."

"I hope not," I whispered back as she shrieked again. "That must be the wailing woman Matilda told us about. Let's just see what she does."

We remained perfectly still as she took a turn around the room then.... to both our horror... began to crawl in bed with us. There was a cold, wet, tingling sensation as she slid through me then settled

65

against my pillow with a long sigh and began to cry. I was lying there... still partially entangled in her... feeling her intense rage, fear and sorrow which were doing all kinds of crazy things to me, when Simon grabbed my hand and yanked me out of bed.

"Come on. Let her be."

To my surprise, I found myself saying, "I can't. I need to know what's breaking her heart. Please. Give me a minute."

He sighed. "Okay. See what you can do and then we're going back to the boat to regroup."

I sat back down on the edge of the bed and tried to touch her shoulder, but she was as insubstantial as fog, and my hand slid right through her. Startled, she opened her eyes. "Who are you? What are you doing here?"

"We're friends who've come to help you. My name is Jodie. What's yours?"

"You need to go before he finds you."

"You mean Geoffrey Blackthorne?"

A puzzled frown creased her pale forehead. "He is not the one. I speak of John Long. The one who calls himself the Bone Man...the plague of the seas. His spirit could return at any time though I have yet to see it. He vanished the day the ships sailed into the harbor. I heard them say he would be brought back to Boston then hanged there for all to see. I tried to kill him once and failed. That time he did not escape."

"Why do you come here...to this room? I thought it belonged to another. The father of Geoffrey Blackthorne or whoever guarded him."

She cut in fiercely, "It belonged to him...to John. It is here I slept with my son when he was out to sea for months at a time committing his monstrous crimes. We'd been on a ship...the Marianne...when he boarded and sank her. Tied the crew to the rigging and laughed at their pleas for mercy as they sank beneath the water. He ransomed or killed the other passengers, but brought us to this God forsaken place where I served his insatiable appetites. My son disappeared one day. I found his shoe at the top of the crumbling cliff and threw myself in after him. I look for his spirit here where I cradled him in my arms and in the sea below. Search for him in the darkness every night. The search has been long, but I will never give up. Now let me be. Let me rest, so I can hold him again if only in my dreams."

She began to fade...growing more and more indistinct until she was gone...*if* she was gone. "What if she's still there sleeping in our bed?" I asked Simon as I stood up and looked down at the damp spot where she'd been a moment before.

"Could be. Another reason to sleep elsewhere. Grab what you need. We're going back to the boat and ask for a different room in the morning since this one is already taken."

None of us...including Bella...wasted much time getting out of there. We were down the hall...the back stairs...and out the kitchen door a short time later. The moon spread its silver radiance over the island and lit the night sky though fast moving clouds that pulsed with lightning were fast overtaking it. Floating over the water below, we were surprised to see what looked like Kongming or Chinese sky lanterns.

"Must be spirits in orb form," Simon murmured as we both watched in awe. "I wonder who they are?"

"Remember the shipwrecks reported off this coast? I bet they are the spirits of those drowned out there," I murmured back.

"You still want to finish out the night on the boat with those floating around and a storm coming?"

"I really wish there was a third option, but better the boat than more of what we've seen so far in this place," I replied.

"If you want, we can make our excuses and leave in the morning."

"There's still Matilda and Ms. Blackthorne to worry about. We'll see how we feel when daylight comes."

Simon led the way down the trail to the tiny harbor where Edith's Gift waited. We were onboard moments later.

"Get some sleep. I'll wake you if anything happens you need to know about," Simon told me over his shoulder as he and Bella headed to the v-berth in the bow.

"I really don't want to be alone just now after all that's happened. Maybe we could share?" I called after him.

I heard him groan. Five steps brought him back to me. He swept me up into his arms then carried me to his berth and set me down there. Remembering the nights of passion we had shared, I knew...sort of...what I wanted to happen despite the circumstances, but it never did. He stretched out and pulled me up against him. We were both asleep a few moments later with my head cradled on his shoulder.

CHAPTER THREE

The boat was rocking and rain was hammering the hatch cover above me, when a soaking wet Simon woke me up to tell me, "Pretty rough out there. Was going to check the weather and found out the satellite phone is missing and the radio has been smashed. What's worse, so has the engine, and we can't even sail out of here. The sails have been slashed beyond repair."

I sat bolt upright startling a still drowsy Bella. "Which means we aren't going anywhere!"

"Yep. Only way off this island is when the supply boat comes."

"Which is almost a week away. So what do we do in the meantime?"

"The job we came here to do. I'll throw together something to eat if you're up to it then we'll head back to the house first lull we get. Let me grab some dry clothes. I'll change in the head."

Wrapped in my blanket, I crawled out of the berth and headed to the main salon. Keeping my balance was difficult as the boat thudded against the dock again and again. I clutched at every handhold I could find till I plunked down on a bench and held on tightly.

69

A few minutes later, Simon busied himself in the galley. My stomach churned, and I begged for my saucepan that he quickly thrust into my hand then told me, "Looks like food isn't in your future. Hope you don't mind if I eat. I'm starving!"

He finished a make do breakfast then sat down next to me. "Wish I knew how much more of this crap was coming," he told me as he tucked my blanket in around me. "Without our radio or phone, we're screwed."

"There's no one on this island but Matilda and Ms. Blackthorne. I doubt either one of them knows enough about boats to sabotage us."

He sighed. "Didn't take much know-how. A smash, slash, and grab. Could even have been a ghost. Remember how much damage was done at Greystone?"

I smiled ruefully. "Like I could ever forget."

"How are you feeling?"

"The way I look."

"That bad, huh? If my eating bothers you, I can go stand in the galley."

"No, you're fine. I might even manage to keep down a few gulps of coffee if you care to share."

"I'll get you some if you promise to use your puke pan instead of anywhere else. Might add that Bella is going to need an emptying soon, so let's hope we get a break in this bastard before too long, or she'll be using the astro turf."

"What time is it? It's still kinda darkish out there."

"Later than it looks and..... Listen! The rains letting up. Coffee can wait. Time to break out the foul weather gear and get going while we have the chance."

It didn't take long to don our yellow, hooded rain slickers. Simon was the first one on deck with Bella and me right behind him. The rain was much lighter now, and the wind had almost died though the waves still battered the boat. While I had slept, Simon had loosened the lines, and the dock was now some distance below us. Reaching it from the moving boat seemed impossible, and I wouldn't have made it without Simon's help.

"Just stay put. You're okay where you are," he told me after I was safely on the dock. "I'm going back for Bella."

I watched him hoist himself up then disappear inside. Some very long minutes later, he reappeared with Bella hanging in a makeshift sling around his neck. "She's not too happy with her new dog carrier" he called down to me. "Stand back. This might be a bit tricky with her wriggling around throwing me off balance."

He timed it perfectly and landed next to me a moment later. "Come on!" he called. "Let's get going! It's about to get nasty again."

I followed him up the trail. He carried Bella most of the way then set her down under the overhang of an outbuilding. While we waited for her to do her thing, he told me, "Look. I know we can't leave till Friday, but the boat is still safe if things get tough."

I grimaced wryly. "Someone or something came onboard and made sure we couldn't get off this island, so how safe can it be?"

"Point taken, but I hadn't locked up. Never occurred to me I would need to on an island. Let's just get back inside the house and feel things out. See how it goes."

"From bad to worse has been my usual experience," I muttered under my breath as Simon scooped Bella into his arms and headed for the house that loomed just ahead.

Darkened by the rain, its stone walls looked even more sinister, and a shudder rippled through me yet again. I didn't want to go back in there, but the boat seemed a worse alternative at the moment.

I was relieved to see lights in the kitchen windows when we reached the back side. A very worried Matilda was waiting for us. "There you be! I was worried sick, I was. You said you would be gettin' up early, and when you didn't come down, I went up to make sure everything was all right. You were all gone, and I feared the worst! That somethin' had snatched you in your sleep."

"We should have left a note. The bed was a bit uncomfortable, so we went back to the boat," I told her with my best reassuring smile. It was more of a half-truth than a lie. Our wet visitor had made it more than a 'bit uncomfortable'.

Simon added, "The boat's been sabotaged. Is there anyone else on this island you haven't told us about?"

Her eyes were enormous as she looked at us both. "I told you about Joe the handyman who comes and goes with the supply boat. Likes it here, he does. He be a strange one for sure, but harmless. The captain blasts his horn when it's time to leave...won't wait if he's not there. Once or twice he stayed on, and we didn't know

72

about it. Camped out somewhere. Don't know how he managed to live."

"Could he still be here? Hiding somewhere?" I asked.

She shook her head. "Had some work for him, but he weren't on the boat last time it came. There's no one on the island now but me and the Mistress. She were up and roamin' about till the wee hours. Is like that when it storms, and it were a howler last night. Came into the summer parlor where I was sleepin'. Gives me the bejabbers when I see her like that in her nightgown with her hair all wild and tumblin' 'round her shoulders. She were talkin' to someone, but I couldn't make no sense of it. Just sat there mumblin' then began to walk about again. I followed her to make sure she came to no harm. Went back to her room just before dawn, and I came in here to make meself a pot of coffee and wait out the rest of the night till it be time to start breakfast for the two of you."

"Wouldn't mind some of that coffee after you tell us the best place to hang these wet slickers and park a damp dog," Simon told her just as Bella gave a good shake sending drops flying everywhere.

"Hang 'em on them pegs by the door. These stone floors won't come to no harm. You can dry her off with that towel over there by the sink. The Mistress is still sleepin' and snorin' like a lord. I kept that horrid parrot's cage covered, so he won't be wakin' her any time soon. Here now. Let me quit me blatherin' and fetch you that coffee and a bit of breakfast."

"I ate on the boat, but Jodie might like some breakfast if her stomach has settled down."

I smiled wryly. "Nothing more than toast with some kind of jelly, if it's not too much trouble. I would really like you to join us right here at this table."

"The Mistress would be pitchin' a fit if she saw us, but I'd like that, too. Grab yourselves a chair. Everything will be ready in two shakes of a lamb's tail."

Simon towel dried Bella then we both took our seats. Matilda was both quick and efficient. Soon I was munching on my toast and swilling down the best coffee I had ever tasted though it could well have been that I was desperately in need of a caffeine fix.

Simon was cradling his cup with both hands when he asked Matilda, "Is there another room we can use since the bed didn't suit us last night?"

"Was it the bed, or somethin' you don't want to mention?" she asked as she watched us closely.

I had to smile. "Seems there was someone else who needed it more than we did. We never got her name. She walked in through the window. Claimed to be the captive of the Bone Man....the pirate you told us about."

Matilda's dark eyes were troubled. "Aye. She's the one I mentioned...why the Mistress really wanted you to sleep in there, so you see her firsthand. Walks around wailin' and weepin' for her son. Fair breaks your heart to hear her. When we finish up, I'll show you another room. Not as fancy and farther from the bathroom. It were put in order not that long ago 'cause I slept there some nights when the attic didn't suit. The Mistress saw the light under the door

74

and told me 'my place was in the servants quarters', so I dared not stay there again. She's the kind to check on a body just to make sure. Crossin' her leads to the worst kind of trouble."

"Like what? As far as I can see, she'd be lost here all alone without you," I told her.

"She gets the devil in her sometimes though she seems frail and all. I'd like to make the switch before she wakes up and has her say. She thinks you're here to rid her of the ghosts. Don't matter none to her what that might cost the two of you in the doin' of it. Just need to change the linens and give it a good dustin', which won't take long."

A short time later, we followed her up the back stairs. She opened the first door on the right and stood aside for us to pass. Bella led the way. It was smaller than the other...the antique four-poster bed and the rest of the furnishings not as grand, but there was a great sea view.

I moved closer for a better look. Massive dark clouds smudged with purple were headed our way pushed by the wind that now whistled through the cracks in the window casement. Distant lightning forked its way into the white capped nearly black sea. A second storm was coming...and coming fast.

"Looks like it will last all day and into the night some," Matilda told us as Simon joined me at the window. "Sometimes it storms fierce like that for days with the wind shriekin' and the waves crashin' over the dock and tearin' chunks from the cliffs. The west side catches the worst of it. The foundation on that wing has started to shift...cave in though the main house should last long enough to see the Mistress out as she wishes."

"From the looks of what's coming, retreating to the boat will be out of the question. We're better off here," Simon murmured under his breath as his hand found mine.

"I guess we'll have to tough it out and see what happens. Our visitor last night wasn't dangerous. Just profoundly sad," I murmured back then turned to Matilda with my brightest smile. "The room is perfect as is. We'll let you get back to whatever you're doing while we complete the move ourselves."

"Beddin' you want is in the linen press next to the stairs. If you don't need me, I'll get her majesty's tray ready then wake her. See you at lunch. She'll most likely not be there."

"Then we'd like to eat in the kitchen with you again," I told her.

She was smiling when she shut the door behind her. We stood there, watching the approaching storm for a while then Simon told me, "I like this bed better. Not a fancy Tudor with Henry VIII vibes, but smaller and cozier, which means...."

"We have to get closer," I cut in as I hid my smile. "Forget what happened last night in a moment of weakness. Same rule applies. Bella sleeps in the middle."

He sighed then pulled me into his arms, tipped up my chin, and kissed me. It was a long time before he murmured, "Are you sure about that?"

Since I wasn't at all sure...since my knees where decidedly weak...since I wanted to melt into him, my contrary self replied,

76

"That...that kiss doesn't change anything. As things stand, we are teammates not bedmates, and I think it would be wise to keep it that way."

One dark brow quirked up, and he smiled. "I sense you are weakening."

"You sense wrong," I replied as I pushed free then added, "Now let's get moving. I'd like to check out the library and the Bone Man's journal when we finish up here."

We had changed the linens and just finished carrying the last of our things into our new room, when we heard a loud scream in the hall. Flinging open the door, we looked down its length and saw Matilda speeding towards the main stairway. Bart the parrot was in close pursuit screaming hoarsely, "Damn the Devil! Damn the Devil!" A grunting, growling sound followed. Something was crawling behind them. It was too dark and the distance too great to be sure, but it looked like Ms. Blackthorne slithering along the carpet with a peculiar sinuous motion. Every hair along Bella's spine bristled and her howls added to the cacophony.

Matilda spotted us and sprinted our way shouting, "Head to the kitchen!"

She was the first one down the back stairs with all the rest of us...including Bart... right on her heels. Slamming the door at the bottom shut behind us, she leaned against it as she struggled to catch her breath. "I don't think she'll be comin' no farther. Never seen her like that. She were like a wild animal...all crazy like...foamin' at

77

the mouth and cursin' worse than Bart then she slid out of bed and came after me."

My own heart was still hammering wildly when I took her arm and led her towards the kitchen. "Let's all just sit down together and see if we can figure out what happened," I somehow managed to tell her.

Simon added, "From what we saw, she could be possessed by a demon though neither of you mentioned anything that would point us in that direction."

By the time we reached the kitchen, Bella had scurried under the table, and Bart had perched on the fireplace mantel. From there, he kept a close eye on the back hall as he muttered darkly, "Awk! She be comin'! Damn the devil."

"I'll make us all a pot of coffee while you two grab a seat," Simon told us a lot more calmly that I suspect he was feeling. What we had seen up there was enough to unnerve even him.

Matilda began to weep, and I put my arm around her shoulders. "We'll figure something out," I told her.

"I can't stay here with that thing! She's had her queer spells like the dog thing when you first come but never none like that. She scared the life out of me, and if she'd caught me there's no tellin' what would have happened!"

"We won't let it happen," I soothed though I wasn't at all sure how we could stop it. "This storm won't last forever, and you can stay with us onboard our boat till the supply boat comes."

It was then we heard the door at the far end of the back hall swing open and bang against the wall. It was Ms. Blackthorne who stomped into the kitchen without her cane. She seemed totally unaware she was still wearing her stained and torn nightgown...that one slipper was missing. Her dark gaze swept us all then settled on Matilda. "Time for breakfast, girl! At once! No more idling about. As to the rest of you, I want to know what you have accomplished to date other than enjoying my magnanimous hospitality."

It was Simon who told her with a continued calmness I had to admire, "Why don't you go to the morning room where we can all sit down and talk about what happened last night."

"Nothing happened on my end. Slept like a baby. And don't be telling me, young man, where to go. I go where I damn well please!" she snapped back. Uttering a combination of snort and huff, she headed towards the morning room.

We were all stunned. She was back to whatever passed for her usual self, but I noticed Bart didn't want to follow her. I didn't want to either but knew we had to learn more about her horrific transformation.

When we arrived moments later, she was seated regally at the head of the table and waved us to our seats. "I assume you've already enjoyed breakfast by this late hour, so you can tell me what you've accomplished your first night here while Matilda serves me."

As we slid into our chairs, once again Simon took the lead, "We've asked to change rooms, and Matilda has offered another option. The Blue Room was unsuitable..."

"And why was that?" she cut in sharply. "It's a perfectly good room. My choice for you. You are not welcome to go about willy-nilly swapping rooms on a whim."

"It was no 'whim'. We were visited by a ghost...a Lady in White...who said she was the captive of the pirate that stayed here for a time."

"She was soaking wet when she floated through the window," I added. "Apparently, she had thrown herself into the sea when she found her son's shoe at the top of the cliff and thought him dead. She's roaming about looking for him. The Blue Room was once hers, and she didn't seem glad to share."

She sniffed loudly. "Haven't seen nor conversed with the like of her. Just saw shadows and shapes, but you made contact and no doubt sent her packing."

"Quite the contrary. We let her sleep and went back to our boat which had been sabotaged by someone," Simon replied as we both watched her closely.

"You told us you slept 'like a baby'," I added, "but Matilda said you were sleepwalking as you often do, and a short time ago...."

I never finished what I was about to tell her as she pulled herself to her feet and glared fiercely at us. "Matilda is a gossip and a liar I would sack if I could. I would not put your faith in anything she says. I'm going to my room now. Tell her...when she *finally* arrives... to bring a tray up to me and be quick about it."

With that said, she swept through the door, and we looked at each other.

"Well, that wasn't at all helpful. It seems Ms. Blackthorne is either lying or doesn't realize she sleepwalks. Personally, I think it's the former," I told Simon.

"She lied about the White Lady. She knew about her and wanted us in that room according to Matilda. Let's get back to the kitchen and tell her what just happened. You told Ms. Blackthorne what she confided in us and that may have serious consequences."

"Like what? She couldn't survive here without Matilda, and I'm sure she knows it."

"You saw that thing upstairs. Did that look like a rational creature who stops to sort things out?"

I assumed that was a rhetorical question that didn't require an answer, so I didn't try to supply one.

At that precise moment, Matilda pushed the service cart through the swing door and looked around. "Where is she?" she asked with a puzzled frown.

"Went up to her room and now wants a tray," I told her then admitted. "I unwittingly may have gotten you into trouble. She knows you told us about her sleepwalking, and she wasn't pleased."

"She might forget. She has spells when she don't remember much of anything."

I pasted on my best reassuring smile. "Then we'll hope for that among other things."

We followed her back to the kitchen where she busied herself making the tray while we drank our coffee and watched. She headed out the door a few minutes later calling over her shoulder, "Be back soon unless she takes another turn, and I don't make it out of there."

"Do you want us to go with you just in case?" Simon asked.

"I'll be watchin' more careful like this time. If I see any signs she's gone bad, I'll run for it. She can't catch me crawlin' along like she did."

"If you aren't back in fifteen minutes, we'll come looking for you," I offered.

"Best be headed off now. By the way, I thought about somethin' earlier when I passed that spot on the wall where a paintin' went missin' you might be wonderin' about. Could be up in the attic under the eaves. There's a heap of stuff there from way back when. I'll take you up there when I get back."

We watched her push her way through the swing door just as Bart screeched, "Rue the day. Rue the bloody day!"

He'd been so quiet I had forgotten about him till then. He was a strange bird in every sense of the word, but was he a prophet as well? Would we all indeed "rue the day"? And then there was the night ahead.

"I know what you're thinking," Simon told me. "You're wondering if old Bart over there is right. He's a parrot not a prophet. Repeats what he's heard and nothing more."

"So where did he hear the things he screeches? Hardly something anyone would teach a parrot these days when 'Polly wants a cracker' seems the norm."

Simon shrugged his broad shoulders and pushed his glasses up. "Nothing we need to worry or wonder about at the moment. Bottoms up on the coffee and then I think we'll head upstairs and wait for Matilda within shouting distance if...."

"The beast returns," I supplied.

Moments later, Bella led the way. By then, the second storm was unleashing its fury on the tiny island. Rain hammered the windows, and the wind shrieked like a lost Banshee wailing for the soon to be dead. We made our way up the back stairs then down the long hall at the top. Reaching the main stairway that swept down into the increasing darkness below, we waited there for Matilda. We didn't have to wait long. The sound of Ms. Blackthorne's bellow of displeasure followed her out the door she slammed shut behind her. Spotting us by the stairs, she hurried our way brushing away her tears as she went.

"What was that all about?" I asked.

"Her eggs didn't suit her. If it wasn't that, it would be somethin' else. But that's normal for her. Not that her words don't hurt. The attic door is down on this end of the hall. Follow me."

Through the octagon shaped window in the alcove at the far end, I saw a lightning bolt plunge into the ink dark water followed by the crash of thunder almost directly overhead. Another followed a moment later as the relentless storm continued to pound the island. Matilda led us to a narrow door tucked into the paneling and almost invisible. Taking a deep breath, she opened it then reached inside and switched on the light.

The steps that led into the cavernous space above were wooden and worn. Tucked in between the small dormered windows along one wall was a row of identical cots with pine wardrobes wedged in between. Most had no mattresses. Those that did were moldy and rat chewed, but the one at the end was covered with a quilt that had been slashed into colorful ribbons.

"That one over there used to be mine," Matilda whispered as she looked around nervously. "He did that after I did a runner that night. The things I told you about are over there in them rooms. If you don't mind, I'll wait here by the stairs with Bella. No way of tellin' what you'll let loose when you open them doors."

"A cheerful thought," I whispered to Simon as I followed him across the wide planked, dusty floor to three doors. The first creaked loudly when Simon opened it. In the dim light that spilled inside, all we saw were stacks of old furniture piled all the way to the rafters. Many pieces were broken as though shoved inside haphazardly with no thought of their value, which could well be considerable by now. The second door opened on more of the same, but the third looked more promising. Inside, there were trunks, crumbling boxes spilling out their contents, and a stack of paintings leaning against the far wall.

"Looks like we might get lucky," Simon muttered as we pushed our way through till we reached them.

"Or unlucky...depending," I muttered back as he lifted the first one and turned it around.

It was a painting of the house done by an amateur hand and signed at the bottom 'Richard Blackthorne'.

"Apparently, the Duke needed a hobby to while away the hours spent on the island," I whispered as I turned around a second painting and then a third. They were both badly rendered memories of his life back home. Behind them was a stack that had been painted over...their subject matter concealed. We had come to the last one, and Simon turned it towards the light. It was an incredible portrait of a young man on a night black horse. His dark hair was ruffled by the wind that swept the long grass and bent the trees around him. He was wearing what I thought was called a red frock coat...buff colored breeches...and shiny black riding boots with turned down cuffs. His eyes were riveting. Black and compelling. A slight smile lifted the corners of his sensuous mouth. It felt as though he was looking...smiling at me...and a shiver raced through me. It was nonsense of course, but there it was. No wonder someone had stashed the painting in the attic. It must have been very unsettling to see it on the wall if everyone else experienced what I did.

"Masterfully done unlike the others. That must be the Duke's son, Geoffrey," Simon murmured. "I doubt he had any trouble seducing the women of his time."

I grabbed the painting from Simon and thrust it back against the wall. "He was a rapist and a murderer by all accounts. I really wish I hadn't seen that."

Simon sighed. "There's a chance...just a chance... you'll see the spirit version of him tonight. From the look of things outside that

85

window, there's no way we can return to the boat any time soon. Neither you nor Bella could handle it."

I grimaced wryly. "So, we stay here and deal with what happens. We managed to get through some very terrifying experiences and out the other side at Greystone," I told him with as much bravado as I could muster. I didn't tell him about the strange effect that portrait had had on me, and I wasn't sure why. All I knew for sure was that I couldn't get out of there fast enough.

"Did you find it?" Matilda asked when we reached her.

"Found more portraits, but no way of knowing which one it was," I lied. "If you have time to show us the way, we'd like to find the library and check out that journal you told us about."

"Glad to. I'm in no hurry to get back to the Mistress, and the rest can wait a bit. Funny how time speeds by these days. Half the time I don't know what hour it is, or how I got there," she told us with a wry grimace.

We followed Matilda down the main staircase and then headed left along the dimly lit corridor. The library was the last door on the end. Stepping inside, I looked around. Very little light found its way through the grimy windows. The top panes were stained glass depicting some myth or fable I didn't recognize. No doubt, they would cast a wash of color over the dusty parquet floor when the sun shone...if it ever did. A large table and four chairs dominated the center of the room that was lined in floor to ceiling bookshelves where ancient leather bound volumes jostled for space. All except one at the far end that contained a splash of colorful covers including stacks of paperbacks.

"Ms. Blackthorne's shelf though I may borrow a few from time to time, since there's nothin' to do here after hours," Matilda explained when she saw my interest.

"You can tell a lot about a person by what they like to read," I replied as I headed that way for a closer look. Most were classics but there was a surprising collection of modern romances that seemed completely out of character from what I had seen of her.

"Certainly an eclectic mix," Simon murmured as he joined me there and lifted out a paperback with a lurid cover. "Seems there is more to the prim and proper Ms. Blackthorne than meets the eye in more respects than one."

"Here it is!" Matilda called to us as she plunked down a thick, leather bound book on the table. "I'll switch on them lights for you then I need to get back to me work."

Pulling up a couple of chairs, we sat down and merely looked at it for a few seconds. Despite its shabby condition, it seemed...well, charged with an energy I couldn't begin to describe. Taking a deep breath, I carefully opened the fragile cover, and together we read the inscription inside: *The Account Book and Personal Journal of John Long.*

The writing was faded but copperplate exquisite. Slowly, I turned the page and together Simon and I read:

This is but a brief account of my travels, ships captured, cargoes seized, and prisoners ransomed intended solely for my

87

personal enjoyment should I ever reach that doubtful state called
'old age'. A reminder of past events to be relived in my senility.

"I imagine he also kept a ship's log somewhere which would be a more accurate reckoning," Simon told me as he turned the page and we read:

Captured the US Carolina on the 5th of June in the year of our Lord 1802. Damage to our ship was light. Lost three men. Two dead...one wounded who would later die. None had been of much consequence having been shanghaied from a brothel in Charleston. An unwilling set of scurvy rascals who never served me well. The son of a wealthy plantation owner...one Adam Carlisle...was onboard. A prize more valuable than the cargoes of cotton and rum.

It continued along the same vein then we came upon an entry that read:

Have more than half a dozen below whose ransom has not been met and are unfit for common labor. Time to clear the decks of useless debris. The sea can have them all.

And so it went...lists of cargoes and prisoners with long time gaps in between...the occasional comment and then:

Celia Fletcher would fetch a handsome price if I choose to ransom her with the rest. Her husband is one of the most influential men in the Colonies, but there is something about her. The fire in her eyes when she defies me...the curve of her proud neck...the prim and proper way she comports herself that makes me want to defile her in every way. I think that must be the way of it though I fear that once I take her I will not release her this side of hell. Her son will be all the leverage I need to bend her to my will.

Hours passed as we read through the pages that followed. We hardly noticed when Matilda left a plate of sandwiches then took Bella for a walk. There were more random entries about Celia. At one point, she had tried to kill him in his sleep, but failed.

She would have slain me with my own blade had I not turned away in time to avoid the thrust. I will not be so careless again. She will yield to me all that she still withholds...her heart...her very soul...or I will sell her son to the highest bidder. A sturdy lad with years of work in him once beaten into submission.

Other entries pertaining to the boy were scattered among the accounts of his captures. He had introduced him to his "trade" though Celia fought long and hard to prevent that.

She shrieks and wails, but tis for naught. As soon as the boy is old enough, he will go to sea with me and learn what needs to be learned.

A long time passed, and then we read:

The boy is a weakling with no stomach for what needs to be done. A few lashes will cure him of that.

There was nothing more about him until a few weeks later when we saw:

The boy is gone as is his mother. Her body washed up along the shore, but not his. So be it.

And so it continued...entry after entry of his captures and kills. Some were so gruesome I had to skip through the pages quickly though the horror lingered. His stolen goods and prisoners were stored 'below' until he found a buyer for the able bodied he couldn't ransom. Everyone else was tossed off the cliffs.

"'Below' must mean the cave under this house where he would have easy access," I told Simon as we neared the end.

"A place I'd like to check out as soon as we can if we can find the entrance."

"I'm sure there is more than one ghost lurking down there from what we read."

Simon smiled grimly. "And the cargoes stored there were soaked in human blood."

We turned our attention back to the journal. The final entry read:

I can see two frigates entering the harbor. American from the cut of their jib and the flags they fly. It appears that the Constitution is one of them. We've crossed her bow before as I well remember. Our speed and shallow draft saved us then, but nothing can save us now. My hidden sanctuary has become a trap. We will fight, and we will die here. I will not leave my island alive to be hung like some dog.

"Ms. Blackthorne seems to think he was captured and hanged on the mainland, but that sounds like he died fighting," Simon told me as he took off his glasses and rubbed his tired eyes.

"He could be another ghost that lingers down in that cave if he didn't go straight to whatever passes for pirate hell," I murmured as I closed the book and pushed it from me.

It was then we noticed the darkness that pressed against the windows. It was way past suppertime, and Matilda's sudden appearance at the door confirmed it.

"Didn't want to disturb you none, so I kept your dinner warm. Supplies are a bit low till the boat comes, so I had to make do. Hope you don't mind. Bella's been fed and walked. Spent the afternoon followin' me around, and I loved every minute of it. The Mistress weren't there to ask about you at suppertime. Has a migraine and wanted a tray."

"Thanks so much for everything," I told her. "See you in a few minutes."

I watched her leave then rose to my feet. "I feel...well, like the evil between those pages is still clinging to me if that makes any sense. I need a hot shower and a change before we go down there," I told Simon over my shoulder as I headed for the door.

"I know what you mean," he replied as he caught up with me and held it open. "We could make it a double and save time. Not to mention hot water, which is in short supply."

"I get first dibs, and you'll have to wait."

"I could race you there."

"Hardly very sporting considering you have legs like a giraffe, and what would Ms. Blackthorne say if she caught us?"

Simon smiled wryly. "It boggles my imagination. I'll let you go first, if you promise not to dawdle."

"Like that ever happens. Let's just get this done. I'm starving."

A short time later, we took the back stairs to the kitchen where a joyful Bella greeted us. Matilda smiled. "She's missed you somethin' fierce, but we got along just fine. Chased Bart into the dining room, and there he stays atop the drapes cursin' and screamin' the last I saw. Sit yourselves down, and I'll serve the stew. As I said, it's not fancy, but it will stay with you...guaranteed!"

When she had finished, she sat down with us and asked what we had found in the journal that had clearly kept us engrossed for hours. Simon and I hit the highlights...eliminating some of the worst accounts...and filling in the sketchy details of Celia's capture and death.

There were tears in Matilda's eyes when she told us, "Near breaks me heart, it does. Poor thing to have endured all that. No wonder she wanders about cryin' and wailin' for her lost lad."

I nodded. "Reconnecting her with her son is one of our top priorities. We're here to help her and the others find their way into the Light where their loved ones are waiting."

"We both witnessed a tunnel come down from the heavens," Simon added. "Those who had gone before descended from this powerful white Light at the upper end and reconnected with those they loved. It was way beyond amazing, and the reason we are here... to release them into the Light."

She brushed away her tears with the back of her hand and smiled brightly. "Oh, my! It sounds ever so beautiful! I will help all I can, but what of that thing that enters the Mistress?"

"We'll figure something out," he told her with a smile.

I had seen the smile Simon flashed her before. It was meant to be reassuring, but hid a powerful doubt. He didn't have a clue on how to deal with what he believed might be a demon.

There was only a thin rim of gray light edging the horizon when we'd finished eating and decided to check on the boat. Grabbing flashlights, we let Bella lead the way down the trail towards the harbor. The storm had passed while we were engrossed in the journal, but there were flashes of lightning off to the west. From the look of it, another cell was rapidly approaching. Down below, I could hear the big waves that still rolled in....the steady 'thud' as they pushed *Edith's Gift* against the dock again and again.

Keeping a tight hold on Bella's collar, I waited on high ground while Simon disappeared into the darkness below. I watched him flash his light along her side then shout up to me, "The fenders are still in place, so she's okay. I'm going to pop inside and check things out."

I held my breath until he came back up top a few moments later and reported, "All good below deck though a few things got shuffled around. Let's get back to the house."

His light bobbed up and down as he scrambled back up on the dock then headed our way at a run. I met him halfway while Bella sniffed among the rocks until she flushed out a ginger tabby cat that hissed loudly then sped away

"That must be one of the feral cats Matilda mentioned," I told Simon as I shone my light that way, "And not the friendly sort like Cinda."

"Bella and Cinda were great friends," Simon added. "I wonder if she'll make another appearance."

"I would love that more than you can possibly imagine," I replied as tears gathered in my eyes. Swiping them away, I added, "I think I just felt a drop of rain. Let's get out of here before the heavens open up."

By then, the wind had picked up again with a keen, cold edge. The house loomed above us...a darker shade of black than the night sky. Suddenly, a light appeared in an upper window. A flickering, reddish light that grew stronger with each passing moment.

"What room is that?" I asked Simon.

"Not sure. Maybe the Red Room, but that's just a guess. Hey! There's someone or something standing there!"

A tall figure was silhouetted against the light and *seemed* to be looking right at me though I couldn't possibly know that. "I bet that's Geoffrey Blackthorne and vote we sleep downstairs with Matilda," I replied as a cold tingling sensation worked its way through me. "We must have stirred things up when we found his portrait."

"We have to confront what we fear, or we'll never finish what we came here to do. You sleep downstairs. I'm going to sleep in our bed and deal with whatever happens."

I shook my head. "Not going to happen. If something snatches you, I could never forgive myself and that goes double for Bella. "

"Bella always had been rather fond of me," he replied with a wry grin I could sense if not see. "Okay. We'll do this together. I won't let anything or anyone hurt you."

"You've told me that before and can't guarantee it. Nobody can no matter how much I wish otherwise."

We took the trail back to the kitchen where Matilda was 'puttin' on the kettle'. "Like a cup of hot chamomile tea before I shut me eyes. Soothes a body, it does. Would you like some?"

We declined...said our good nights...and hurried up the back stairs to our room. A fire had been lit, and the bed turned down. It was warm and almost cozy *if* I could forget what I had seen in the window just a few doors down...*if* that had not been the Red Room...*if* the figure we had seen was not Geoffrey's. Those were a lot of 'ifs' I hoped were true. I could still feel the strange pull he had exerted on me when I saw his portrait and feared what the night would bring.

"At least the power is still on, and we won't be fumbling around in the dark," I somehow managed to murmur as cheerfully as possible.

He nodded then pulled me into his arms. His dark eyes were intense as he told me, "I meant what I said. I'll do my best to keep you safe. If things get to the point where I can't do that, I'll get you outta here."

I tried to smile but failed. "The same goes for me. I have your back. But right now, this team of two needs to head to the bathroom, which is just a few doors down from where we *might* have seen Geoffrey."

A short time later, we were back in our room where we locked the door...stuffed in the rag...then climbed into bed with Bella snuggled between us.

"A penny for your thoughts and feelings," Simon whispered as he reached across the space between us and grabbed my hand.

"A penny is next to worthless these days, and you don't want to know."

"Then just tell me if you feel up to doing this? Can see all this through to the end?"

"As I said before, I like Matilda more than ever and want her to be safe. I feel sorry for Celia and want to reunite her with her son, and then there's you. I won't let you do this alone."

"All of which doesn't exactly tell me what I want to know."

I sighed. "Just go to sleep. I'll be awake for awhile and will let you know if something happens."

"Since I can't get a straight answer out of you, I might as well," he replied then rolled over on his side. Only moments later, I heard his soft snore.

I lay there for a long time listening to the crackle of the flames...Bella's occasional dream induced 'woof'...and, of course, Simon. The storm had arrived and fierce bursts of wind driven rain rattled the windowpanes in their ancient casements. Lightning slashed across the sky and thunder boomed directly overhead, but I wasn't all *that* worried. The house had withstood storms for centuries though parts of it were now falling into the sea according to Matilda. There were other things more pressing to fear…a long list of them. I tried to divert my thoughts from where they were headed as drowsiness over took me. The steeple clock on the mantel had just chimed ten times when I drifted off to sleep.

I'm not sure what woke me, but something had. I slid up in bed and looked around the room. Nothing had changed. Simon and Bella were still fast asleep. The storm had somewhat abated. The fire still burned brightly…and then it happened. The candles on the mantel lit one by one illuminating the painting above it. It had been a seascape. Now it was the portrait we had seen in the attic. The dark figure on horseback seemed to be smiling at me and then to my profound horror stepped out of the painting and floated my way. I wanted to scream...I wanted to shake Simon...even Bella awake, but I couldn't move any part of me as he came closer and closer whistling some tune I didn't know.

His dark gaze pinned me against the headboard as he took a seat on the edge of the bed.

"You are very lovely with your beautiful gray eyes and hair of flame. I want you...every bit of you."

I tried shaking my head...opening my mouth...but again nothing happened. I simply sat there like a lifeless doll though the horror I felt must have shown in those gray eyes, for he next whispered close to my ear, "I will take my time with you. Seduce you until you beg

97

me to pleasure you. The kind you could never know with the one lying there. You are mine. Remember that should you weaken. Betray me with him, and he will die."

I managed a muffled 'no', which made him smile. It was a most beguiling smile.

"A kiss and then I'll be gone...for the nonce." and with that said Geoffrey leaned down and kissed me. It was the lightest of touches and yet it burned. "Now sleep. This will seem but a dream in the morning, but I will be back. Believe that. You are meant to be mine for eternity as you must already know."

CHAPTER FOUR

I don't know how, or when I fell asleep. It was Simon who woke me with a kiss. "Wake up, sleepy head. Time to get moving."

I murmured something incomprehensible even to me as another image flickered through my mind. Other dark eyes. Seductive, beguiling eyes without the smile I saw in Simon's.

"You look all befuddled. Did you have a bad dream?"

"That painting over the mantel became Geoffrey's portrait. He stepped out of it and sat on the edge of the bed then told me I belonged to him. That I must never betray him, or you would die."

"It was a nightmare conjured up by all we've seen and heard since we came here," Simon scoffed. "Best cure for one of those is to jump into a new day, so climb out of bed...or better yet...stay where you are while I head down to the bathroom and get cleaned up."

"What about sticking together."

"It's broad daylight if you don't count the thick cloud cover. You should be safe for a few moments. I'll make it quick."

After grabbing a change of clothes, he left while I looked around the room. Nothing had changed. The seascape above the mantel was still there. Bella was sleeping next to me. I didn't feel...sense any ghostly presence. I slid deeper under the covers and sighed. A new day was beginning on Blackthorne Island, and I feared what it would bring.

Sleep was beginning to overtake me once again when Simon returned to report, "All's quiet out there. No howling beast crawling down the hall or Geoffrey Blackthorne lurking about. I'll walk you to the bathroom and stand guard outside."

"What happened to 'it's broad daylight and should be safe'?"

"I can risk me but not you. Time to get moving. Bella needs her morning walk if we can get her out of that warm bed."

My shower was quick. The hot water soon became tepid and then cold. I toweled off then scrambled into my clothes. A short time later, we all headed down the backstairs towards the kitchen. The smell of coffee reached us first then Matilda's cheerful greeting.

"Grand to see you," she called as she gestured to the table where three cups were waiting. "Heard the plumbin' bangin' so knew you were up. Coffee has almost finished its perk. Will be starting breakfast soon. Checked on the Mistress a bit ago, and she's still asleep after her ramblin' about last night. Went outside, she did, which don't happen but once in a while. Walked right up to the cliff edge. Me heart was in me mouth wonderin' what she was about and how to stop her without givin' her a fright when she turned around and walked back up to her room. Climbed right into bed, she did, wet to the skin and all. I should have woke her and got her a dry gown, but...."

Her hesitation had me supplying, "You thought it best to let it be considering what we saw yesterday. A wise decision in my book."

I helped as much as she would let me with the breakfast preparation while Simon took Bella for a walk. They had just returned when Bart flew into the kitchen and perched on the mantel squawking hoarsely, "Blood! Blood and bones! Awk! Blood and bones! Where's my dinner?"

Matilda smiled ruefully. "Let me get him a bite to eat and some water. Not sure where he's been all night."

"Heave ho. Down below," was his reply

Once fed, a screeching Bart disappeared down the back hall while we ate breakfast and made plans for the day.

"I'd really like to see that cave," Simon told me. "If it's as dark down there as most caves are, we might see some activity. The question is: How do we get there? There must be an entrance somewhere in this house."

"Never come across it whilst I were cleanin'," Matilda told him as she poured us all a second cup of coffee. "There's a lot of this place I've not been in. Rooms not worth messin' with since there's no one to use them. You should have seen it before they did what little they did to fix it up. Make sure you stay clear of the west wing. That's the side the sea's claimin' bit by bit, and it's not safe. It be easy to get lost until you get your bearings. Sometimes even when you think you have 'em."

"Thanks for the warning, but I won't take it off the table if we don't find the entrance elsewhere," Simon told her.

"I wouldn't be unhappy if we never find it," I added. "That cave must be a nest of horrors."

"Probably just full of ghosts who did no wrong. Prisoners who couldn't escape while alive and didn't escape after death for whatever reason. We're here to free them. That's why we have to go down there," he reminded me as if I needed it.

Before I could summon a reply, a fragment of a tune I had heard somewhere drifted through my mind and then I remembered. It was the one Geoffrey had whistled when he visited me in my nightmare.....if it really was one. More and more, I had my doubts. It had felt all too real.

Simon interrupted where that was headed. "What's wrong? You look sort of weird."

I shook my head. "It's nothing. Just remembering my dream."

"That's all it was. Best spend your time forgetting it."

"I hope I can," I managed to murmur as Matilda rose to her feet and headed towards the swing door.

"While you two finish eatin', let me check on the Mistress and see what she fancies this mornin'," she called over her shoulder. "Be back in two shakes."

"Do you want us to go with you?" I asked.

"No need. I'll be right as rain," she called back.

"She's a lot perkier than I would be if I had to go up there," I told Simon who was dribbling syrup over the last pancake.

"She's pretty amazing. Still here after all that's happened. You don't see that kind of loyalty very often. Soon as I finish this we need to start looking. Where's the most likely spot?"

"When they laid the foundation for this house, they must have broken through to the cave at some point. Your 'most likely' could be anywhere including the forbidden west wing."

Simon sighed. "We could cover a lot more ground if we separated, but that's not going to happen. Just a couple more bites and we'll head down the main hall as far as it goes then systematically work our way back towards the kitchen."

"Or the reverse, since we're already here," I had to point out.

So, that is what we did. Room after room turned up nothing. Those that Matilda hadn't cleaned were layered in centuries of dust, damp, and rat droppings that interested Bella who sniffed around for their origin. Past the main staircase, the ceiling had collapsed in several, so Bella was left in the hall while we took our chances without result. The function of some were apparent...offices...study...summer parlors or winter parlors...there was enough for both and some to spare. That was even a grand ballroom shrouded in darkness behind its crumbling velvet drapes. Other rooms had no apparent function. Just empty, forgotten spaces succumbing to centuries of neglect. We took our time in the library looking for sliding or pivoting bookcases but found none.

"That doesn't mean there's not one here," Simon pointed out.

"It just means we haven't found it yet. It will take days...even weeks or months to explore all of this place, and, if the entrance is well hidden, we may never find it. How about a break for lunch and a cup of coffee? Maybe take Bella out for a bit?"

"The best idea I've heard all morning. Walk first...lunch second."

We left by the front door. Almost immediately, Bella spotted something in the long grass and gave chase. We followed her... trying to keep her in sight... and found ourselves on the trail that led to the derelict house we had visited two nights ago. I wondered if it would look different in daylight. Less evil. Maybe sort of ordinary. Just another old enormous, rambling cottage the elements had claimed. Not that it mattered. I had no desire to find out after what we had already encountered there.

"For an old girl, she still has some speed," Simon told me as we watched an ear flapping Bella continue her pursuit. "If I'm not mistaken, there's a bit of blue sky just up there to the left."

There was...a mere smidge....but it offered hope the sun still existed when I was beginning to have my doubts.

"We've found nothing so far and only brushed the tip of the iceberg room wise," I reminded Simon as we saw a tongue lolling, tired Bella trot back our way.

"At the rate we're going, we may never find it, but your 'iceberg' analogy, weird as it was, gave me an idea. There's every chance this cave opens on the sea. Maybe at low tide we can check out the cliffs... use the sailboat's inflatable to get close to shore."

"Are you crazy?" I asked him sharply. "The waves would smash us against the rocks, and we'd be joining the ghosts of Blackthorne Island."

"I've handled it in some pretty rough water. You can...."

"Not going to happen," I cut in before he could finish. "Let's get some lunch and decide where to look next."

***

A short time later, we were eating lunch when Matilda asked if we had found the cave entrance. Simon told her where we had searched and turned up nothing.

I was half listening when a sudden thought occurred to me. "Like idiots, we've been focused on the walls. What if the entrance is in the floor?"

Simon grimaced wryly as he slipped a tidbit from his plate to a waiting Bella. "There could be a trap door under the rugs in any of the rooms we've already searched."

"Not to mention all those we haven't."

"We need to go back for a redo," he told me. "Let's finish up here and get going."

Armed with our flashlights, we left Bella with Matilda and began our search anew. One by one, we reentered the rooms we had previously checked and rolled back the heavy, dusty, rat chewed rugs. A long time later, we found a hidden iron ring in a room where the ceiling had collapsed along the far wall.

"Are you ready to do this?" Simon asked me as he watched my reaction closely.

I took a deep breath before I answered. "We came here to do a job that I'm more and more convinced needs doing."

"Then here goes," he replied with a grim smile as he seized the ring. At first, the trap door refused to budge then swung open on a prolonged and eerie screech. Together we flashed our lights into the gaping hole. A rickety wooden staircase descended into the profound darkness at the bottom.

"Still with me?" Simon asked way too cheerfully in my opinion.

"Like glue," I told him hoping he didn't notice the slight quaver in my reply.

"Thata girl," he murmured as he began his descent. "Stay where you are until I make sure this staircase is safe. It has quite a wobble."

Leaning over the edge, I watched his light dim with distance then heard him shout, "Come on down. It's a long way, so be very careful. The railing is none too solid and there's a step missing here and there. I can smell the sea and hear breakers, so there must be an outside opening somewhere close."

A shiver shot up my spine as I slowly began my descent. Every step brought an increasing awareness that we were far from alone.

I had reached the bottom where he pulled me close and whispered, "I have a strong sense we're being watched. Are you feeling it, too?"

"Yep. There's something down here. Something dark and evil." I whispered back.

"Perhaps the source of whatever possesses Ms. Blackthorne from time to time."

"You mean a you know what that starts with a 'D' I don't want to say out loud kind of thing?"

"Could be," Simon replied with a grim smile. "Let's just keep moving. "

We flashed out lights around the huge space chiseled out by water leaking down from above and a voracious sea over eons of time. Primitive wooden doors led to other rooms, but we followed the reflections that flickered on the walls and ceiling...the sound of the crashing waves... to another chamber where mounds of long dead seaweed had washed inside. Tangled amongst them were scattered remnants of the boats that had been wrecked on the rocks offshore. We were threading our way through when something brushed against me leg. To my horror, it was the skeletal hand of some poor soul lost to the sea. Embedded in a veil of seaweed, his empty eye sockets seemed to watch me as I gingerly stepped around him. Sweeping the area with my light, I soon discovered he was not alone. Others had been washed inside. Most were a scattering of bones, but here and there more 'vacant' eyes seemed to chide us for intruding...for being alive.

Noticing my reaction, Simon told me, "Just some poor guys who didn't make it. Nothing to be afraid of."

"I wonder how many of their souls linger here."

"We could hold a séance down here and find out."

I think my heart stopped for all of three seconds before I managed to say, "Please tell me you're joking?"

"I was...sort of. Just a thought to tuck away," he replied as we reached the opening and looked out on a ribbon of white sand beach that the low tide had created.

I stepped through and looked around to get my bearings. "Look! There's the dock!"

"Which made it that much easier for Captain Bones to unload his stolen goods and bring them here," Simon added as he yanked me back inside. "Might mention, standing *under* a crumbling cliff is another good way to get yourself killed. Let's go check out what's behind those doors."

We retraced our steps back to the main chamber and flashed our lights around then headed to a narrow door that stood ajar. A broken, antique padlock lay on the floor next to it. Inside, smashed wooden crates were scattered amongst old trunks that spilled their time and damp rotted contents onto the floor. Rats had nested in one and fled at our approach.

"Looks like someone looted this place and took whatever was valuable" I murmured as I picked up a broken doll from the floor.

Terror and sadness washed over me the moment I touched it. The little girl who once loved it had come to a bad end, and I gently tucked it back in its trunk.

"Might have been those who put a stop to John Long's reign of terror, or maybe looters who came afterwards," Simon told me as he headed for the door. "Let's see what else we find in the other rooms."

What we found was much the same. Empty and broken casks...smashed crates...the scattered bits and pieces that had belonged to the now long dead. The last room was different. Blanketed in a strong feeling of despair, hopelessness and grief, it was larger than the others and jammed with the remnants of mildewed, straw pallets. A hole in the floor must have served as their toilet. Shackles were embedded in the stone wall along one side. One set still held the skeletal remains of a man dressed in tattered knee breeches and rat gnawed buckled shoes. Thin strand of black hair still clung to his skull, and his lower jaw had fallen to the floor. An overwhelming sense of rage engulfed me and sent me scrambling from the room.

I was leaning against the wall on the other side of the door when Simon joined me. "What's going on? Why did you run out of there like that?"

It took me a moment before I could answer. "It was a cumulative experience and the chained man was the topper. I'm okay now. I just need to get out of here."

He waited at the bottom of the stairs as I sped to the top. A few moments later, he joined me there then dropped the trap door back into place.

My heart was still hammering wildly when I told him, "I promised to see this through with you. We have a deal, but *please* don't ever go down there again."

"I can't promise that. Tell me exactly what happened."

I drew in a long, slow breath then told him, "The dead just seemed to keep pulling at me in a way I've never experienced before and never want to again. That's as close as I can come to explaining it. Let's get back to Matilda and Bella. Back to the living...at least for awhile."

I was very glad when we reached the kitchen, and its almost normal atmosphere. Matilda was working on dinner while a hopeful Bella begged for scraps.

"Did you find what you were lookin' for?" Matilda called to us over her shoulder.

"Yep," I replied with a wry grimace, "and a bit more than we bargained for."

"Let me pop this in the oven, and you can tell me all about it."

She joined us at the table a short time later, and we gave her the edited version of what we had found. Grisly details were omitted.

"'Tis indeed a dark tale to be told of this old house and them who haunt it...pirates and murderers and such...then there's himself who touches me at night when he can find me."

"Still?" I asked.

Her black curls bobbed up and down as she nodded. "Aye, but he doesn't chase me down any more when I run like a rabbit."

I didn't tell her of my own experience with Geoffrey. I chose to think Simon was right. It had only been a dream conjured up by all we had seen and heard. I'd only been half listened to Matilda as she rambled on when something she had said caught my attention.

"I'm sorry. Would you repeat that?"

"Just sayin' in them books I read, there's always secret doors behind wardrobes and such. Could be one in the Mistress' room. The wardrobe in there be original to the house, and the workmen couldn't budge it when she wanted it moved."

I remembered the one in our room with an increasing sense of horror. The need to know if it hid a secret entrance became a compulsion. Scrambling to my feet, I snatched up my flashlight...tossed Simon his... and headed down the back hall at a run. I took the stairs two at a time and reached our door a moment later with Simon and Bella right on my heels. Throwing it open, I sped to the huge French armoire that took up most of the sidewall.

"Come on, Simon! Help me move this thing!"

"You know you are behaving like a crazy person. What's with you?"

"I need to know if something has access to where we sleep at night."

"Ghosts can walk through doors, so you can't mean them."

"What about Ms. Blackthorne when she's possessed? She doesn't like us all that much and has an armoire that doesn't move. Put the two together and it spells very unwelcome nighttime visitor."

Simon sighed. "If it makes you feel any better, we'll check it out."

Bella watched from the comfort of the bed while we both pushed against it with no results.

"Okay. That didn't go exactly great," Simon needlessly pointed out. "Let's check inside and see what we find."

Opening the door, we shoved aside our clothes and flashed our lights over the back wall with its row of ornate clothes hooks.

I stepped inside and rapped on the panels then reported to a stooped Simon who was hovering over my shoulder, "That sounds hollow to me."

"Yep. I'm going to yank and twist those hooks. One of them might be some kind of release mechanism."

Nothing seemed to work until he reached the last one on the far end. The back panel pivoted open and a burst of fetid air that smelled of death and decay wafted out from somewhere.

"Well, that did it," Simon murmured as he flashed his light into the dark opening.

"I wonder where it leads."

"One way to find out. Are you up for it?"

I blamed an abundance of adrenaline for the 'yes' that popped out of my mouth.

"Okay. Let's check it out."

111

Bella tried to follow us, but Simon shut her out. "Looks like we could head left or take those stairs that look interesting," he told me as he flashed his light into the darkness below.

"Or forget about the whole thing," I suggested…not that he listened.

He led the way down the wooden stairs that creaked and groaned under our weight then down a very narrow passageway that threaded its way between the stone walls. Cobwebs fluttered in the breeze we created. Centuries of dust and debris littered the floor including a partially decomposed rat which…I hoped… was the source of the smell. Side corridors branched off in all directions, and here and there, a wooden staircase led up into the darkness overhead. Paneled doors punctuated the sides at random. Peepholes were more common. Checking out some of both, we discovered more empty, derelict rooms and little else.

"Whoever built this place had a penchant for voyeurism," I whispered. "These passageways are an absolute maze that could lead anywhere in this rambling mausoleum."

"Yep. Let's keep going this way and see where we end up," Simon whispered back.

My adrenaline rush had deserted me by then, so I told him, "Maybe we should turn back. We could easily get lost in here."

"Not if we keep going straight. Come on. It's amazing down here."

"We should have found a way to mark the staircase we came down, so we'll know which one it is when we turn back... which will hopefully be soon," I murmured.

"Good idea, but too late now. We should be able to follow our footprints in all this rubble."

So, we continued on and ended up at a 't' intersection where I told him, "Okay. Time to turn around and get out of here. This whole place is creeping me out."

"Oh, come on! Just a wee bit farther. See! I'll mark the wall this time, so we can't get lost," he coaxed.

He flashed his light to the right and headed that way. I reluctantly followed but not before I told him, "Look! If something horrific happens, it will be on you."

Though still harboring all of the usual cobwebs, dust, dirt, rat droppings, peepholes, doors, and the occasional long dead carcass, this passage seemed more traveled, and I wondered why. I knew the answer would only add to my growing terror, so I put it down to my overactive writer's imagination and let it go at that.

Simon soon punctured my bubble. "Looks like someone's been through here a few times judging from those prints in the dust," he murmured as he bent down and examined them more closely. "Too indistinct. Could be human or something else entirely."

"A something else like Ms. Blackthorne who may have easy access to where we sleep," I pointed out.

"Too true. Maybe we can do something about that when we get back. Look! There's just one more door before we come to a dead end."

"Poor choice of words."

"Let's check it out then turn back."

Neither of us was too surprised to see it open on yet another room devoid of furniture and layered in dust.

"We could be anywhere inside these walls," I told him. "What are the chances we'll actually find a room we recognize?"

He laughed. "I didn't see the skeletal remains of those lost between the walls if we don't count the rats. I really want to see if we can find our way to Ms. Blackthorne's room, which means we need to head up to the second floor. We'll double back and hope my sense of direction isn't as bad as yours. I'll continue to mark our route, so we can retrace our steps if necessary."

We headed to the intersection then made the turn that would take us back the way we had come and continued on till Simon told me, "I think there's a chance we might be in the general area we need. There's a stairway over there. Let's head up and see what we find."

What we found was more of the same until we came to a door that had once been sealed up. Blocks of stone lay scattered about, and we picked our way through them carefully.

"I bet this leads to Geoffrey Blackthorne's prison. If so, we've almost come full circle," Simon told me as he slid it open, and we flashed our lights inside. As he had predicted, it was the Red Room and empty as far as I could tell.

"Now that we know where we are," I suggested. "I think we should stop crawling around in these walls."

"Come on. It's a bit of Gothic fun and not much farther to Ms. Blackthorne's room now that we have our bearings. I really want to see if her armoire is another entrance to these passageways like you thought."

"If it turns out I'm right, we need to do something about it or find another place to sleep."

We continue on down the passage between the walls. Simon counted the doors, and we made only two mistakes before he whispered, "This must be it. We need to be very quiet from this point on."

He opened the narrow door slowly, and I followed him inside the huge armoire past a pile of shoes and hanging clothes that smelled of mothballs and lavender.

"Looks like you were right," he whispered as he eased one door open a mere crack, and we looked around. The gray light of late evening shone through the windows. All was quiet. The bed was empty.

"She could be in her bathroom," I whispered just as a door on the far wall popped open.

Ms. Blackthorne swept into the room humming a tune, which became a muttered, "Now where did I put my shawl. Can't go down for dinner in this drafty pile of stones without my shawl and wool undies."

She continued to mutter under her breath as she searched the pile of clothes she'd left on a chair, but I wasn't really listening. I remembered that tune. It was the same one Geoffrey Blackthorne was whistling when he stepped out of the portrait. A shiver ran through me. Was he the one who possessed her and not a demon?

Simon and I both heaved a sigh of relief when she found her missing shawl then grabbed her cane and 'thumped' her way out the door. We both had been afraid the armoire was the next place she'd search.

"After we've finished checking out this room, we'll leave the conventional way," Simon told me as he plucked a cobweb out of my hair.

"More than fine by me," I replied with a sigh of relief. "Since we're here, let's see what we can find."

Our search turned up nothing helpful except a badly drawn sketch of something right out of a horror movie. If I squinted the right way, it looked a bit like Geoffrey Blackthorne...the long dead version.

"She must have drawn it," I whispered. "Perhaps trying to recapture someone she saw?"

"You know who it looks like as well as I do, which makes me believe that *he* is the one possessing her," Simon replied as he folded it up and shoved it in his pocket.

116

"I might add that the tune she was humming was the same one he was whistling in my all too real nightmare. What are you going to do with that sketch?"

"Not sure exactly. Maybe just let things play out and see what happens."

"Whatever that means!" I replied with a flash of irritation. "If you show it to her, she'll know we've been snooping in her room, and the consequences are bound to be ugly."

He smiled wryly. "Yep. Now let's get cleaned up and changed before we turn up for dinner."

"The best idea you've had so far. Crawling around inside those walls has given me a big case of the 'ick'."

I was the last one out of the bathroom after a quick shower and change. Simon was waiting for me in the hall. "Do you think I still smell like dead rat?" I muttered sniffing the end of my still damp ponytail.

He leaned closer and took a sniff of his own. "You smell about the same."

My gray eyes narrowed. "Which means?"

"What I said. Let's go."

We took the back stairs down to the kitchen where Matilda was loading the serving cart with the first course. An excited Bella ran to meet us. We both hunkered down to pet her as Matilda told us, "Bart flew out the door when I took Bella out and hasn't come back. The Mistress has been askin' about him, and I been afraid to tell her. It don't take much to set her off, and she be already in a right bad

117

mood especially with you being late and all. Been keeping things warm, but she be tired of waitin' and wants to be served now."

"Thanks for the warning," I told her with a smile. "And thanks for looking after Bella. We'll trod lightly" then added in a whispered aside to Simon, "Yet another reason to keep Geoffrey's sketch under wraps."

He was smiling enigmatically as we headed down the short hall and through the swing door. Dressed in her usual black everything from shawl to shoes, Ms. Blackthorne sniffed loudly and waved us to our seats. "In my day, it was customary to be punctual for meals. I'd almost eaten without you. Now tell me what progress you've made with this ghost hunt."

I was more than surprised when Simon pulled the sketch from his pocket and told her, "We found this in your room. Did you draw this? Do you know who it is?"

She rose awkwardly to her feet then shouted, "How dare you enter my room and forage through my personal belongings! How dare you...."

"We dare because we are here to do a job," Simon cut in more calmly than I would have. "There isn't an inch of this island...this house...that should be off limits. Now answer my question: Who is this?"

She sat down hard sending a billow of lavender scent our way. "I've never seen that before and don't want to see it again. It's monstrous!"

"We think it's the dead version of Geoffrey Blackthorne," I told her as I watched her closely.

"And how would you know what he looks like living or dead?" she snapped back.

It was Simon who replied. "We found his portrait in the attic. Did you draw this sketch?"

"Quit badgering me! I know nothing of it! Matilda!" she shouted thumping her cane on the floor. "Attend to me at once! That blasted girl's wits have gone woolgathering most of the time. Never around when I need her. Matilda!"

The swing door banged open, and Matilda entered the room at a run. "I'm here!' she managed to utter before she was silenced with, "Bring a tray to the front parlor where the company is nonexistent and therefore less offensive!"

"Perhaps we should just pack up and leave this place. Oh, wait! We can't do that can we? Someone sabotaged our boat," I reminded her with a trace of sarcasm…well, maybe more than a trace.

Her eyes narrowed to mere slits as she pinned me in her gaze. "Don't test me, girl! Finish what you came to do, or stay on your boat till it's time to leave and do nothing. Your choice."

It was Simon who told her, "There are people...spirits we care about in this place who need our help. Trying to accomplish that may well prove to be more dangerous than you can possibly imagine. Your attitude doesn't improve the situation."

To our surprise, she smiled...a bit grimly...but it was there. "You young people have more spunk that I gave you credit for. Yes, that

119

is my sketch drawn from memory of a nightmare I had. Perhaps I will remain seated, and you can fill me in on what you've uncovered to date."

So, that is what we did. Of course, there were things we omitted like the network of secret passageways that took us to her room. Hopefully, she didn't already know about them, and I was holding the good thought. I also didn't tell her about my dream. To date, the only one who knew about that was Simon, and I wanted to keep it that way. We did mention the figure we had seen in the Red Room's window, which horrified her enough.

We had nearly finished when Matilda opened the door letting in Bart who landed on a smiling Ms. Blackthorne's shoulder and pecked at the jet earring she was wearing.

"Where have you been, you old rascal?" she asked him affectionately.

"Awwk! Dead and gone! Dead and gone! Fetch my shawl!"

Matilda told her, "Flew in… he did…when I opened the door to sweep the stoop. Didn't mention he'd been gone before, Ma'am, 'cause I didn't want to worry you. He's been fed and watered, but didn't eat much. Maybe he just wanted to see you."

"Of course, he did! He's my darling pretty boy, aren't you?"

"Where's the gold? Awwwk! Hoist the sail! Over the side with ye, matey!"

Their strange conversation continued, and I whispered to Simon, "The more I listen to Bart, the more I wonder if he came off a pirate ship. Is there such a thing as modern day pirates in these waters?"

"Boats have gone missing from time to time, and there have been reports of others being followed...threatened."

"All of which you neglected to tell me about when we made this deal."

He smiled ruefully. "Yep. Sorry about that, but would you have gone through with this if I had added that to the mix?"

I knew in my heart that no matter what the dangers were, I wouldn't have let him do this alone, but told him an emphatic, "No!" then added, " Let's take Bella for a walk. It looks like there's another storm coming, and this may be our last chance to check on the boat before all hell breaks loose again."

"Agreed. You do know there are a couple of other possibilities as far as Bart's concerned."

"Such as?"

Simon shrugged. "Someone thought teaching him that Long John Silver imitation was cute or....."

"Or what?"

"Maybe he's possessed by one of those who haunt this place. Just saying."

"Now that's a comforting thought!" I replied tartly. "Let's excuse ourselves and leave Ms. Blackthorne to her tête-à-tête with the formerly missing Bart who may be a long dead pirate."

We stepped outside a few minutes later where a joyful Bella spotted a flock of terns and gave chase. Night was fast approaching and lightning lit the western sky where fast moving black clouds were headed our way. The sound of the rising wind and restless waves hammering the cliffs accompanied us as we took the path down to the harbor where Simon checked the boat and reported all was in order.

"I really, really wish we could sleep onboard tonight," I shouted down to him from the dock.

"The offer is still on the table," he replied as he climbed up next to me. "If you can stand the pitching and rolling, you can stay here with Bella, and I'll sleep up at the house."

"And you remember my answer. Let's get back inside and see what we can do to secure the armoire doors. I noticed neither one of us mentioned the passageways to Ms. Blackthorne."

Simon grinned wryly. "And I think we both know why. I might mention yet again that no matter what we do to secure those doors, it won't stop a ghost."

"Like I didn't know that already to my regret."

We rounded up Bella and headed back. I was sure Simon felt as reluctant I did to reenter the grim looking mansion that seemed to mushroom from the rocks and earth it stood on. I glanced up at the window where we had seen the figure...the Red Room. He was there again, and I felt the same kind of strange pull...as though he was looking right at me...telling me he would be coming for me soon. Every molecule in my body seemed to scream, "Don't go back in there!", but that wouldn't happen. Simon needed me, and I wouldn't let him down.

Matilda was waiting for us when we came back inside. "I had me ear to the door when you were talkin' to the Mistress about what you seen, and it fair gave me the shivers. It must be himself up there in the window, and it might be him you saw at the old place. When the boat comes, I want to be on it, but only if you can convince her to come with."

"Maybe we can send the spirits into the Light and cleanse this place, so you both can stay," Simon told her. "That's the job we came to do."

Matilda smiled weakly and brushed away her tears with the back of her hand. "I don't know how much more I can handle. I hardly sleep at all now."

"Maybe we can put a cot in our room, and you could...." I began, but she cut me short.

"I couldn't be doin' that! That wouldn't be at all fit and proper!" She tried to add a second smile but without much success.

"Just so you know, the offer is always open," Simon told her.

We talked for a while longer then said our "good nights" and headed up to our room where Simon sat down on the bed and leaned back against the headboard. Patting the spot next to him, he told me, "We need to get started tonight. We have a sense of what we're dealing with...now we need to do something about it. What do you think about a séance up here instead of in the cave?"

To say I was horrified would be a colossal understatement. "I think it's a bad idea. You saw what happened at Greystone, and

Wendy was experienced in that kind of thing. What if your séance makes things worse?"

"How much worse can they be?"

"Lots worse!"

He grimaced wryly. "I'm open to ideas at this point."

I tried to think of something and came up with...well, nothing. "When do you plan on trying all this?"

"The midnight hour. Now let's look for the key to that armoire... *if* there is one. That should stop a possessed Ms. Blackthorne if she plans a visit. Tomorrow, we'll unload our equipment from the boat and set up some cameras and EVP recorders for a start. They will give us an even better idea of what we are dealing with here."

We found the key was under the mantel clock. After he locked the doors, Simon burnt some sage and recited the prayer of protection as we walked around the room.

"And will that really help?" a hopeful me asked

"The sage thing works unless the spirits are deeply entrenched, which I fear they may be here."

"And the prayer? Evil still found us at Greystone."

"That's where faith comes into it. We survived the horror there."

"And now we're facing yet another one," I murmured.

His dark eyes were troubled when he told me fiercely, "I wish I hadn't brought you here...kidnapped you, but I was desperate. You kept shoving me back whenever we got close, so I came up with this harebrained scheme."

I sighed. "It's okay. I might have protested a lot...maybe a whole lot...but I would have come anyway before I'd let you do this on your own. And besides, I've learned to sail. Left the safety of the shore and was out on the sea that I loved, which was quite frightening sometimes, but awesome in every sense of the word. We have a job to do for Matilda...the trapped spirits...and even for old Ms. Blackthorne who is possessed through no fault of her own."

I was about to rattle on when he swept me into his very strong arms and kissed me. It was the gentle kind and then he whispered close to my ear, "No matter what it takes, I won't let anything happen to you. I promise."

He released me far too quickly, and I hid my disappointment by saying, "I've lost count of how many times you promised me that, so by now you know my reply. About that séance? Who's the medium going to be?"

"That would be you. As you no doubt have noticed, spirits seem attracted to you. You'll be great."

I was far from convinced of that, but managed to say, "Okay, but I'm going to need a refresher course."

We decided to try for some sleep before midnight, but remain dressed in case we had to leave in a hurry. Simon fell asleep with his usual ease while I lay there listening to the wind shriek as it swept the rocky island...the crash and boom of thunder...Bella's occasional 'woof' and Simon's usual snoring. I tried courting sleep by closing my eyes and counting to a hundred backward. When that didn't work, I slid up in bed and watched the flickering flames in the grate...the dance of light on the ceiling...while I kept a watchful eye on the seascape above the mantel. At some point, sleep must have claimed me, for the next thing I knew Simon was shaking me awake.

"Almost midnight and we have some things to set up, or were you planning to sleep through till morning?"

"I wish," I managed to mutter as I glared at him under half closed lids then pulled his pillow over my face. From under it, I added a muffled, "I think this is a very bad idea."

"It's the only one we have," he told me. Following a brief struggle, he yanked the pillow off and peered down at me. "Up you get and make sure you are wearing your St. Benedict medal."

My sigh was both deep and prolonged. "It's tucked under my sweater."

"Great. We have the candle we need and can use that little table in the corner."

"We only have the one chair," I pointed out.

"I'll grab it, and you can sit on the edge of the bed."

It took only a minute or two to set things up while Bella watched from a warm spot on the hearth. It was almost midnight when I lit the candle he'd placed in the middle of the table.

"Okay, I'm trying to remember how Wendy did it," I told him as we joined hands. "She started with the protection prayer, which you will have to handle since I only remember bits of it, and it needs to be done right."

126

"Okay, I'll do that part. The rest is on you. '*We pray that the power of Love encircles all those gathered here. That it will protect us and guard us from all evil and prevent any attachments that would follow us. May that Higher Power light our path and guide us through whatever may come our way this night and always.*' Now we both ask for the protection of a Greater Power."

So, that is what we did...each in our own way. "Now what?" I asked. "Wendy was the real thing. I haven't got the foggiest notion of what to do next."

"Do what your gut tells you."

My *gut* told me to take a deep breath to steady my nerves and try calling them. "If there are any spirits with us here tonight, please let us know." Nothing happened though the temperature *might* have dropped a bit. I tried again with the same result.

"This isn't working," I whispered.

"It's colder," Simon whispered back.

So, I hadn't imagined it, I thought, just as four things happened. The fire in the hearth flared up then died back down to mere embers. Bella howled piteously then dived under the bed. The casement window flew open, and the wind rushed in billowing the drapes and threatening to extinguish the violently flickering candle, which was now our only source of light. A tall pillar of utter blackness followed the burst of wind into the room.

"How is that for a dramatic entrance?" an all too familiar voice asked as a glowing figure began to take form. "Pray tell, why have you two summoned me here on this stormy night? Or was that for the general populace and not me in particular?"

Once again, I couldn't seem to move…mouth included. Simon's hands tightened on mine when he replied, "I'm Simon, and this is Jodie. We're here to help the spirits trapped on this island."

"I was not addressing you, Sir! My queries were intended for her. She is quite lovely even with her mouth agape like that, isn't she? Courtesy demands I introduce myself, but I am quite sure you both already know who I am…Jodie in particular," he told us as he took a seat on the windowsill and swung one booted foot back and forth. "There are others here. A lot of others such as the pirate who moved in uninvited and his mistress…Celia?…who weeps and wails incessantly much to my distaste. Did you know he used to be known as Gentleman John when he began his career? That changed after he landed here. He became…well, you saw the evidence of his moral perversion and greed below. I know you did. I was watching. Everyone changes who comes to this island. There is a pervasive, ancient evil here. You yourselves will change given enough time."

I had found my voice by then and had to know, "What changes them? Who or what is this ancient evil if it isn't you?"

"I will now take my leave of you and let you find out."

"Wait!" I cried as he reverted into the pillar of black smoke and shot back through the window. To my absolute horror, I found myself dashing after him until Simon caught up with me and spun me around. "What do you think you're doing!" he shouted as he gave me a good shake.

I stared blankly at him for a moment before I could reply, "I wanted to follow him and haven't a clue why."

I was shivering violently, as he drew me into a hug. "You would have died if I hadn't stopped you. I'm taking you to the boat. What I just saw scared the crap out of me. You were...."

"No!" I cut in sharply as I shook him off. "I'm fine, Simon. Really I am. We have to finish this. Didn't you hear what he said? The island changes people. Look at what it's done to Ms. Blackthorne though that *might* be Geoffrey's doing and not some ancient evil. She'll never leave here willingly, and we can't abandon Matilda. More importantly, I can't abandon you. We're stuck in the middle of this mess, and I don't see a way out unless we go through with our plan...together."

Simon sighed heavily. "You are one hard headed little idiot, and I love you for it. I just thought of something...about this ancient evil thing. There's a chance that we might be dealing with an elementary spirit."

"Which is?"

"I've heard them defined as depraved souls who have separated themselves from their divine spirits prior to death and ...by doing so...gave up their chance for immortality. Some people confuse them with elementals that are linked to the four forces of nature...fire...earth... air...and water which are usually benign like mermaids."

"Can they possess people?"

Simon smiled grimly. "They could indeed. If so, we have two more problems: finding *and* getting rid of him if that's even possible."

My own smile was equally grim. "So add him to the possible demon and all the rest though Geoffrey may have been lying. Maybe he was trying to scare us by adding a new horror to the mix."

"I think that's the last we'll see of him tonight. Do you think you could get some sleep?"

"I could try, but first we need to make a trip the bathroom if you know what I mean."

***

We were back in bed a short time later...all except Bella who remained hidden beneath it. Simon fell asleep almost instantly. It took me awhile, but I had just dozed off when I felt a gentle tug on my hair.

"Stop it, Simon," I muttered then opened my eyes a mere slit. We had left the lights on, but now it was dark. Only the dying fire lit the room silhouetting against its feeble light a tall figure in a long black cloak. I had no doubt who it was. Geoffrey had come to keep his promise. I screamed and screamed again until he silenced me with his hand then whispered close to my ear. "Your friend will not hear you...not now...perhaps not ever if you continue to produce that horrid noise."

I peeled away his fingers and managed to shout, "What have you done to him?"

"Nothing permanent. Now come. My need for you grows stronger."

Feeling a strange compulsion to do exactly what he said, I yanked the covers up over my head and muttered fiercely, "Not going to happen."

He pulled them back, despite my best efforts to stop him, then smiled down at me. "Come. No more childish attempts to elude your fate. If it is games you look to play, we can do so in my room where it is not so...*crowded*. Refuse me again and he will die."

"If you want me to cooperate in any way...no matter how distasteful...you had better not hurt him or Bella and let's throw in Matilda and Ms. Blackthorne while we're at it."

He sighed and rolled his eyes. "Anything else?"

"Not at the moment. I do need to ask you a question and would appreciate an honest answer if you have that in you."

I could see his white teeth flash in the near dark as he smiled. "Ask away. I promise nothing."

"Since there seems to be a clutch of supernatural beings lurking about, I need to know if you are more than a ghost."

"Which means?"

"Are you a vampire?"

"And pray tell, what is that?"

"An undead who sucks the blood of the living to survive."

He laughed. "I assure you I am very, very dead and I never 'lurk'. Now enough stalling and come along," he told me as he took my hand and yanked me to me feet. "Since we're here...and for a bit

131

of fun... I'm taking you to my room by way of the scenic route through the passageways you were exploring."

"But the Red Room is just a few doors down the hall," I found myself telling him to both my horror and surprise.

"That is not our destination, though perhaps I did detect a welcome eagerness in your suggestion?"

"You detected wrongly!" I replied with a shudder.

He smiled wickedly. "You are but teasing me, now tis time to go. I can pass though the locked armoire, but the key is required for your passage. Where is it?"

"Find it yourself!" I snapped.

"Look at Simon over there sleeping like the dead. I can make that happen. My *not permanent* can become very permanent should I so wish."

"On the mantel under the clock," I reluctantly muttered.

"Then make haste and fetch it, so we can depart."

Compliance was the only option under the circumstances, so I did as I was told. A howling Bella tried to follow us through the armoire, but he slammed the doors in her face. I don't remember much about the journey through the dark, narrow passageways...just the smell...the cold...the feel of his body pressed against mine...and then we were inside a room I hadn't seen before. The bed was enormous with twisted posts like gnarled trees that rose to a canopy embroidered with dragons. Their eyes seemed to glitter. The side curtains were covered in more of the same and gathered back with long, silky tassels.

He was watching my reaction when he told me, "Never liking to be fettered by mundane tasks...lost in his books, painting, and other pursuits, Father put me in charge of the reconstruction that took a great many years, so I made a few changes. He never knew about this particular room, which became my sanctuary or the other that served its purpose. The only ones who knew were the two burly louts who guarded me constantly when I had free rein on the island, and those who toiled to produce and furnish it. There were others...women who shared it with me from time to time. All were well paid in coin or pleasure to keep my secret. A bonus since they hated him enough to do most anything I asked no matter how bizarre it seemed in their eyes. A hatred I had come to share as well. There is more to the tale, but I will spare you that for now since I have other things more pressing on my mind."

He swept me into his arms and pinned me with his dark, smoldering eyes. His smile was playful as he added, "Now I will make you mine in every sense of the word. Ravish you until we are both sated. How does that sound?"

His gaze was compelling, and I felt my will begin to buckle, but somehow managed to blurt out, "I think I'll pass. I'd like to leave now! This very second!"

"How can you wish that when I predict we will be such great lovers?" he asked as he dumped me on the bed where I landed against a hard lump buried under the covers that...to my surprise... crunched a bit. Stretching out next to me, he leaned on one elbow then told me, "I know what you heard about me...the rapes...the murders...but believe me none of that was true. They were willing...far more than willing...and quite alive when last I saw them. The real killer escaped justice though I came to know who it was in time. But enough about me, Jodie. No, we will need to do something about that name. Jodie isn't fit for a goddess, and you are all of that. Those amazing gray eyes with the black rings around the irides...your silky hair of fiery copper...your magnificent, delectable body...and then there's your indomitable spirit that requires a bit of taming. I don't suppose you've seen Willie Shakespeare's play *The Taming of the Shrew*?"

"I won't be tamed, and I am most definitely *not willing*! I want you to let me go," I shouted as a strange lethargy crept over me.

"'The lady dost protest too much, methinks' to quote from another of his plays. You are making things far more difficult than need be. Let me make love to you. Show you the moon...the stars...the fires of hell and the light of heaven in my arms," he whispered as he seized my now flailing fists and pinned them above my head.

I brought my knee up sharply and caught him somewhere that produced a grunt of pain just as the door burst open. A snarling Bella jumped up on the bed as a furious Simon tossed holy water on Geoffrey then made a grab for him. The struggle that followed was brief. Simon was left grasping thin air when a cursing Geoffrey disappeared. His disembodied voice called from the red mist that slowly engulfed the room. "I shall call you Serilda. It is a Teutonic name that means 'a maiden in battle armor', for that is an apt description of you, my prickly little hedgehog. Until we meet again."

He was gone then...poof...just like that mist and all. I was shivering violently when Simon gathered me in his arms and lifted me off the bed.

Snuggled against his warmth, I told him, "He had put you in a deep trance of some kind. Told me he would make it permanent if I didn't cooperate, so I had to come. How did you get here?"

"Bella kept barking, licking, and pawing me till I woke up. She tracked you through the passageways to a hidden stone door he had left ajar. I marked the way back. Now let's get out of here."

With Bella's help and Simon's scratches, we found our way back to our room where he switched on all the lights then tucked me in bed. I had a strong impulse to climb under it as I had often done in the past before Allison rescued me. Under there, I had felt safe. There was nothing about 'here' I could say that about.

Simon climbed in next to me. "Please tell me we got there it time! He didn't hurt you, did he?"

"No," I murmured. "Just whispered evil, sweet, seductive nothings in my ear, but he did tell me he's not a vampire, so we don't have to add that to the mix."

He laughed. "Well, at least that's something if you believe him. Now go to sleep. Bella and I will keep watch though I doubt he'll be back again tonight."

"I might mention you said that before."

"I was wrong, and it almost cost me you."

Brushing a wayward strand of hair off my cheek, he planted a kiss in its place then pulled me into his arms. Bella jumped up and stretched out across me feet. They were both trying to keep me safe, but I had a feeling it wouldn't be for long.

CHAPTER FIVE

Simon shook me awake the next morning. I groaned and opened my eyes slowly. It was almost a shock to see a tiny patch of sunlight streaming through the window.

"I let you sleep in a bit after what you went through last night," Simon told me as he yanked back the covers. "But Bella needs walking, and I couldn't leave you up here alone. Come on. There's probably coffee waiting."

I slid into my sneakers and followed him out the door. With an impatient Bella leading the way, we had almost made it to the back stairs when we heard a 'bellow' from the hall behind us. Ms. Blackthorne had spotted us and was headed our way thumping her cane emphatically with each step.

"That was a perfectly hideous night! Screaming and screeching and barking going on loud enough to wake the dead," she told us around each puff as she struggled to catch her breath. "And I'm looking at the culprits. Wild orgies are not permitted under my roof, is that abundantly clear?"

For some reason, neither one of us wanted to mention what really happened, so Simon told her, "Duly noted. We will try to keep it down in future."

Her loud sniff of disdain followed us as we continued on. She was clearly 'displeased' with us, and I had to wonder how that would play out.

I waited in the kitchen with Matilda while Simon took Bella out for a quick walk. There were tears in her eyes when she told me, "I wasn't sure I'd be seein' you again after what I heard durin' the night. I wanted to come help, but I couldn't. I tried…honest I did, but I'm not very brave. If somethin' bad had happened to you...well, it don't bear thinkin' about."

Gathering her into a hug, I told her, "It's okay. You're a lot braver than you think to still be here after all that's happened. Geoffrey took me to a hidden room, but Simon and Bella saved me, and all is well. Ms. Blackthorne is thumping her way to the morning room by now, so let me help you fix breakfast."

"Tis all ready. Been keepin' it warm in the oven not knowin' when...or even if...you would be down," she replied as she brushed away her tears with the back of her hand. "Bart's missin' again, and I don't know how I'll be tellin' her."

"He turned up before, so I wouldn't say anything till you absolutely have to."

By then, Simon and Bella had rejoined us. He headed for the coffee pot while Bella headed for her usual spot under the table. I told Matilda we would prefer eating in the kitchen instead of joining

Ms. Blackthorne in the morning room, so we served ourselves from the dishes she sat out while she loaded the cart and headed down the hall.

"Maybe we should have gone with her. Ms. Blackthorne is already in a foul mood and likely to take it out on her," I told Simon as I buttered a muffin.

"At least, she wasn't possessed the last time we saw her. Matilda can manage. We need to focus on bringing what we need from the boat and setting it all up, which means going back down to the cave."

My sigh was of the resigned variety. "There's sure to be a lot of paranormal activity down there based on what I was feeling, but that's true of this whole place."

Simon smiled ruefully. "Yep. We'll have to pick and choose the most likely spots, which will include the Red and Blue Rooms as well as the one Geoffrey carted you off to. It will be daylight when we set up, so things should be quiet. Once it gets dark, we'll monitor all the remote feeds in the safety of our room."

"Which wasn't all that safe last night," I reminded him needlessly.

"Look. I would give anything to keep you out of this, but you are the most....."

"Stop right there! We've gone over this before plus we have a deal. I hate this whole thing, but you stood by me at Greystone...rescued me last night... and I'm here for you. Period. End of discussion."

His sigh was deep...he even threw in a groan. "Okay, another cup of coffee, and we get busy. Looks like the weather is actually cooperating for a change."

And so the day began. We lugged everything we needed from under the boat's v-berth and carried it up to the house. We had just returned to the kitchen after our second trip, when Simon told me, "Okay. We should have everything that's absolutely necessary. We'll set up the cameras in the cave first and work our way back up. They're in that black case with the wheels and the blue one on the table. Most have audio capabilities but three don't, so we'll need the EVP recorders in that bag over there, which you can carry. I'll manage the rest."

We asked Matilda to keep Bella with her then headed down the hall towards the room with the trap door. Except for the 'squeak' the wheels were making, it was very quiet...eerily so as though the house itself was watching and waiting to see what happened next. I remember experiencing the same thing at Greystone and found myself wishing Allison and Cinda were there to protect us. There wasn't a day that went by that I didn't think about them...miss them...and....

Simon broke into my thoughts with, "We're here. Are you ready to do this?"

"As ready as I'll get."

He pushed open the door, and I followed him inside. "We'll leave the cases up here since they're too heavy and cumbersome to lug down those stairs. There are some canvas duffle bags inside the blue one we can sling over our shoulders. It's going to take more than one trip," he told me as he laid his cases on the floor and snapped open the lids. After re-bagging what we would need, he handed one to me. "Is that too heavy for you?"

"Nope. I can manage."

"Great. Come on."

Wielding our flashlights to ward off the unrelenting darkness, we climbed the rickety staircase into the cave below where we left our duffle bags and went back up for a second load. After we'd brought everything down, we set up the remote full spectrum and infrared cameras on their tripods. One was placed by the cave entrance...another in a storage room...two in the main cave covering the stairs and several more in the room where the straw pallets had been found. We were positioning a camera in front of the chained man when I felt a tug on my ponytail and a whispered "Serilda" close to my ear.

I had felt someone watching me since we entered the cave, and now I knew it was Geoffrey, which really came as no surprise all things considered. I didn't mention it to Simon. I wasn't sure why. Maybe I was afraid he would try to make me leave, which wasn't going to happen.

After we had finished the set up in the cave to Simon's satisfaction, we headed upstairs where we placed a camera in both the Red and Blue Rooms. A third was slated for Geoffrey's hidden sanctuary, so we returned to our room and retraced the route Simon had marked last night. While he set up the camera, I waited outside in the passageway fending off a too inquisitive rat. I had no desire to go back in there...no wish to see it ever again.

"I wonder what's down that way," Simon murmured as he rejoined me a short time later and flashed his light to the left where the unexplored darkness waited.

"All of this is Geoffrey's modification, so it could lead anywhere."

"Come on. I'm curious enough to see where this goes."

I sighed but followed him down the narrow space between the walls. Cobwebs brushed my face...dust rose from the stone floor with each step as we continued on. We passed a staircase to our right and decided to explore it later. A few feet farther brought us to a dead end.

"Looks like this is as far as we go," Simon murmured as he flashed his light over the stone wall in front of us.

"That makes no sense," I murmured back. "Why add this extra bit only to end like this? That wall must open somehow."

"Worth a try. You take that side, and I'll take this."

Minutes passed before I found the concealed latch that sent the wall pivoting inward with a loud screech. We flashed our lights inside.

"It's just an empty room. I wonder what its purpose was?" Simon mused.

"Maybe we should just go back," I suggested as a familiar unease worked its way up my spine.

"Fine by me. No…wait! There's something over there in that corner. See!"

I swung my light that way. The skeletal remains of a man wearing a silk dressing gown lay curled in the fetal position against the wall. Wisps of gray hair clung to his skull.

A wave of dizziness washed over me, and I clutched Simon's arm for support. "Who do you think that is?" I whispered.

"Could be Geoffrey. He went missing, remember? We don't know how old he was by then."

"He had this place built...this was his turf...so why would he be here?"

"Good question. Wait out here while I take a closer look at this door."

Slipping through, he examined the other side and reported, "This was a trap. There was no way out of there. Someone lured that guy down here and left him to die a slow, hideous death."

"I think it was his father. Who else would he hate enough to do that to?"

"I think you might be right. He saved him from the gallows only to imprison him here for the rest of his life. For him, that might well have been a fate far worse than death. Let's get out of here."

We decided to see where the staircase led and were surprised to see that the paneled door at the top exited into the Red Room.

"How very convenient for him," I murmured as I pulled a cobweb out of my hair and dusted off my pants. "A direct connection to his sanctuary and the death trap for his not so beloved father. I wonder why he didn't take me that way last night instead of the 'scenic route'? Maybe it was just some demented form of foreplay. That the delay...the anticipation of the yet to come...aroused him even more, which is something I don't want to even think about."

"I wonder if he lured some of the female staff down to that room. There must have been quite a few over the years who served both him and his father. Quite probably, a great many of them would have succumbed and kept their mouths shut. He wouldn't risk killing them under the circumstances."

"I might mention, he denied that. Said they were all 'quite alive' when he last saw them."

"And you believed him?"

"No. I had to wonder why his father would have kept him prisoner if there wasn't a reason. Living on this island must have been hellish for him, too, unless you believe Ms. Blackthorne's version. That he was a recluse who wanted to escape the world as he knew it. Let's get out of here and back to our room."

It was on our way there that a sudden errant thought came out of nowhere. One I didn't like. "You said all that equipment we just set up would tell us who's here, so we could identify and help them, but I think there is more to it than that. We're not just here to release these spirits, are we?"

"Look. I've not been entirely honest with you," he replied with his most disarming grin. "I am putting together a documentary on hauntings like this, and..."

143

"You lied to me?" I cut in sharply.

"Well, let's just say I didn't tell you everything. Yes, we are here to release the spirits, but I also want to capture on tape everything that happens here. We lost everything we'd recorded at Greystone, and I realized what a great documentary that would have made especially the reunions at the end when they all went into the Light."

"So, you want to exploit them, is that it? Add to the reputation of Simon North the famous ghost hunter."

"It's not about me, and I'm not a ghost hunter famous or otherwise! A documentary like that would make a powerful statement. The kind the world of disbelievers needs to see."

"I thought I knew you, Simon. Thought your heart was in the right place. Thought you might be...."

He grabbed my shoulders and looked deep into my eyes. "You're not listening to me! I know I didn't tell you everything, but I wasn't sure how you'd react. After I complete it, you'll see it first. *If* you don't like it...*if* you think I've exploited them, it will never be shown. You have my solemn promise."

My smile was weak, but it was there, and I wondered how I could have ever doubted him. Was it the beginning of the change Geoffrey had warned us about? The very thought terrified me, so I brushed it off. "Okay. I believe you, because I *have* to believe the Simon I know would only do the right thing. Saying that, I think tonight we need to have a séance in the Blue Room and see if we can contact Celia. Tell her about the Light where she'll find her lost son then ask her to spread the word. She must know everyone who haunts this place by now."

"If you're up to it...really up to it... that sounds like a good idea," Simon replied as he watched me closely.

I offered my brightest smile. "It's a place to start. Remember how great my first one went?"

"Yep, which is why I had to ask."

***

The hours passed quickly. Ms. Blackthorne insisted we join her for dinner, but was distant...preoccupied and said very little which suited me just fine. Bart was back, but I sensed a change there, too. I wondered if they both somehow knew what we planned. Perhaps tapped into the ghostly undercurrents here and believed something terrifying would be the result? Ms. Blackthorne seemed to confirm what I was thinking when she paused in the doorway on her way out just long enough to announce, "The devil will be abroad tonight and woe to all who cross his path."

Matilda was waiting in the kitchen when we'd finished eating and told us, "I hope you don't mind, but I already walked Bella. It's so good to have a warm, furry friend to share the stars with when I had no one before. This place gets awful lonesome. Now tell me what you've already done and what you plan on doin.'"?

Simon's answer was a bit vague, but seemed to satisfy her and then she said, "You'll be stirrin' up a pot of trouble, that you will.

Be careful or the pair of you won't come through the night. Perhaps it would be best if I kept Bella with me?"

I was all too afraid she was right and was glad when Simon agreed. The conversation dwindled then died, so we grabbed the last of the cases and lugged them up the back stairs to our room.

"I wish we had placed a camera in Ms. Blackthorne's room," Simon told me as he dropped the one he carried on top the bed and snapped open its latches. "I'd like to see what possesses her."

"That makes one of us. What's all that stuff?"

"It's a Network Video Recorder and, of course, a monitor so we can view what's recorded. The NVR can receive feeds from up to sixteen cameras without wifi which we certainly don't have here. Let me hook everything up."

"What about the three EVP recorders that are recording the voices? Can you tap into them remotely at the same time?"

"We'll have to collect and listen to them later. We're keeping one with us at all times."

It didn't take long to set up the monitoring station then ready the Blue Room for the séance after which we tried to get a bit of sleep. I drifted off almost at once and had a mix of vivid dreams all of which included Allison, Cinda and Henry. I was crying when Simon woke me up.

"From the few words you were mumbling, I think you just had another dream about Allison, right?" he asked.

I nodded, sniffed, and swiped away my tears. "Your grandfather was there, but mostly it was flashes of what happened at Greystone

146

mixed with my memory of when she took me from the group home and offered me a place to live. Just before you woke me, she was holding Cinda as she told me, 'I'll always be close if you need me.' Do you think she's here now, Simon?"

"I wouldn't be a bit surprised," he told me as he pulled me into his arms. "Same with that old cat of yours. They both love you very much. Try to get some more sleep if you can."

A warm feeling of safety and peace settled over me, and I smiled. She was here. She had to be unless it was the comfort of Simon's arms.

I fell into a dreamless sleep cradled against his shoulder. He woke me just before midnight. "Wake up, teammate. Time to go if you are still sure you want to do this?"

I touched the St. Benedict medal I wore around my neck before I replied. "Needs to be done, and, according to my dream, we have our protectors."

Simon smiled grimly. "Let's hope you're right. We'll need every one of them if the devil is on the prowl tonight like Ms. B seems to think."

"And she very well might know him personally considering what we've seen of her so far," I added as I slipped into my sneakers.

We grabbed the EVP recorder we had decided to use, our flashlights, and extra batteries. At the last minute, Simon snatched up a pair night vision goggles then we both headed down the hall.

It was almost warm in the Blue Room where we had lit a fire earlier while we were setting things up. Its flickering flames provided all the light we needed as we took our seats across from each other.

Simon placed the recorder and flashlights within easy reach then told me, "All right. You know the routine. I'll say the prayer for protection again unless you want to?" I shook my head and he continued. "Okay. I'll light the candle, and we'll begin."

Its light cast his face in eerie relief, and I remembered thinking the same thing when Wendy held her disastrous séance at Greystone. He didn't look like Simon any more. Just for a moment, he looked almost inhuman and then it passed. I was letting my imagination run amok again, and this was not at all the time or place to let that happen.

Simon switched on the EVP recorder then took both my hands in his. I prayed with him then added my own part at the end. All the while, I kept hoping that feeling of peace and safety I had experienced earlier would return, but it didn't happen. I reminded myself that Celia seemed harmless, but the Red Room was just though the door on my left. What if Geoffrey was in there listening to us...perhaps even watching us?

My rambling thoughts must have lasted for some time because Simon whispered, "Are you okay?"

I nodded and grabbed his hands tighter. "Just great. Let me get started." I took a deep steadying breath and called, "I need to talk to Celia. Celia! Can you come to us?"

There was no answer, but I persisted. "Celia, we have something wonderful to tell you. Something about your son."

The room seemed to grow colder, and I knew Simon had noticed it, too. "Celia...." I began for the third time when, suddenly, the casement window flew open, and a soaking wet Celia floated through. Seaweed clung to her long wet hair that trailed over her back and shoulders. Her image was wavery and uncertain as though we were viewing her underwater or behind a thick lens.

Her eyes pinned me with a glance that was hopeful, sad, and angry. "Have you called me here to torment me with the belief I may find him?"

I shook my head then told her, "We believe his spirit is waiting for you in the Light. That you will find him there not in the sea where you have searched so long."

She floated around the room then returned to hover just above us. "What is this Light of which you speak?"

"A tunnel drops down from above...a bridge between heaven and earth. Those who have gone before descend from there to claim those they love then take them into this brilliant white Light and what lies beyond. Simon and I have both seen it. That's why we came here. To tell you and all those like you who are trapped on this earthly plane what we know about this Light...about the unconditional love that awaits you on the other side."

"You truly believe my son is in this place?"

"Yes! He's there. I know it. You need to spread the word...tell the others, so they may learn that freedom is within their grasp."

Her frown was doubtful, but her eyes were filled with hope. "How does it come? This tunnel of yours?"

"I'm not exactly sure. I *think* it comes if you believe...truly believe and want it with all your heart. But you must let go of this place first."

"But this is all we know!" she protested as her eyes darted back and forth between us.

"That's why the letting go and believing are so important. Perhaps I can help you with that. There are those I love up there who might show you all the way. Please go tell the others."

"I will tell them all. There are many. Some from the ships that wrecked off shore. Some from those John kept prisoner and tortured below. They roam these halls from time to time or float about the island under the stars. Some never leave the cave...or so I have heard. I have not been down there since he brought me up here to this room, but I will do this for you if you promise you have not lied."

"I have only spoken the truth. It's your chance to find your son. Please tell the others that....."

My voice trailed off as she zoomed back out the way she had come. The temperature began to rise then plummeted again as Geoffrey Blackthorne passed through the connecting door from the Red Room.

He was dressed all in black from his velvet frock coat to his knee high Hessian boots. His long dark hair brushed his broad shoulders, and one equally dark brow was raised quizzically as he looked us over slowly. "Another one of your parlor games has produced unfortunate results. You want them to leave, and I want them to stay except one or two who have become tiresome. Is that abundantly clear?" he asked almost pleasantly, but his smoldering eyes told a different story. He was really pissed off!

"Why should it matter to you if they leave here?" I managed to ask though his nearness was disturbing in all kinds of ways.

He shrugged. "I have my reasons. Perhaps they simply keep me entertained in this drear place. None are leaving here including you, Serilda. Nor you," he told Simon who was watching him closely. "At least, not among the living."

I could feel Simon's hands tighten on mine, but his voice was almost calm when he replied, "And how do you plan on stopping us?"

Geoffrey moved a step closer. His smile was almost playful in a dark kind of way. "Oh, that won't be a problem. I might mention the holy water burned a trifle, but did little else. Unless you have a great many other tricks up your sleeve, I will do whatever I want with you."

"You're envious, aren't you? Resent that the others will find their way to heaven while you're stuck down here?" I asked hoping to divert him from where he seemed headed.

He shrugged again and took a second step closer as he pinned me with his dark gaze. "I already told you I was innocent of the crimes laid at my doorstep."

"Then why did your father imprison you here? You were going to rape me last night...admit it!"

To my surprise, he laughed," Would that have even been necessary, my Serilda? I could feel you weakening. I have told you that I raped no one. While alive and held prisoner on this island, I dallied with a housemaid or two...perhaps even a dozen. One loses count. All believed in my innocence. Father had ordered that only the male staff deal with me directly, but they had been curious enough to risk bringing me this and that. It was easy to earn their trust...take them to my sanctuary and enjoy them. Long after my death, some of the pirate's female captives served me just as well, but they were all willing. Every last one."

"And what about Matilda?" Simon asked. "She is frightened to death of you!"

He smiled. "Those are ill chosen words on your part. She was never in danger. I but toy with her when I can. Boredom is commonplace in my world and watching her scurry about amuses me. To date, she has come to no harm and with good reason."

"Which is?" I demanded to know.

"Perhaps I took pity on the frightened little wren. Perhaps there is another reason I do not care to share at the moment."

The next question was Simon's. "What about that thing that possesses Ms. Blackthorne and maybe even Bart from time to time. Is that you?"

His smile deepened. "Perhaps it is I...perhaps it is another. The ancient evil already mentioned. You asked his name, and now you'll have it. He is known as the Dark Man…a title well earned. His spirit was here when we first came so very long ago and remains to this day. Look to him as the source of all the horrors that happened here. The one who changes those who live here if only for a short time. Not all. Just those he chooses. I told you about John Long who had been a different man until then. A privateer working against the enemies of his country became a savage pirate who did as he damn well pleased and the devil with the consequences."

"Why aren't you afraid of him, if he is all you claim?" I asked.

One dark brow quirked up again, and he smiled ruefully. "We have an understanding the nature of which I do not care to divulge."

"I think you are afraid to be alone with him…if there is a 'him'," Simon replied. "The others serve as a buffer. That's why you don't want us to release them."

"That is as patently absurd as Serilda's 'envious' supposition. Believe what you want and pay the price of your ignorance," he drawled as he slowly began to fade…then vanished.

Simon sighed. "Well, that stirred up a bit more than we'd bargained for, but the camera must have caught some great footage."

"Do you think there is anything on the EVP recorder."

"Don't know. Let's listen."

No audio had been recorded beyond our last words. I was about to switch it off, when a deep voice whispered hoarsely, "I am coming for you."

Goosebumps raced up my arms, and I dropped the recorder that Simon caught before it hit the floor.

"That didn't sound like Geoffrey," I somehow managed to say.

"That might have been this so-called Dark Man...*if* he does exist," he murmured.

"Might mention, I don't think it's *you* he's coming for. That would be me."

"We just need enough time to finish what we came here to do and then we all get the hell outta here and wait on the sailboat till the supply boat comes. Let's get back to our room and check what the other cameras we placed are taping."

We reached our room without further incident. Grabbing a seat in front of the monitor, we watched the activity going on down below. Orbs drifted in from the outside then morphed into skeletal apparitions dressed in the tattered remnants of bygone clothing. Others joined them who looked more recently dead.

"There sure are a lot of them," I murmured.

Simon nodded. "Yep. Look at the old fisherman over there in the corner. He looks freshly dead and quite lost. As though he can't quite figure out how he got there."

"And what to do now that he is. Looks like all of them are pretty much in the same fix though most have had a much longer time to sort it out."

They all seemed to drift about aimlessly...wailing and weeping...mumbling to themselves and occasionally to each other. Most were garbled bits the audio couldn't pick up. Suddenly, they all scattered as the pirate crew drifted through the cave entrance carrying crates and barrels...chests and large trunks. They headed to

154

the storeroom where the camera recorded them stacking and storing their booty before they faded then disappeared. Moments later, the same thing happened again...same apparitions...same load of captured goods...same everything.

"What's going on?" I asked.

"It's a residual haunting. They're caught in an endless loop repeating the same thing again and again totally unaware of their surroundings. Like an old film reel being played over and over."

"Can Celia reach them...talk to them?"

"I don't really know. The living can't. Perhaps the dead can."

We continued to watch and listen to the monitor. In the room with the straw pallets, more apparitions churned about in a mad frenzy. Some were in orb form, but there were others who had fully materialized. A woman wearing the remnants of a bloodstained gown wrung her bony hands and wailed mournfully. Two young children huddled in one corner with their weeping mother. A white haired man wearing a tricorn hat, tattered shirt, and knee breeches paced the length of the room repeatedly shouting, "God's teeth, you swine! Do you know who I am?"

"Another residual?" I asked.

"Yep. He's been at it for centuries judging from his clothes. Must have been someone important in the Colonies whose ransom wasn't paid."

There were others like him...caught in their loop. All looked lost. Most looked insane. The chained man remained silent and unchanged when we had expected more from him than that.

155

"That's enough for now. Tomorrow we'll spend the day going over everything frame by frame, or as much as we can humanly handle," Simon told me with a sigh. "It's going to be a very long day, so get some sleep."

"I've been thinking."

"Oh, oh!"

"Just listen! That voice on the recorder sounded a lot like the ghost's we saw at the cottage though a bit raspier. Maybe he is the Dark Man."

"I think Geoffrey was lying. That this guy doesn't exist."

I shook my head. "Say he was telling the truth. If he is an ancient evil that was here before Geoffrey and his father came, he might have been the one who built that primitive stone hut that became their temporary home. It all fits. It explains why he haunts there though, apparently, he doesn't confine himself to that location."

"You might actually be right," Simon replied with a thoughtful frown. "Maybe we should camp out there and see what happens. Have another one on one encounter instead of viewing it all through a remote yet to be placed camera."

"You're joking, right? From Geoffrey's description and what we've already seen of him, I vote we never...ever go back there again. Period. No discussion allowed," I told him sharply.

He smiled and tweaked my ponytail. "Get some sleep. We'll talk about it in the morning."

I groaned. Like sleep was even possible after hearing that.

CHAPTER SIX

The next day, we got an early start then watched and listened to the feed from all the cameras on the split screen monitor. The voices we heard from those with audio housed a mix of pain, fear, anger and a hopeless longing that somehow they would be rescued...find their lost loved ones...or simply die. Their screams, moans and wails wove in and out among the images we had captured. It continued until the first gray light of dawn found its way through the cave entrance then they all faded and were gone.

The camera in Geoffrey's secret room had picked up nothing. The Red Room's only activity was just before the séance. A glowing Geoffrey had been pacing the floor until he heard us enter the Blue Room. He listened at the connecting door to our conversation with Celia...smiled grimly...then burst through. After that, there was no sign of him anywhere.

"He knew about the séance and was waiting for us," I murmured.

"Yep. Let's just finish up and call it a wrap."

We were both completely drained...mentally and emotionally... by the time Simon shut down the equipment. Darkness had already claimed the island, and we were way late for supper when we headed to the kitchen where an excited Bella greeted us.

It was Simon who made our apologies. "Sorry we're so late, but it was some pretty engrossing stuff."

She grimaced wryly. "I can just about imagine though I don't want to. Seen mor'en enough to put a fright in me. Supper is still warm and in the oven. I was about to bring it up to you, and now you've saved me the climb. The Mistress pitched a fit about you not being there for supper, but she's gone back up to her room. Come on. Sit down. It's nothin more than stew again. The supply boat should be here in two days weather permitin', and I'm none too sure it will. Clouds buildin' again. Looks like we could have us a real bone shaker as early as tonight."

"Does it do anything else but storm around here?" I had to ask.

She laughed. It was the kind of laugh that didn't seem to get much use, and I wasn't too surprised. "We get some sun, but it mostly it be rain, wind, and fog for days on end. Sometimes them fog banks are so thick you can't see much of anything even up close. Now let's get some hot food into the pair of you. Don't worry about Bella. She's already been fed. Love havin' her company, and I think she enjoys mine though she kept lookin' for the two of you to show up."

Matilda joined us while we ate, and we filled her in on what we had found so far. It was straightforward with no editing followed by Simon telling her, "We want you to stay with us on the boat when we've done what we can to release the spirits here. Even if we accomplish that, it may still be far from over. This Dark Man entity complicates things."

158

Her eyes were troubled as her gaze swept us both. "That be the scariest thing yet. This Dark Man...and you think he might be in the cottage?"

We hadn't discussed Simon's camping plans again, and I really, really hoped he had changed his mind, but that hope was dashed when he told her, "Could be though he apparently doesn't confine himself to that location. I want to take some equipment and spend the night out there."

"Personally, I think that's a very bad idea," I told him more sharply than I intended.

"And I second that," a wide-eyed Matilda added. "Anything might happen to you and from the sounds of it, all of it bad."

Simon leaned back in his chair. "If this Dark Man is the root of what's going on here, we need to know more about him. We'll get the hell outta there at the first sign things head south."

"*If* we have time," I pointed out. "You saw that entity the last time we were there, and you couldn't get out of there fast enough. If he is this Dark Man, he's even more powerful than we thought. What chance do we have against him?"

Simon's smile was an attempt to reassure me that didn't come close to working. "Okay," he told me. "Let's just eat and put all this on hold for a while. I'm famished!"

I didn't want it 'put on hold'. I wanted it forgotten but kept my mouth shut...at least for now. After we ate, we grabbed our flashlights and took Bella for a walk. I wasn't too surprised when we headed towards the cottage. Bella had been running on ahead but turned back when it loomed in the distance. Silhouetted against the star filled night sky, it looked more sinister than ever though I had to wonder how much of that was due to what we had learned. Did the Dark Man dwell within those walls as I very much feared? Was he the ghost we had already seen there, or some other horror yet to be confronted?

I yanked Simon to a stop then pleaded, "Please don't do this! Celia is working on the plan to release those here and then we're gone when the boat arrives in two days. Let's not stir up more trouble than we can possibly handle. Let's just focus on...."

He cut in with, "I don't exactly know why this needs to be done. Call it gut instinct. Call it what you want, but I'm going in there tonight. You are not...I repeat 'not'...going with me."

"Like you're going to stop me! We're a team. Where you go, I go. When you die a hideous gruesome death, I will be right behind you. End of discussion."

His sigh was heavy. It was now too dark to see his expression, but I knew what it would be. A mix of anger, frustration, worry, and maybe...*just maybe*...relief. "Then let's go back and grab what we need," he told me then added, "I really wish you weren't such a hard head."

"Well, I am, and you're stuck with me for the foreseeable future however short. That's the deal we made."

"Fine. Have it your way. We'll leave Bella with Matilda then go to the boat. I need to grab a few things."

***

160

A short time later, we took the trail down to the harbor. Lightning flashed along the horizon and distant thunder rumbled like the warning growl of some savage beast. A wicked storm was fast approaching. Another horror added to a night of horrors, I thought, as I waited on the dock while Simon disappeared below. He came back up moments later and handed me a duffle bag...went back and returned with an aluminum case.

"More holy water, sage and my last camera. First time out since it's been repaired," he told me as he climbed up on the dock. "Let's see if Matilda can supply a Thermos of coffee and maybe a blanket or two we'll need at the cottage. It's going to be a long night."

"Or maybe not," I told him as we headed back up the trail. "We are...no arguments permitted...leaving immediately if things start to get hairy, right?"

He mumbled something I couldn't hear, so I pulled him to a stop. "Right?"

I could hear his sigh. "Look. We've been over this before. If you're scared, stay out of it."

"Tell me you're not scared!" I scoffed. "You'd have to be an idiot not to be!"

"Then maybe I'm an idiot. It won't be the first time."

"Meaning?"

"This isn't the time to....."

"Meaning?" I persisted.

His second sigh was deeper. "I had to kidnap you to spend some time with you in hopes of...in hopes of..." A third sigh followed and then he continued, "I've been an idiot about you from the first moment you fell off that ladder into my arms. I've been as patient as a man can be, and it doesn't seem to matter one helluva lot to you."

I knew where this was headed. He loved me, and by now I knew I loved him, but I wasn't ready for the kind of commitment he deserved. I didn't know if it was my trust issue or simple fear that things would inevitably go wrong, which pretty much amounted to the same thing in a roundabout way. All I knew for sure was that he was right. This wasn't the time or place to talk about it, so I told him, "Storm's getting closer. Let's get this done, if I can't change your mind."

"Nope," was all he said.

I knew he was angry with me, but there was nothing I could do about it, so I sped up the trail leaving him to follow. When we reached the house, Bella ran to greet us as Matilda watched from the open kitchen door. Welcome light spilled into the night, and it seemed like a small haven. One I didn't want to leave.

"If you two still plan on doin' this, I'll fix you some sandwiches and coffee to take with," she offered as we filed past her.

"Sounds great," Simon replied with a smile. "Could use some blankets, too, if it's not too much trouble."

Matilda scurried to get things ready then kept Bella when we left a short time later. He led the way, and I reluctantly followed. We had gone some distance when he called back to me, "I'm as mad as hell at you right now, so I won't be talking to you for the foreseeable future."

"Fine by me," I shot back though it was far from that. A silent, angry Simon was a side of him I hadn't seen before, and it bothered me more than I cared to admit. Time would sort it out. Right now we had to get through the night.

We continued up the trail flashing our lights in front of us. The silence between us remained though I was more than ready to end it. His distance made me feel...well, alone in a way I hadn't felt since he came into my life. The storm was much closer now, and I could hear the waves slamming into the cliffs below. The temperature had dropped, and the wind now whipped the long grass on both sides of the trail into a frenzy then howled through the rocky outcroppings like a long lost soul. Leaning into it, we reached the cottage that looked even more sinister now that I knew about the Dark Man. It was pretty much the last place I wanted to be, yet I followed Simon inside. I had no other choice.

The smell was worse...the dark more intense, and our flashlights did little to push it back.

"Okay, you can grab a seat on the floor unless you want the rat chair. A third option would be holding the flashlight while I set up the infra-red camera," he told me, "or...better yet... just hand me one of the night vision goggles from you duffle bag."

"So, you're talking to me now?"

163

"Only when necessary. Let's just see how this plays out. We can always beat feet outta here, okay?"

"Okay. But I'm not going too far from this door or what's left of it," I replied as I dug through the bag and handed him the goggles he wanted then donned my own.

Looking through them, an eerie green light flooded the room, and I remembered the first time I'd worn them at Greystone. While Simon set up the camera, I spread out a corner of my blanket on the stone floor and pulled the rest up over my shoulders. It was already cold, and a manifestation would drop the temp even lower.

"Okay, that should do it," Simon told me as he spread his blanket next to mine. "Last chance to leave."

"And get struck by lightning. Listen to it out there!" Right on cue, a bolt struck nearby and its loud boom of thunder made me wince.

He tucked my blanket under my chin then smiled at me. "Bet you never thought you'd be safer in here than out there. Let me grab the Thermos. We both could use something hot to drink."

"So, you've forgiven me for whatever?"

"Let's just say it's all been put on hold. So, tell me what you've sensed about this place so far?"

"It's just an ancient tomb that smells of dirt, dust, rat poop, mold and decay. No ghostly presences on my radar"

"But the night is young," he reminded me needlessly.

We shared the coffee as we huddled together on the floor. An hour passed, and I was having a hard time staying awake. Two hours passed, and I had almost succumbed when Simon gave me a shake.

"Shhhh!" he whispered. "Something is forming at the top of the stairs."

I squinted in that direction. He was right. A green glowing mist had gathered at the edge of darkness. Ever so slowly it began to take shape...first a column...and then a man. It might have been the same one we had seen before though details were impossible to make out. He was little more than a churning mass that slowly descended the stairs. Closer he came...then closer still. I could see his face now. Only bits of mummified flesh remained though enough to see he had once been human and not some demon straight from hell. His red eyes embedded deep in their bony sockets never left me as he spoke in a hollow sounding voice that could have come from the pit of hell, "What is it you wear upon your countenance that makes you look so strange? You are not the one I seek as I once thought. Why are you here when I told you I would come for you?"

Before a terrified me could reply, Simon asked, "Are you the one they call the Dark Man?"

He laughed. The really sinister kind that sent chills racing through me, though that could have been due to the plunging temp as he came even closer. "Is that how I am known? How interesting. But it suits me," he replied then told me. "I know not who you are, but sense you might understand who I *truly* am though why I should care baffles me. Come!"

Against my will, I scrambled to my feet and was headed his way when Simon pulled me to a stop. I tried to shake him loose just as the Dark Man touched me. A wave of sensations...sights and sounds...washed over me. There was a deep abiding sense of loneliness, rage, and hate. A feeling of contentment...even joy followed by despair and regret. Interwoven though it all were images of ships...the dead and dying...sea birds...wild flowers...waves crashing against the cliffs...an endless deep blue sea that turned blood red...a sky that soon darkened blotting out the stars. The idyllic was mixed with the horrific until everything was blighted...dead...as empty as a cast off shell.

"How awful that must have been for you," I whispered to him just as Simon snatched me up, slung me over his shoulder, and ran outside into the storm.

"I felt sorry for him, Simon...pitied more than feared him," a still badly shaken me told him as he set me on my feet.

"That pity almost cost you the unimaginable. Look. We're both drenched to the skin and need to get back to the house without getting struck by lightning if that's even possible. Thank God for these goggles, or we couldn't see a thing. Let's make a run for it!"

We were nearly half way there when a lightning bolt struck far too close. Its companion boom of thunder shook the ground beneath us.

"Come on!" Simon shouted as he grabbed my arm and made a dash for the shelter of a ruined outbuilding that loomed off trail in the distance. Reaching it, he led me to a dry spot in the far corner.

166

"That last strike almost got us. It can travel through the ground as far as 60 feet, and we weren't much farther away than that. Hey! You're shivering. Come here," he told me as he gathered me into his arms. "I'm worried about you. If I hadn't stopped you back there, you would have gone with him just like you tried to do with Geoffrey and almost died."

"I'm far more confused than you are, Simon," I murmured against his wet shoulder. "Both he and Geoffrey exert a strange pull on me that's hard to resist. Maybe...just maybe they are one and the same. That this Dark Man is someone Geoffrey made up for some sadistic reason. He likes to play games. I know what I felt...saw when I was touched back there, but maybe none of it was real. Maybe he was moving me around on his chessboard. Manipulating my sympathies."

"You could be right. If you're up to it, maybe our next step is to confront him with what we suspect. I think we would both feel better if we could take this Dark Man off the table and had only one evil to deal with. Let's just stay here till we get a break in this storm."

Some minutes later, it had moved on just enough that we decided to risk it though another cell was rapidly approaching. For a distance of about twenty-five feet, everything around us was lit by the eerie green light from our goggles as we sped back to the trail then on to the house where light from the kitchen window streamed into the night. Stripping them off, we stood just inside the kitchen door as a joyful Bella greeted us, and a worried Matilda clucked,

"Let me fetch you some towels and somethin' to wear 'fore you catch your death then I'll put on the kettle for some hot chocolate. Came out here to make some for meself then saw Bella scratchin' at the door and howlin'. She knew you were comin' before you got here, she did. Just mighty glad you're back safe and sound. Wait there. I'll be right back."

She scurried out of sight and returned moments later with the promised towels and two long black robes. "These belong to the Mistress. She has three of 'em 'cause she dribbles when she eats and then there's Bart poopin' everywhere. Been laundered and might suit for a quick change out of them wet clothes," she told us with a warm smile. "You can use the bathroom back there in the scullery. The Mistress had one put in when she couldn't always make it up them stairs in time, if you get my meanin'"

The kettle had come to a boil by the time we had slipped into our robes and returned to the kitchen where we looked each other over. It was Simon who said what we were both thinking. "We look like members of some dark cult," he whispered.

"Yep, though yours exposes quite a bit of fetching ankle," I whispered back. "We're going to have to find some place to sleep because I don't want to go upstairs again. Not till morning when the sun is shining *if* it ever does from the sound of what's still going on outside."

Matilda had overheard us. "No need if you don't mind sleepin' a bit rough. I planned on usin' the back parlor tonight. Got a fire goin' in there, so it should be right cozy. Let's get some hot chocolate in the pair of you, while I fetch some extra blankets and flashlights in case we need it. The lights have been on and off since you left."

All three of us followed her down the halls a short time later. As we passed each closed door, I had a sense someone was on the other side...listening to us...perhaps even watching us. Judging from her low, rumbling growl, I think Bella sensed it, too. Half way down, the sconces flickered twice, and we held our breath. A moment later, they went out. The darkness was intense, and we were thankful for the flashlights Matilda had rounded up from somewhere.

"It's just down this side corridor all the way to the end," Matilda told us when we had made our third turn. "Not much has been done on this wing, so be careful how you go."

I was glad she had warned us. The hall runner was a trip hazard and piles of discarded items were scattered everywhere. More than one housed a rat that scurried away at our approach. A thin rim of light shone under the last door, and we followed Matilda inside where I looked around in surprise. It actually looked inviting! Twin, tufted settees bracketed the marble fireplace where a cheerful blaze roared. A thick, blue Aubusson rug covered the floor...a beautiful four paneled oriental screen graced one corner...and there was even a window seat piled high with cushions and blankets.

Matilda had been watching my reaction then smiled, "The Mistress doesn't know about this. It's my special spot. Did it all myself. Lugged stuff from here and there she wouldn't miss. Tis one of the places I sleep since I left the attic. There's a place for us all. I like the window seat, so I can see the night sky."

And so it was settled. Bella found a spot by the hearth. Simon and I took the settees, which were as hard as bricks though I didn't mention it. I felt safe in this room, which was far more important than my comfort.

I had just plumped up my pillow, tucked the blanket up around my neck, and was drifting off to sleep when Matilda, suddenly, scrambled to her feet shouting, "It's the Mistress! I just saw her go by the window. We have to stop her! The fastest way is through the west wing."

Grabbing our flashlights, we shut Bella inside then sped after her. We managed to catch up with her just before she headed down a side corridor we hadn't seen before.

"Be careful through here!" she shouted as she hurried on. "This whole side of the house is starting to slide off the edge!"

We had gone some distance when I saw what she meant. The hall took a downward slope and large, gaping cracks criss crossed the floor and walls. Chunks of plaster had fallen from the ceiling, and all the doors were racked…some hanging by one hinge.

Simon grabbed my arm and pulled me to a stop. "Go back! I'll handle this!"

I shook my head...broke free and sped after Matilda who had already reached the outside door and disappeared from view. Wind driven rain drenched me as I stepped through a moment later and flashed my light around. There was little earth remaining in front.

Just a sunken, crumbling rim no more than four feet wide. Below, I could hear the waves chiseling away at the cliff...stealing what little remained. Off to the left, most of the foundation had already been undermined and now overhung the edge. It wouldn't be long before the west wing would be claimed by the sea.

Simon had caught up with me by then and flashed his own light around. "Watch where you go, or you won't like where you land," he warned me needlessly as we hugged the side of the house and moved on.

Our path widened. Just ahead, I caught a glimpse of white illuminated by a flash of lightning, and we ran that way. A second bolt lit the scene, and I saw Matilda struggling with a frenzied Ms. Blackthorne. We had almost reached them when she plunged over the edge almost pulling Matilda with her.

Reaching her, I gathered her in my arms as Simon shouted to be heard above the boom of thunder...the wind and waves, "She's gone! There's no way she could have survived that fall."

"Let's get back inside. This storm is getting worse," I shouted back just as a jagged bolt split the darkness directly overhead illuminating the scene with its strange white light. It looked like a set from some horror movie. None of it seemed real...couldn't possibly be real...and yet it was.

It was a frightened Matilda who derailed my thoughts with, "Best make a run for it. That one could have got us. I'll take you to the south door."

We sped after her as she headed back to the house then followed her to the parlor where we had been warm and cozy only a short time ago. Once inside, a tearful Matilda stoked up the fire then told us, "I tried to stop her. Hold on to her, so she wouldn't jump. She kept sayin' he wanted her to do somethin' bad she wouldn't be doin', so she was goin' to end it. She weren't a kind soul, but I miss her. Maybe we'll find her body washed up come mornin', so she can have a decent burial in the dress she fancied for the occasion."

A heavy silence fell over us as we all shed our wet things behind the screen then wrapped up in the blankets. A short time later, a still badly rattled Matilda was asleep on a settee while Simon and I sat on the window seat and watched the fire as the storm slowly moved on.

Simon was the first to speak. "Now there's just the three of us."

"Bella makes four."

"Yep. Let's see what tomorrow brings. We have to get through just one more day."

"And night," I added.

"Do you think you could get some sleep if we curl up here on this almost comfy window seat?"

"Maybe, though I wouldn't count on it."

He pulled me to my feet, stretched out, then patted the spot next to him. I curled up against him and was asleep a short time later where a dream was waiting.

I wasn't sure where I was. Some place lit only by a red, glowing mist that kept shifting around me. Someone was standing there watching me. A tall, indistinct 'someone' who whispered hoarsely, "Come with me. I know you want to."

Was it the Dark Man or Geoffrey? Were they one and the same as we thought? All I knew for sure was that I wasn't about to comply.

"Simon!" I screamed as he came closer and fear swallowed me whole.

"Simon!" the entity mocked. "He can't save you. No one can. Not even that one behind you."

I looked around, and there she was. A glowing Allison...an angry Allison who headed his way shouting, "I will not let you harm her!"

"I will use her as I please, and you cannot stop me," he shouted back then vanished.

I was crying when Allison pulled me into her arms. "That is a creature of immense evil. Use your wits and be very careful," she warned me then she, too, disappeared.

CHAPTER SEVEN

I remembered nothing after that until Simon woke me then said, "It's just past dawn and the storm has passed. Matilda left to check on the generator though I told her that was a bad idea. That we should stick together, and I couldn't leave you. Do you want to try for a bit more sleep?"

I shook my head. "I had another nightmare. Allison warned me to be careful. That we were dealing with an immense evil."

"If sleep is off the table, let's go see how Matilda is making out."

Wrapped in our blankets and flashing our lights in front of us, we let Bella lead the way down the still dark halls. Without her, we would have been hopelessly lost. We had reached the main hall and familiar turf, when the lights came back on.

"Well, that's a plus," Simon told me. "Matilda must have fixed the generator."

When we reached the kitchen, we found her busily making coffee as she called to us, "Got lucky, we did. The generator just needed a reset. Happens a lot after the kind of storm we had last night. When you go upstairs to get out of them blankets, would you fetch Bart?" She paused to take a deep breath then added, "I can't bring meself to go in her room after what happened, and the poor bird needs lookin' after. He'll be in his cage, so he won't give you no trouble. He was right fond of the Mistress in his own way."

"How about some of that coffee first," I told her with a wry smile. "I'd really like to see more daylight before we go up there."

I delayed as long as I could then left Bella with Matilda and followed Simon up to our room. "We need to change quickly," he told me as headed to the armoire. "I want to check on the boat as soon as possible. We'll dress in here to save time. I promise I won't peek though I have seen every inch of you by now."

A few minutes later, we were headed down the dimly lit hall to Ms. Blackthorne's room. Once again, I had a weird sense we were far from alone that only increased when we passed the Red Room. "He's in there now. I know he is," I whispered to Simon.

"Do you want to confront him while we have the chance?" he whispered back. "Find out if he's been playing some sort of sick game like you think?"

"The word 'no!' springs to mind. Let's just grab Bart and get outta here."

We had reached Ms. Blackthorne's room by then, and Simon opened the door. The pale light of early morning fingered its way through a small gap in the drawn drapes as I switched on the lights and looked around. The bedding had been slashed. Her clothes ripped to shreds and strewn on the floor. All the bits and pieces she had cherished had been dashed against the walls and scattered everywhere. Only Bart's cage remained untouched. I picked my way through the debris till I reached it. Afraid of what I would see, I lifted the edge of the cover and peeked inside then breathed a sigh of relief. He was still alive and greeted me with a forlorn, "Awwwwk! Gone for good. Gone for good. Poor bird. Poor bird."

Simon had joined me by then. "Look at all the feathers he's plucked out! No doubt stress induced."

I grimaced wryly, "No wonder if he heard or even saw what happened up here. Shhhh! Listen! Did you hear that?"

"That what?"

"A whispery kind of 'what' coming from the armoire."

175

"Nope. Didn't hear a thing. Maybe it's just your imagination?"

"Maybe I should speak a bit louder, so all can hear," a familiar voice called as Geoffrey began to materialize. He was dressed as he had been in his portrait and smiling as he struck his riding crop against the side of his boot. "It seems the Dark Man came to see her last night."

"Unless it was you. Slashing things to ribbons in a fit of pique seems to be your style," I told him as he strode to the window and looked out.

He turned my way and pinned me with his dark gaze. "Believe as you wish. It matters not. Let's just say whoever it was had a task for her that involved you. She refused which infuriated him, and you see the results. I watched you both witness her demise from a distance. Rather dramatic of her. Throwing herself into the sea to escape him. Of course, she's still here somewhere. No doubt confused and rather lost. Perhaps not yet accustomed to her current state."

It was Simon who asked, "Why are you here? Why materialize when it is almost daylight?"

He smiled darkly. "I wanted you to know that you will be spending the night here with me and not elsewhere as I heard you planning. Someone both human and alive left you a surprise," and with that said, he vanished.

"I don't like the sound of that," Simon muttered as he lifted the cage and headed for the door. "Let's get Bart delivered to Matilda. I want to check out the boat."

With Bella in the lead, we headed down the trail. The sun had risen higher washing the land, sky and sea with its rose and lavender light. A salt scented breeze reached us as we rounded the final bend that had shielded our view of the harbor. We both stopped in our tracks. The boat had vanished.

"What the hell!" Simon shouted as he took off at a flat out run with me close on his heels. As we drew closer, I saw jagged pieces of her fiberglass hull and rubber fenders bobbing about in the waves.

I waited on the trail, with a firm grip on Bella's collar while Simon made his way down what little remained of the wave washed dock. Reaching the spot where she'd been tied, he examined the lines still attached to the pilings then snagged a floating fender. "They've all been cut! She didn't stand a chance in that storm. Smashed against the dock again and again until her hull was shattered, and she went down. She....."

He didn't finish what he'd been saying...just stood there looking down into the water for a long time then, slowly, headed back to me. His eyes were wet with tears...his mouth set in a grim line. Tears filled my own eyes. Even though I knew how pitifully inadequate my words were, I managed to tell him, "I am so sorry, Simon. I know how much she meant to you. I wish there was something I could say...do."

He took a deep shuddering breath then said a lot more calmly than I knew he was feeling, "She was the last bit of Grandpa I had. I could see her down there. Under the water."

"There's only three of us left on the island. I don't believe Matilda did this. When would she have had the time? She was with us."

He shook his head vehemently. "We don't know when they were cut! She could have done it while we were at the cottage."

"Saying that timeline is right," I protested. "Why couldn't it have been Ms. Blackthorne? She was the one possessed by that evil thing."

"She was an old lady who could barely walk!" Simon scoffed.

"Until she was possessed. Who knows what she was capable of doing then. You saw her crawling down the hall on all fours like some wild beast."

"Wait a minute! I just thought of one other possibility."

"Like who?" I asked in surprise.

"This handyman who was a bit strange, remember?"

"I think his name is Joe. You think he's still on the island?"

"It's a long shot, but there's a whole lot of this place we haven't explored yet. Might be worth a look."

I frowned thoughtfully. "How would he manage without food, water and shelter?"

"Geoffrey said it wasn't a ghost which means we have three choices. We've pretty much ruled out two, which leaves this Joe, *if* he's here."

"We didn't rule out Ms. Blackthorne or even Matilda entirely," I pointed out, "and maybe Geoffrey lied to throw us off the track."

"Meaning?"

"He could be the one who did it. Cutting a few lines would be easy for him."

Simon shook his head. "It's a possibility, but my gut tells me it was someone alive not dead."

"Your gut could be wrong."

"Yep, but I'm doing this my way. We're finding this Joe. If he's not on the island, I will need to dig deeper for the answers I need."

***

Matilda was standing in the doorway when we got back. "What's wrong?" she asked as her gaze swept us both. "Something terrible must have happened!"

It was Simon who told her. "The boat's been sunk. The lines were cut. Is there any chance this Joe you told us about is still on the island?"

She frowned thoughtfully. "Last time he came on the boat was near on a month ago. If he's been here all that time, I might not have known. He's stayed on before with no one the wiser like I told you before." She paused and then continued, "Thinkin' on it, them supplies seems to be gettin' lower than expected...not much...so I scarcely noticed. Maybe he is here after all."

"We're going to check out the island and Bella can help," he told her. "Is there anything of his lying around?"

"Might be something in the outbuildings. They be all over the island. Leftovers from the work camps according to the Mistress. He's a queer one to be sure, but why would he do somethin' like that?"

"Not saying he did, but what other choices are there?"

I knew where that was headed and was about to intercede when I noticed Bart's cage was missing and asked about him.

Matilda sighed heavily and shook her head. "Doin' right poorly. Refused to eat. Just paced back and forth on his perch bobbin' his head up and down and screechin' somethin' fierce. I put him in the scullery and covered him back up to calm him down. Been quiet for a while now."

"Maybe you should check on him and make sure he's okay?" I suggested as a niggling unease washed over me.

"Could do. Be right back."

We watched her disappear down the back hall. She was sobbing when she returned moments later. "He's dead. Just lying there on the bottom of his cage. What could have happened to him?"

We followed her back to the scullery where Simon lifted the cover and peeked inside. "Hard to tell. Maybe died from the stress. No telling how old he was."

"I couldn't stand the horrid old thing poopin' on everything and bein' a nuisance with such language and all, but seein' him like that is right upsettin'."

"Find me a towel to wrap him in, and I'll see he gets buried as soon as I find a shovel," Simon told her as he opened the cage door and gently lifted him out.

Tears filled my own eyes as I looked at the small mound of orange and green feathers that had once been so full of life. Perhaps he had died of grief. Far stranger things have happened.

***

Matilda had opted not to go, so there was just the three of us when we left a short time later. I was carrying Bart as we checked out several outbuildings till we found one that looked promising. Its roof had collapsed on the backside but was covered with a tarp, and the door had recently been repaired. Bella led the way inside where she scared up a rat and chased it into the huge woodpile stacked along the far wall.

"There's a shovel over here," Simon called to me as he made his way through the clutter to a row of rusted tools.

"Hey! I found an old flannel shirt on this peg," I called back as I lifted it down. "Might be Joe's."

Simon joined me and examined it closely. "Little more than a rag, but looks too clean to be hanging here for long. Let's see if Bella can pick up his scent off it."

"Here's hoping, but first we need to take care of Bart."

We buried him not far from there. It was a sad moment as I stood there looking down at the small grave we'd covered with rocks. Another death and I hoped his tiny spirit would re-connect with Ms. Blackthorne's wherever she was. They had loved each other in their own way.

"Come on, Jodie! Let's get going," Simon urged as he held the shirt under Bella's nose then told her, "Go find him, Girl!"

She sniffed, whined then sat down. It wasn't going well.

"Looks like it's up to us," I told Simon. "Where should we start first?"

"We'll check any remaining outbuildings then the cave. There might be some place down there where he could hide that we missed. If the tide's out, we should be able to get in there without going back through the house."

"There's also the cottage. We only saw a small part of the layout, but I can't imagine he would like his roomie."

"Yep. We'll save that till last."

One by one, we searched the remaining stone buildings scattered around the island. Most were barely intact. None looked like a likely place to shelter, and then we found one possibility that was far enough away from the house Matilda wouldn't notice if it was occupied. Simon and Bella were the first through the door. I was right behind them and looked around once my eyes adjusted to the darkness. In the far corner, tattered blankets covered a mound of dry bracken. Pried open, empty food cans littered a makeshift table. A blue canvas cushion from our sailboat lay on the floor next to it.

"Well, that settles that," Simon muttered. "This Joe is the one who sank our boat. Probably did the other damage, too. He's hiding on this island, and I'm going to find him."

"At what cost? You are forcing him into a corner, and he'll fight like a trapped animal."

"You don't think I could take him?" Simon asked as he pushed his glasses up on his nose. "You think I'm some wuss who can't handle himself?"

"That's not it," I hastened to tell him. "He may have a knife, judging from those cans over there, and is desperate enough to use it. I don't want you hurt. We're leaving tomorrow. Let's drop this and focus on what we came here to do in the time we have left."

"Hell no!" a clearly pissed off Simon shouted. "He sank my boat and...."

"And what? You're going to beat him up?"

"If it comes to that, and I'm hoping it does! Now I'm going to find him. Are you coming or not?"

There wasn't any other option, so I went. By then, Bella had picked up a fresh scent that interested her enough to follow it. It led to the cliff edge where it looked like Joe had been robbing the nests. We found his long dead campfire not far from there. The skeletal remains of birds and what could have been rats were piled next to it. I wondered why he hadn't let Matilda know he was still on the island instead of living like some wild beast? And why had he sabotaged then sank the boat? There was no earthly reason for it unless he was being controlled by some *unearthly* entity just like Ms. Blackthorne.

"He must know we're after him by now and has gone to deep cover and.... Hey! Look at that!" Simon murmured as he bent down to examine a very large shoe print in the soft mud. "That's as fresh as they come...and there's another one over there. It looks like he may be headed towards the cottage. We'll dig him out of there!"

A feeling of intense dread settled over me. "Like I already mentioned," I told him hastily. "We have more important things to focus on like releasing the spirits here and getting off this island when the boat comes tomorrow."

Simon managed the first smile I'd seen that morning. One I didn't trust. "You're right. We'll get back on track, but first I need to check out the cottage. If he's not there, I'll let it drop."

I tried my best to dissuade him, but he resorted to his usual ploy: I could wait outside with Bella, which wasn't going to happen.

A relentless Bella stayed on his trail all the way to the cottage where she disappeared inside. We were close behind when she headed towards an open door in the back wall just left of the stairs. A long hall lit only by a window at the far end stretched ahead.

"I wish we had brought our flashlights," I murmured as I opened a door on my right and peeked inside. Very little light found its way through the broken window. The usual dirt, dust and cobwebs were everywhere, but I felt no sense of evil...just an intense longing edged with rage.

Hastily, I closed the door and hurried on till I caught up with Simon and Bella who were checking out a large room that had once been a library judging from the empty shelves and the few rat chewed books scattered across the floor.

Simon picked one up and examined the cover. "The Study of Birds and Their Habitat," he read, "or what is left of it after the rats

184

had a feast. Must have been left behind when the others were carted over to the big house. Let's check out the rest of this place."

"There must be a kitchen. What did they use for water?"

"Probably a cistern to catch rain water. The set up would have been crude considering the times, but it would suffice. Are you picking up any sort of vibes?"

I nodded and was about to tell him what I had experienced earlier when Bella bayed and took off at a run. She headed down a side hall, and Simon ran after her with me right on his heels. We ended up in a storage room that still contained the shattered remnants of crates, trunks, and barrels. Most were stacked in one corner, and Bella headed that way. Suddenly, a tall figure sprang out from behind them and bolted for the door. He didn't make it. Simon tripped him as he passed and pinned him to the floor.

"I've got you now, you son of a bitch!" he told him fiercely. "Why did you sink my boat?"

He struggled briefly then lay still. His face was badly scarred from his jaw to his temple...his gray beard long and unkempt. In his eyes, there was a mix of terror and resignation, and I felt a wave of pity wash over me.

"You're hurting him, Simon. Let him up. Give him a chance to tell his side of the story."

There were tears in those eyes when he looked my way. "He made me do it. Said he would hurt me if I didn't. I didn't want to get hurt no more."

Simon pulled him to his feet. "Okay. You weren't responsible for your actions. I'll buy that. Who is this he? Is it Geoffrey Blackthorne?"

He shook his head then whispered, "He's here now...listening. The other one. He's been watching you since you came to the island. He wants her to stay. That one over there and aims to have her. He...."

He never finished what he was trying to say. Gasping for air, he clutched at his throat as his face grew dusky, and his eyes protruded. He was being choked to death, and there didn't seem to be a thing we could do to stop it, but I had to try.

"That's enough!" I shouted. "He's done what you've asked of him now let him go. Now!"

Suddenly, Joe was yanked upward till he hit the ceiling then dropped to the floor where he lay motionless. Rushing to him, I searched for a pulse, but there was none.

"You killed him!" I screamed as Simon grabbed my arm and pulled me towards the door whispering urgently, "Let's get out of here!"

Demonic laughter followed us as a terrified Bella led the way with Simon and me close behind. The dark hall seemed endless. Finally, we reached the door, and Bella sped through. Simon was shoved after her, and I was yanked back inside. A dry, suffocating wind engulfed me as I was pulled into the bowels of the cottage.

I must have passed out briefly, because I awoke in a strange room we hadn't seen in our exploration. I was lying on the stone floor and feeling cold...unbearably cold...and tired as though all life had been drained from me. Silhouetted against the light coming through the window behind him, a tall, dark figure stood in front of me.

"I brought you here not for the reason you fear though I would not rule it out entirely," he told me. "I have not had a woman in a very long time."

I struggled to a sitting position and managed to say, "I want you to let me go!"

"Not yet. Maybe not ever. I let you see who I was...what I once felt before I became deadened inside. You are here because you alone might understand what I am about to confess though confession may not be the right word."

"I don't think I want to hear this."

"You do not have a choice, my dear. So, how shall I begin," he mused. "Ah, let me start by telling you I freely admit I am a monster. I will not burden your sensibilities by revealing the atrocities I have committed. Some said I was in league with Satan, and I did not refute it. It caused my enemies to fear me and fear is a useful thing. I was a man of power and influence who could not be disposed of in the usual way, so some of my more *inventive* foes decided to maroon me on this island. A trusted servant drugged my wine, and I was whisked away. Confined in a wooden crate aboard ship until we reached this place. They left me here with nothing to sustain me. Left me to die slowly...day by day.

187

"At first, I was enraged beyond measure and spent my time railing against my fate...hating those who had condemned me to a lingering death. But anger and hate were a poor diet indeed and, without food or water, I soon began to weaken, so I learned to hunt the birds and seals...found a way to capture the rain. I ate seaweed for the nourishment it offered, fashioned my house from the stones and clay...the salvaged timbers and all sundry from the shipwrecks off the coast that had washed onto shore. Even found things to clothe me...blankets to keep me warm in the trunks of the dead...or *soon* dead. I killed those few who survived. All but one woman who pleasured me for a time till she died in childbirth. Then I, too, died one day.

"I had welcomed death thinking it would free me from this place, so imagine my surprise to find myself still here and alone until the Duke and his son arrived in their ships and took over the island...my home that I had fashioned with my own hands. Their workmen made it into this monstrous pile they called, 'barely livable but it would suffice for a time'. I listened and learned that the son had been found guilty of raping and killing women. He would have hanged had his father not freed him from Tyburn and brought him here. I came to have a fondness for him."

He paused for a moment then continued, "This Geoffrey was a kindred spirit in some ways. Marooned, in a sense, as I was. A man of lust and passion. His seduction of the serving wenches amused me, but the rest is his tale to tell. Over time, their grandiose mansion was left to the elements...deserted until the pirates came, and I believe you know how that turned out. Under my influence, Gentleman John became a ruthless savage slaying without mercy except for the one he kept. Someone called Celia as I remember. They were all immensely entertaining for a time and then they were gone, too, leaving but their rubble and ghosts behind in the cave below...Celia to wail and mourn."

I found myself asking when he paused a second time, "What do you want from me?"

He shook his head. "I wish I knew. I only know that when I first touched you, you sensed...saw how long I have suffered. Felt compassion for me...perhaps even empathy. I have come to think that you alone might understand that I was forced into these circumstances against my will. That I became a monster out of necessity...because of what was done to me."

"Sounds to me like you were a monster before you came here. Before you killed innocents without mercy! Committed atrocities you won't 'burden me with' because they would paint an even grimmer portrait of who you are. I admit to feeling sorry for you briefly, but that's over! You are a far cry from a sympathetic figure in any sense of the word!"

"But perhaps deep inside, where only *you* can see, there is some redeemable quality however small?"

"If you promise to let me go, I might take a closer look though I really doubt I'll find it."

"You might be surprised. I was a little boy once. Cute, precocious...loved by my parents until..."

His third pause had me asking, "Until what?"

"They died in a fire. Many thought I was to blame since I had been known to play with it from time to time, but nothing was proved. I went to live with an elderly aunt. The insufferable Agatha Holtmore. Ms. Blackthorne reminded me of her. Maybe that was why I let Geoffrey toy with her a bit...shame her...while I watched. I made her do my own bidding till she defied me by choosing death. She's still here somewhere and will pay for her sin in due time."

He was clearly now enjoying the grisly tale he was spinning, which gave me an opportunity to slide closer to the door. I had only gained a few feet when he pounced on me then lifted me by my shoulders till we were face to face…if one could call it that. In rapid succession, *that* face began to change. It was Ms. Blackthorne who now peered at me then Joe...and then a whole lot of others I hadn't seen before. All were smiling slyly until they vanished.

"You see how I am but one yet many when I have wished it so? " he asked with a sly smile of his own. "Perhaps I will possess the body of the young man who even now is searching my home for you. You called him Simon. How would you like me to possess this Simon? I could even enter that dog of yours, for animal possession is even easier."

I was way beyond terrified but wasn't going to let him see it. "None of that would induce me to see you in a favorable light which is what you want. Let me go. We'll be off the island tomorrow, and you can have it all to yourself once again."

He set me on my feet. His red eyes never left mine as he murmured, "I have heard what you plan. The long dead have been my only companions, and now you want to take even them from me leaving me alone again with the wind and the waves as I have been for centuries. The fierce storms that tear at the cliffs. The moon silvered grass that ripples like water in the slightest breeze. The birds and the seals...the clouds that tear across the sky or lie stretched across the horizon in an endless band. The long empty nights that both embrace and suffocate me."

I sighed. "Enough of the poetic, self-pitying lament. I am not going to feel sorry for you again. We're going to release as many as we can. They need to reunite with those they love and leave this place of horrors."

"So it must seem to you. So it seemed to me once. I can't let you do that. I want them here. All of them...the insane and the sane...the lost and the wicked...the good and the bad. They belong to me. I would add you to them. Perhaps I will let Geoffrey have you first as a special boon. He is still young and his appetites far stronger than one as ancient as myself."

"Not going to happen," I told him as I made a dash for the door. I was out in the hall and running when I heard him call after me, "This is quite enjoyable. The tiger and the mouse. Now run like Satan himself is after you, for he may well be. Darkness strengthens me, so I will come for you in that royal mausoleum once the moon has risen."

191

CHAPTER EIGHT

Bella found me first though Simon was right behind her. Kneeling on the floor, I gathered her wriggling, joyful body into my arms then Simon drew me into a fierce almost rib cracking hug. His voice was hoarse with emotion when he asked, "Are you okay?"

"Fine for now. Please get us out of here as fast as you can," I begged. "He let me go...the Dark Man who is definitely not Geoffrey...but he could change his mind at any time."

"I marked the walls, so we could find our way out. Let's get going."

We found our way outside and hadn't gone far when Simon pulled me to stop. "I need to know exactly what happened back there. Don't omit a singe thing."

So, I told him all I remembered ending with, "This Dark Man doesn't want the spirits to leave here. Even talked about possessing you and maybe even Bella."

Simon smiled grimly. "We'll have to make sure the first happens and the second doesn't. Let's get back to the house and figure out what to do next."

**

Matilda had seen us coming through the kitchen window and ran to meet us. "Did you find Joe? Was he on the island?"

"He's dead," Simon replied. "Back at the cottage. We'll tell you all about it when we're inside."

"Looks like a little friend followed you back, though I've never seen it before," she told us as she pointed to something just behind us. "And it seems to have taken a real fancy to Bella."

I looked back over my shoulder. A black cat was head butting a happy Bella as her tail wagged furiously. It was Cinda. I would know her anywhere! Calling her name, I was headed her way when she 'meowed' once then vanished.

Simon had seen her, too. "She knows you're in trouble and came to tell you she's close by."

"Which means Allison is here, too," a teary eyed me managed to reply. "She won't let anyone hurt us."

I found myself wishing I was wearing her mermaid pin, but I had left it behind when I met Simon at the Flying Bridge. It was heavy and there'd been no place to pin it on my sundress. She had given it to me when I was a troubled, angst-ridden teen, and I had come to think of it as a shield that would ward off all harm. I touched the St. Benedict medal I wore around my neck. The forces of good had to be enough, or we would never leave the island.

Back in the kitchen, Matilda brewed a fresh pot of coffee. Soon we were all sitting around the table enjoying a cup, which seemed so every day ordinary after my nightmarish experience just a short time before. Cradling mine in both hands, I told a slightly edited version of what had happened to Matilda. To say she was horrified was a colossal understatement.

"May the good Lord protect us all," she murmured. "What are we to do? How can we keep safe until the boat comes for us?"

"Which is what time exactly?" Simon asked.

"All depends on the tide. Needs to be high to make it over some of the rocks. The captain has scraped bottom before and won't have a go at it before then."

Simon smiled grimly. "I have an idea on how to keep us safe. I've never tried it before, so I don't know if it will work. A ring of salt supposedly protects those inside it. We will need to place white candles in its north, south, east and west quadrants then hope and pray for the best."

"And where will we do this?" I had to ask. "It won't be inside these walls after dark. That's when he said he would come for me in this 'royal mausoleum'."

Simon watched me closely as he asked, "What do you propose?"

"It's going to be a clear night from the look of things. Why not outside? That way we can see the tunnel of Light when it comes for all the lost souls Celia is gathering up, *and* I won't feel trapped within this house."

Matilda had been listening. "Tis a wondrous thing you be doin'. The Mistress might be among them. How can I help with the readyin' of it all?"

"For starters, we'll need that salt I mentioned and lots of it. Can you supply it?" Simon asked.

"There be plenty in the storeroom. Should be enough if this circle's not over big. Let me fix us all a bite to eat first."

194

I helped make the sandwiches on autopilot as I mentally sorted through all that had happened at the cottage...what might happen that night. A circle of salt seemed like poor protection, but at least we would be outside under the stars instead of in a place imbued with evil.

Simon was equally quiet while we ate saying only that he needed to grab the equipment he would need for the set-up from upstairs since we'd left his last camera at the cottage when we made our hasty exit. Leaving Bella with Matilda, we headed that way a short time later. First stop was our room where I told Simon I was going to pack my things and bring them down with us. That the rest of the time I spent on the island would be outside and not in some Gothic nightmare of hidden doors and secret passageways saturated with centuries of evil.

"Okay. If that's what you want, that's what we'll do. Pack up your stuff, and I'll pack mine," he told me. I was half expecting a 'but' to follow, but there was none.

I threw everything I'd brought with me into my suitcase and oversized shoulder bag then set them next to the door. Simon did the same as he told me, "I'll haul down the recorder and set it up in the kitchen to receive the feeds after we get the cameras from the Red and Blue Rooms. Are you ready to do this?"

I really wasn't but nodded anyway and followed him out the door. A strong sense of something I couldn't quite name surrounded me growing stronger with every step I took. It almost felt like the house itself didn't want us to leave. That it wanted us to stay forever...absorbed into its very walls until those walls fell into the sea.

Those dark thoughts carried me along until we reached the Blue Room where Simon told me to wait in the hall. I didn't pull the 'team' card on him. I was more than happy to do just that.

The door was open, and Simon was only a few feet away, but I was still uncomfortable. This time it felt like someone was watching me. An invisible 'someone' who was very close. Suddenly, I felt the solid press of his body as Geoffrey whispered, "All packed up and ready to go, I see. But you will never leave me, Serilda. You are mine forever."

I pushed him back then shouted, "We need to get out of here, Simon! Now!" There was no answer from the Blue Room. "Simon?" I tried again with the same result.

I was about to head inside and yank him out, when he appeared in the doorway then asked, "What's wrong with you this time? What happened?"

He sounded far more irritated than concerned, and I didn't like it. "He was here! Geoffrey!" I told him. "He said I 'was his forever'."

"And that put you in such a big flap?" he replied absently as he stuffed the camera he carried into his duffle bag.

My eyes narrowed. "It wasn't *you* he threatened. It was me. I can be in as big a *flap* as I want."

He sighed then told me with exaggerated patience, "Listen, Jodie, tell me what happened in a succinct manner without the drama I don't need."

My eyes narrowed a second time. Simon was behaving very strangely. "Okay. Geoffrey was here. He wants me and won't let me leave. Is that succinct enough for you?"

"That will do. We have a plan. A good one I hope. He's not here with you now. I am. Let's go back to our room and regroup. You can rest while I watch the monitor before I pack it up. I want to see if we caught anything else on the cameras below we didn't get to see last night."

"I'm not *resting* in that room. I'm grabbing my stuff and heading downstairs. You do what you have to do."

He shrugged then said, "Suit yourself, but I'm really disappointed in you."

Back in our room, I was headed out the door when I had second thoughts. Something was going on with him. I had seen his quiet pissed off side just a short time ago, but this was different. Was it stress or had the change begun Geoffrey had warned us about? I remembered the Dark Man's words. Was he possessed by him or even Geoffrey? There was enough of Simon still there...at least the tech head worried about his documentary...but the rest of him was a cold stranger. But if what I suspected was true, none of it was his fault. Leaving him wasn't the answer. Finding a way to save him *was*, so I told him, "All right. I'll stay long enough for you to watch what we missed then we're both out of here."

"Fine. Just stay out of my way and let me do this."

He quickly scanned the camera feeds past the point where we had last viewed them. I was watching the monitor over his shoulder. There was more of the same frenzied spirit activity we had seen earlier then...simultaneously...all the cameras blinked and went dead.

"They must have drained the batteries this time," Simon murmured as he pushed his glasses back up on his nose then sighed. "But I already have some great footage plus what I hope to capture tonight. The grand finale!"

It was my turn to sigh. "Look. I need to ask you something, and I want a straight answer."

"Go for it."

"Are you possessed?"

Even his laugh was unfamiliar. "Why would you ask such a thing?"

"Because you don't seem like yourself. You're not the Simon I know."

"And you have too much imagination for your own good," he snapped as he pulled the EVP recorder from the duffle bag and thrust it into my hand. "Listen to it while I check out a couple of these frames. It will just take a few minutes, and we'll go right after. I promise."

I didn't want to...not even a little bit...but I rewound the tape and pressed 'play'. There was only silence for a very long time and then I heard a hoarse all too familiar voice say quite distinctly, "She is yours...for now. I will not interfere. Perhaps I will enter you, so we can both enjoy her with your young and vigorous body long dead as you may be."

Simon took the recorder from my nerveless fingers and replayed the spot again then let it spin on.

The next voice was Geoffrey's. "We have a pact. You may do what you want with the other."

The Dark Man laughed then replied, "Remember our agreement, or you will pay the price. There is much about her that interests me. No one else has ever sensed....."

I strained to hear the rest, but static drowned out his plans for me. "Okay! Do you understand why I need to get out of here?" I told Simon as I headed towards the door. "I'm carrying my stuff down to the kitchen where I will remain until it's time to head outside. I will never come back up here again."

"Fine by me. Take your bags, and I'll lug down all the rest without your help if that's the way you want it. Now let's get moving since you're in such a big hurry."

I snatched up my things and headed out the door. I had just passed the scullery when I heard Simon coming down the stairs behind me. Carrying two of the equipment cases, he brushed past me without a word then plunked them down inside the kitchen and retraced his steps. He was headed back upstairs alone, and I felt guilty because I didn't want to go with him. He hadn't really answered my question...just waltzed around it. From what I was seeing...hearing... it seemed more and more unlikely that Simon was still himself.

Inside the kitchen, I grabbed a blanket off the pile Matilda had gathered. Wrapping it around me, I found a spot on the floor close to the door and leaned back against the wall. Bella joined me there as Matilda told me, "You look dead on your feet, if you don't mind me sayin'. Why don't I take you back to the parlor where you can get a proper nap?"

I managed a smile I was far from feeling. "No thanks. I'm fine here. Had another encounter upstairs and really want to be somewhere close to an outside door that I can bolt out of if necessary."

"I understand. How 'bout I put the kettle on and fix you a nice cuppa tea?"

"That would be great," I replied just as Simon arrived for the second time.

Dropping another case on the table, he told me, "Look. I understand all this must be scaring the crap out of you, but we're so close. Every piece of solid evidence we have of the afterlife is.... Well, you know what I mean. Do you think....?"

"I *think* I am going to enjoy some tea and a nap. Right here with Bella. You can do what you want."

"This isn't like you," he snapped.

"And you aren't like you, so we're even."

He was cursing under his breath when he stormed back down the hall. I didn't care. All I could feel was a growing sense that I was right. It was then I realized how quiet Bella had been when

200

normally she was so excited to see him even when he'd been gone a short time. Had she also sensed Simon wasn't Simon any more?

Matilda brought me my tea then left to pack her own things from wherever she kept them. I wasn't really comfortable and was sure sleep was impossible, but I was wrong.

It was nearly dark when Simon shook me awake. "We've still got lots to do, so nap time is over. Up you go!"

He pulled me to my feet then told me, "Sorry if I've seemed distracted...abrupt...but I have a lot on my mind. Let's just see how tonight goes."

He almost seemed himself. Had I been wrong to think he was possessed? I was very much afraid that was more wishful thinking, but I clung to it as I gathered up the pile of blankets and headed outside where the shadows were closing in.

A leashed Bella and Matilda were already there, and she called to me over her shoulder, "Come this way. Simon and I picked out the perfect place while you were sleepin'. It's right over this hill."

I followed them to a flat grassy spot with a view of the sea that the setting sun had painted a blazing red and orange. I stood there mesmerized by its beauty then shivered. The light would soon be gone. Night was almost here and with it all that I feared.

"See!" Matilda called again as she scooped Bella into her arms. "Here's the salt ring Simon put me in charge of. Watch where you step, so you don't disturb it none."

She shortened Bella's leash and fastened it to a stake inside the circle as I carefully stepped over its rim and joined them. "This will keep her safe with all the commotion goin' on," she told me then added, "Look! Here comes Simon with the cameras and such. Went back and got him the one from the Red Room, so he'd have two. We talked a lot while you slept. His film sounds like a grand idea. I'm so happy to be a part of it."

"Let's just see if we survive the night," I told her with a flash of irritation. She seemed to be on his side now...whoever he was... and I found it disturbing.

Simon had reached us by then. His eyes glittered with excitement when he told us, "I've set up the NVR Recorder in the kitchen to receive the camera feeds. They both have audio. We all just need to stay calm and together. Tonight should be one helluva ride."

He was whistling as I watched him fasten the cameras to their tripods. He had always been my safety net and now he was a stranger. Possibly a dangerous one. Tomorrow and the boat seemed a long time away.

I forced myself to focus on spreading out the blankets. Matilda helped me flatten an end the wind had flipped over then told me, "I need to go grab the candles and lighter. Also, made more sandwiches for supper. Be right back."

She refused my offer to help, so I sat down next to Bella and whispered in her ear, "I don't think our Simon is here any more. What do you think?"

My question was answered a few minutes later, when Simon dropped down on the blanket next to us, and Bella uttered a low menacing growl. "Okay. That's enough of the masquerade," I told him. "You never gave me a straight answer, so I'll ask it again. Are you possessed?"

I wasn't surprised when he laughed a second time. "You know, this place has changed you. You're not the Jodie I met and fell in love with. You're like...well, like some kind of paranoid crazy person I can't depend on anymore. Here's a question for you. If I was possessed, why would I want to release the spirits when both Geoffrey and the Dark Man want them here?"

"I don't know. Maybe some part of Simon is still in charge. But I know how I feel...and look at Bella! She's afraid of you!"

"Enough already. We're both running on empty for lack of sleep and scared. Let's just get through the night and outta here in the morning. Okay?"

"How can I do that if I can't trust you to have my back?"

"Look! Here comes Matilda, and I don't want her to see us like this. Just smile and be nice like you used to be."

Like I had something to smile about. There wasn't a single word he had uttered that convinced me I was mistaken, but for Matilda's sake I would try. Rising to my feet, I helped her with the picnic basket and lantern she was carrying. Soon we were all tucking into PB&J sandwiches and hot coffee she poured from a Thermos twice the size of the one we'd left back at the cottage. She'd just finished and sat down on her blanket, when she cried, "Oh, look over there! It's that black cat again."

To my immense joy, Cinda was standing just at the edge of the deepest shadows. Her tail was twitching... her eyes glowing brightly as she stared at me then vanished. A wave of both sadness and disappointment washed over me and then I heard her soft, rumbling purr and felt her settle in my lap. She wasn't gone. She was with me, and so was Allison...or so I believed. They were there to watch over us. Protect us from evil. Maybe soon...some how...some way...Simon could be reclaimed and the island's horrors nothing more than a memory I would never forget no matter how much I wished otherwise.

Bella was the only one who sensed she was there. Tail wagging, she flopped down at the end of her leash and watched us closely as I stroked Cinda's soft fur and looked around me. The sun had long since vanished, but the day's last gray light still lingered off to the west. A full moon was rising, and the brightest stars now dotted the fast darkening sky. It felt peaceful when I wouldn't have thought that even remotely possible in a place like this.

Simon broke into my reverie with, "Like to get closer to midnight before we begin. Not sure it makes that much difference, but historically that seems to be the witching hour and a powerful spate of time. Sleep if you can. It will be a while before any of us get another chance."

At his words, Cinda jumped from my lap, and I felt a profound sense of loss even though I knew she hadn't abandoned me. We all would need both her and Allison if we were to survive the night. It would be good versus evil and there was no guarantee we would win. To divert my thoughts from the dark place they had gone, I asked Matilda where she was from.

"I was born over in the UK. Me da was a customer at the flower shop where me mum worked over there, and he brought us to the States when I was fourteen. That's why my accent is a bit Brit...a bit Yank and everything in between. He left us at Christmas some ten years ago or so. Said he had a surprise for me he had to fetch then took a runner and never came back. She died two years ago. Dropped dead in her tracks comin' back home from the paper mill where we both worked."

She paused to swipe at her tears then continued, "Needed to get away after that, so when I saw the advert for this job I caught a bus and went for the interview. Thought there would be a lot of others, but not many wanted to live this isolated like with no shops and all. Ms. Blackthorne said 'I would have to do', and here I am. She were a hard one to deal with...a bossy boots to be sure and downright cruel sometimes...but I came to care about her, like I said. I couldn't leave the poor old thing all on her own no matter how bad things got here. I'd almost changed my mind about that and then you came."

"Now we just need to release the ghosts, and we can all leave together, if nothing changes those plans in what will be a very long night," I added with a sigh.

Silence hung over us as I watched the flickering lantern, or the now star crowded heavens. The moon continued its trek across the sky casting a silver path across the endless sea and brushing the wind tossed grass around us with its radiance. My thoughts wandered back

205

to Greystone and how close Simon and I had come to losing our lives...where Cinda did lose hers. I thought about Millie who had also died there...about Allison who had been with me throughout it all.

By then, I had become increasingly drowsy… and *might* have slept for a while… when Simon announced, "Let's get started. This waiting is taking a toll on all our nerves. I'll light the four candles at the quadrants and switch on the cameras while you two take your places over there in the center."

Yawning, I scrambled to my feet and joined Matilda there. The shadows pressed close from all sides, and I had a strong sense someone was there…watching us as though we were merely players on a stage meant for his amusement. There was no way to tell if it was the Dark Man or Geoffrey. It could well have been just my imagination.

Meanwhile, Matilda had stuck a single while candle in the ground and lit it. I knew what that meant. Simon confirmed it a few moments later when he rejoined us. "From what we've seen so far, the best way to summon the spirits is another séance, Jodie, whether you like it or not."

"Which I don't, but it needs to be done."

"You're in charge, so handle it."

"Okay," I murmured as he extinguished the lantern. "Let's all join hands."

A strange kind of energy shot up my arm when I took his. I tried to jerk it back, but he held on tightly. Not wanting to frighten

Matilda by persisting, I took a deep steadying breath and began, "*We pray that the power of Love encircles all those gathered here. That it will protect us and guard us from all evil and prevent any attachments that would follow us. May that Higher Power light our path and guide us through whatever may come our way this night and always.* Now we are supposed to add our own...."

"We'll skip that part tonight," Simon cut in sharply. "Let's just begin."

So, that's what I did. Taking yet another deep breath, I called, "Celia! Celia, the time has come if you and the others are ready to do this. Please let me know that you hear me."

The candles flickered though there was now no wind. "Okay, if that was you, please try to materialize...become visible."

The candles flickered violently then went out one by one leaving only the moon and stars to light our circle. A spire of white light appeared that slowly transformed into Celia. Her dark hair and white gown churned about her as though tossed by a violent force.

Her eyes were bright with both excitement and hope when she told us, "They are coming! All those from above and below. John is among them. He had been chained to the wall all this time when I had thought him taken away and hanged by those who came here. We are all terrified of the Dark Man who would keep us in this place, but we have come to trust you. A spirit from this Light you spoke of came to us...a woman with red hair and a black cat. She told us that what you said was true. That through this tunnel we would find those we loved and lost. I hope to find my son among them. See! They are ready now."

All around us, orbs of light had appeared then slowly morphed into the vague shapes of men, women, and children. They were dressed in the tattered remnants of clothes that spanned centuries...the rich and the poor... lords and ladies...servants and sailors. Many were the ones we had seen on the cameras...the frenzied ones from the cave...but others I hadn't seen before. They advanced to the edge of the salt ring in total silence. Only, the sound of the waves and Bella's whine could be heard. Their mouths gaped open in quiet entreaty and hope filled their eyes as they waited to see what happened next. I prayed I wouldn't fail them. That they hadn't come in vain.

I wasn't at all sure what to say, so I spoke from my heart, "You must overcome your fear. The Dark Man cannot keep you here. It's time to reunite with your loved ones who have been waiting a very long time to take you home. You must want that with all your hearts, and a tunnel of Light will descend from the sky linking heaven and earth. They are waiting for you there. You must believe. Look up, pray, and believe!"

All eyes turned to the night sky...all but mine. I sensed then saw a black fog creeping up the hill around us. Slowly, it came closer until the spirits saw it, too.
Screaming...crying...praying...cursing, they scattered like leaves in a hurricane. Now just the four of us remained inside our protective circle.

Simon's hand tightened on mine. "We're safe here. Just don't break the circle no matter how bad it gets. You, too, Matilda. Just hang in there. We'll be fine."

The fog was closer now, and inside I saw a dazzling core of pulsing red light. A familiar dark figure was silhouetted against its brightness. He had almost reached us when he called, "I told you they could never leave, and yet you persisted. A transgression I won't forgive."

By then, I had had enough. He had sickened me with the tale of his life, and now he may have destroyed the one chance the others had to find their way back to those they loved. Yanking my hands free, I sprang to my feet and faced him squarely. "How dare you speak of forgiveness! You are nothing but a sadistic monster who thinks he has won. We won't give up! We will try again aided by those far more powerful than you. The power of Good shall overcome...."

"Evil?" he cut in before I could finish. "Who's to say it won't be the other way around? That Evil trumps Good? Come with me willingly, and I will spare those with you."

I don't know exactly what I expected from Simon, but it was way more than his silence. Spinning around, I saw him standing there lit by the Dark Man's core of brightness. Something was pouring from his gaping mouth...a glowing blue 'something' that began to reshape into Geoffrey just as Simon slumped to the ground. My heart was beating frantically as I dropped down next to him. He was still breathing but just barely.

209

"Don't waste your time on him," Geoffrey told me as he took out a lace edged handkerchief and dusted off his glowing frock coat. "He is still alive and will remain so...for a time. I let a *revised* version of him surface long enough to play with his toys, because they were part of his persona and...quite frankly...beyond my understanding. Needless to say, all that he has done will be destroyed in due time. Come with me, my Serilda! You are mine until the Dark Man claims you as is his right. We have struck a bargain where you are concerned, and I must honor it."

I jumped to my feet and backed away which brought me perilously close to the edge of the ring. It hadn't worked so far with Simon aka Geoffrey, but I hoped and prayed it would keep the Dark Man out. I was wrong. His swirling dark fog drifted over the salt quite easily and engulfed me. I was close to the flame red center that gave no heat as an intense feeling of sadness...longing...and then emptiness washed over me just before blackness claimed me.

CHAPTER NINE

I groaned and opened my eyes slowly then looked around in the dim light. I had expected to see the Dark Man, but it was Geoffrey sprawled on the bed next to me looking astonishingly handsome in a black, silk dressing gown. Propped up on one elbow, he was toying with my hair and smiling as I looked up into his dark eyes.

"Before you ask, you are once more alone with me in my secret chamber...at least for a time."

"What's happened to the others?" I demanded to know as I struggled to a sitting position only to be shoved back down.

"They should be fine...for now. The Dark Man will be quite busy for a time dealing with the chaos you caused. His puppets...his toys are quite out of control, and that is something he will not tolerate."

"So, he brought me here and left me with you?"

He grimaced wryly. "Would it were so. He dumped you in my arms after you swooned then left. Bringing you here was no mean feat though I did take the short cut this time. I had forgotten how much a living woman weighs having not swept one off her feet in a very long time."

To my surprise, I found myself saying, "I've wondered how you manage to feel as real as living flesh when you are a ghost?"

"A gift I have that most others do not. Tis past time for me to show you how very *real* I am," he replied with a seductive smile as he traced my lower lip with his forefinger.

I shoved his hand away then told him, "Just let me go. Let me get back to the others and off this island. If you touch me...try anything with me, I'll make you more than sorry. I defended myself from predators when I was growing up and improved on those skills with lessons in the martial arts that could hurt or kill you if you weren't already dead." I was more or less babbling...stalling for time and he knew it.

He sighed heavily. "As entertaining as it is to hear you ramble on about your past accomplishments, we do not have that much time before he claims you. So...."

A plan began to form in my frantic mind as I cut in with, "*So, we can't have that, can we? You could have me all to yourself if we got rid of him. You would be Monster #1 on the island instead of #2. Doesn't that sound great?*"

He laughed then leaned over me. A kiss followed. The ravaging, hungry kind I had never experienced before. It both frightened and stirred me, which frightened me even more. Was my traitorous body betraying me?

The silk robe had parted exposing his muscled chest feathered lightly with black hair, and I shoved against it with all my strength, which seemed to have no effect at all. "Not now! Not when he can intrude at any moment!" I found the willpower to shout then added, "Let me help you rid yourself of him. Together we can do it, but it can't be down here. There must be some place he's more vulnerable." I was clutching at straws, as they say, and hoping for the best.

He rolled on his back and sighed. "You must think me a fool. I know a diversion when I encounter one, but I am interested enough to hear you out."

"Okay. You're right about the diversion, but think about it. Wouldn't it be great to rid this island of him? You and the others have been under his control since forever."

"By and large, he and I have managed to exist somewhat amiably. We never wanted the same thing until you arrived and that changed. You still hold my interest, so pray continue with your plan."

"This is what is called a long shot, but when he had me in his clutches I felt this profound sorrow that must be caused by something or someone. Let's hope it's a *someone*. What if we find whoever it is and....fill in the blank here 'cause I am running out of ideas."

"Hmm. Let's see," he murmured. "If it is a 'love' thing...which your words suggest... perhaps whoever it may be could be persuaded to take him elsewhere."

"Like where?"

He laughed. "I supplied my bit. Now it is your turn to continue the plot."

"Okay. Let me think. Hell comes to mind, but that may be wishful thinking. Why don't we just try it and see how it plays out?"

He rolled over and sat on the edge of the bed. "You've quite ruined the mood, so tell me how you plan to accomplish the impossible?"

A memory resurfaced. "He told me he had kept a woman alive who had been washed up on the island. That she had died in childbirth having what must have been his baby. She might be the source of his sadness even though I doubt that someone like him could ever love anyone in a healthy kind of way. But say that I'm wrong about that. That he did love her. They would have shared the cottage though I didn't feel her presence there. As a ghost, she could be anywhere, but the cottage might serve as a conduit. A means to summon her."

"I have never rambled about willy-nilly. Would not know how to begin, but come. I find myself quite liking the idea of having you all to myself for as long as you please me."

My eyes narrowed to mere slits. "And if I don't?"

His smile was beguiling. "Why worry about that impossibility? Up you go. We have much to accomplish if we are to save your friends and finish our little dalliance that may well lead to something far more."

I didn't want to think about what that might mean, so I focused on following his now glowing figure as he hurried down the passageways between the walls...some of which I had never been down before... and then we were outside under the star filled heavens. Grabbing my arm, he half lifted half pulled me along at an incredible rate that quickly brought us to the cottage. Remembering all too well what had happened the last time I was there, I hesitated to step inside which he soon remedied.

"He could be back here at any time," he told me as he yanked me over the threshold. "Do what you must and do it fast."

As I looked around, I wasn't at all sure where to begin. The bed she had died in would have been somewhere within this room. If she hated him, as she surely must have, there would be no reason for her to return, but I had to try.

214

"I don't know who you are, but we need your help to free all the spirits trapped on this island by him. Please come! We need you desperately!"

There was no answer, so I tried again. It was on the fourth try that I heard a long drawn out sigh in the far corner...a second followed and then a woman spoke in little more than a husky whisper, "I have come albeit reluctantly at the prodding of a woman with a black cat. She was quite emphatic that I should answer your summons despite never wanting to set foot in this place again."

"That would be Allison and Cinda though I can't begin to imagine how they found you."

"Time and distance as you know it does not exist on the other side. Beyond that, I have no way of conveying what I barely understand myself. My name is Alice Nightingale. Who are you?"

"I'm Jodie and this is Geoffrey Blackthorne."

She began to materialize then...just a pale blue wisp who said, "He is one of us though quite solid from the look of him. How is it you can see us?"

"I'm not at all sure, but I can. Sometimes to my immense regret. What is your story? I know what the Dark Man said, but I would like to hear your version."

The blue wisp began to take on a vague shape as she scoffed, "The Dark Man? Is that what he calls himself? He is Osbert Hendricks marooned here by those who hated him...hated him as I did. I was returning from England where I had been visiting my sister when a storm blew up out of nowhere and drove our ship off

215

course. I was scared...terrified as were all the rest onboard with good cause. We were shipwrecked on the rocks offshore. I'll never forget the horror...the sound of the ship being torn to pieces...the screams of those around me mingling with mine. Some of us were washed ashore still alive or barely so. He...he killed the others with a club. Battered them to death. I remember their vacant open eyes staring up at the sky...their shattered skulls...the blood...."

She broke off for a moment as she struggled with her tears then continued, "He kept me alive. Nursed me back to health despite how much I wanted to die. He never spoke beyond what was necessary and then one day he did. It was a tale of horror...of what he had done to survive. I tried to block it out but could not. He wanted absolution I think. Forgiveness for his sins, which I could not grant him. Would *never* grant him even if it was within my power to do so. I was his unwilling companion...the object of his lust and then I became large with child. At first, I hated what was growing inside me...wanted to rip it from my womb...but as I felt it quicken I came to think of it as mine alone. That he had no part in it. That its birth would ease the unspeakable horror of my days."

She had fully materialized by then. Wearing a filmy white gown that floated around her like cobwebs, she was almost as tall as me with pale gold hair that cascaded nearly to her waist. Her gaze swept the room and then she sighed. "I remember it all so well to my eternal regret. Many hours I struggled to give birth and then I lost consciousness and never awoke to here...this place. I found myself back at my parents' house and there I remained until now. They

216

never knew I haunted them. With time, their spirits joined me one by one, and we are happy in our own way though changes have come we can do nothing about. I have always wondered what had happened to my baby. Had it been born alive and well? Was it a little boy or girl? Perhaps you know?"

I shook my head. "All I know is that he told me you had died in childbirth. Nothing about the baby." I remembered reading about the horrors of Allison's birth...Millie's loss and gut wrenching grief. I thought about Celia's never ending search for her dead son. "I believe you will find your baby in the Light if you leave with the others. I'm still hoping it will happen tonight if we can get him out of the way long enough. He doesn't want them to leave and that includes me and my friends."

"He has the power to stop them. That much I know of him, for in death he would be more powerful than in life. Tell me about this Light and your plan."

"There is a tunnel of Light that connects...."

"Hurry it along," an impatient Geoffrey cut in as he grabbed my arm. "He will soon be looking for both of us since I have broken faith with him and now kept you over long."

"This can't be hurried," I replied as I shook free then told her what I had told the others.

Hope filled her eyes as she moved closer...then closer still. "Perhaps a merciful God will let me find my baby. Help me bring my parents into this Light, so we can all be together forever. What do you want of me?"

217

"Can you think of any way we can stop him?"

"I believe he came to love me over time though he never said as much for which I was grateful. Let me think on it, and I will give you my answer."

"There is no time for reflection!" Geoffrey told her sharply. "He will end this before first light while he is at his strongest. It may already be too late for the one she calls Simon... not that I care overmuch."

"But why would he hurt him?" I cried. "It's me he wants!"

"It pleasures him to kill," he called after me as I headed out the door at a flat out run.

He caught up with me and spun me around. "If you would permit me to carry you again, we would arrive much sooner."

I sighed. "Whatever it takes. Just hurry!"

Moonlight traced the contours of his handsome face as he smiled enigmatically and scooped me up in his arms. "Would it were I you would risk so much to save. Let it be known, my intentions towards you have changed."

"And why is that?" I found myself asking out of curiosity instead of settling for 'grateful'.

His smile deepened. "You are not some baggage to seduce and discard. You are too...well, real though that does not suffice to describe you. I have watched you since the moment you set foot on this island. When I initially possessed Simon, I sought to damage your trust. Make you hate and even fear the dark Simon he'd become, so that when I claimed you he would not be in your thoughts and heart. That has since changed. Were it possible...if I hadn't made a pact with the 'devil'...I would have stayed within him and lived his life with you. Been the man you know and love though there are aspects of him I would have had trouble emulating. As already mentioned, his penchant for gadgets and such is beyond my comprehension."

"You would never have been able to pull it off," I told him. "I would always know my Simon no matter how hard you tried. Now let's get moving!"

He sighed. "I fear you both see and listen with your heart, but sometimes that heart can be blind. A word of warning only."

"There's no time for riddles," I snapped at him. "Get going or put me down and let me walk!"

"Very well," he murmured. "Milady's wish is my command...at least for now. Perhaps my baser instincts will claim me later."

***

We arrived back at the circle where Geoffrey set me on my feet. There was no sign of the others.

"Simon must have recovered and is looking for me. He would have taken Bella with him, and Matilda might have joined them," I called to Geoffrey who was now kicking at the salt ring with the toe of his boot and smiling grimly.

"There is another more likely possibility," he told me. "The Dark Man has them all."

219

"I won't think that! I can't think that! I bet Simon believes you're the one who took me, so he'll check out the Red Room first and then your den of iniquity below."

"Where you had been but a short time ago," he reminded me needlessly. "Let me know what you find. I don't want to be involved from this point on believing what I do."

"Because now you're afraid of the Dark Man like all the rest of us?"

"Terrified better describes it. I have angered him by breaking our arrangement and, in doing so, the truce we have shared for centuries. Retrieving your Simon is akin to snatching a bone from a rabid dog."

He had vanished before I could reply. Grabbing the lantern off the blanket, I lit it and ran back to the kitchen where I flipped the light switch on the wall. Nothing happened. The power was off again. Had the generator failed, or was it something more sinister?

Swapping the lantern for a LED flashlight, I searched through the cases Simon had stacked by the counter and grabbed a bottle of holy water. Simon had tossed it on Geoffrey with no apparent effect, but it was one more weapon in my next to nothing arsenal.

I was running full tilt when I sped up the back stairs. All around me, I heard whispers and saw flashes of light. The spirits had returned and were waiting to see what happened next. I could not...would not fail them or the others though the how of that had yet to be determined. If Geoffrey was right...and there was every chance he was... I would be confronting a very powerful, angry entity hell bent on doing all of us immeasurable harm.

My troubled thoughts carried me down the hall to the Blue Room and its connecting door. Flinging it open, I flashed my light around Geoffrey's former prison that was profoundly cold and empty. I searched for and found the hidden door in the paneling then hurried through without hesitation. As I made my way down the narrow passageway between the walls, I had a strong sense the spirits had followed me but didn't stop to check it out. Every moment counted. It seemed like forever before I reached his hidden sanctuary where a red light fingered its way beneath the closed door. Taking a deep breath, ignoring my trembling legs, I yanked it open and stepped inside where a horrific scene awaited me.

A seemingly lifeless Simon was suspended in mid air while the Dark Man sprawled in a nearby chair manipulating him like a puppet dangling from its invisible strings. There was no sign of Matilda or Bella, and I feared the worst. "Put him down!" I screamed as I sped his way and tried to pull him free. "What have you done to him? Where are the others?"

He shrugged as he continued to jerk Simon about. "He is still alive. As to the others, they are somewhere within these walls. I once made a marionette out of a stable cat when I was a lad much to my mother's chagrin. I had quite forgotten how entertaining it can be. How did you manage to elude Geoffrey and where can I find him? He has much to answer for."

"Find him yourself!" I spat back which was probably not the wisest course, but by then I was furious.

"Tut tut! You are in a flap yet again, aren't you. I will release your Simon if you come willingly and do what you are told."

I shook my head and shouted, "Let him go! Let us all go and you can have your miserable island all to yourself!"

"Ah, look at you. The warrior woman rushing to everyone's defence useless as it may be. By the by, the other souls you tried to save have been persuaded to stay despite your best efforts to convince them they were free to go."

"They're already terrified of you. What new inducement have you added?"

He smiled slyly. "I told them I would eat them...swallow them so they could never leave me. I wonder why I hadn't thought of it before," he mused as he rose from his seat and headed my way.

Every fiber of my being screamed at me to run, but I stood my ground. "And could you do that? Would it work?" I managed to ask hoping he didn't notice both the quaver in my voice and that I was stalling for time.

To my surprise, he smiled...it wasn't the pleasant kind. "Perhaps. Perhaps not. But as a threat, it was most effective. Now what do I do about you?"

His nearly fleshless fingers gripped my arm searing my flesh...or so it felt, but I dredged up a grim smile of my own from somewhere. Shaking free, I told him as calmly as I could manage, "I'm not afraid of you, Osbert Hendricks. Release Simon. Now!"

At a wave of his hand, Simon collapsed to the floor at my feet where he opened his eyes and squinted up at me. "Forget about me! Just get the hell outta here!" he whispered hoarsely, but, of course, I didn't listen.

"Not going to happen. We leave here together or not at all. How badly are you hurt?"

"Shaken up mostly and not sure where I am or how I got here," he replied as I helped him to a sitting position.

"What happened to Matilda and Bella?"

"Don't know. I was in the Blue Room when everything went blank."

"You were possessed by Geoffrey until ....."

A bemused Dark Man had only been half listening and now cut in sharply with, "How is it you know my name? There is only one who did, and she is no more."

"Alice was here," I replied as I watched his reaction closely. "I spoke with her at the cottage. She is waiting there for you."

I was astonished at the shift of emotions behind his ravaged, bestial face. Disbelief...fear...hope...longing...and then he simply disappeared. He was headed for the cottage, and I both hoped and prayed Alice had done her 'thinking' and come up with a plan to save us all. Meanwhile, we had to work fast. Every minute was precious.

I helped an unsteady Simon to his feet and led him to the door. "Where do you think Matilda would take Bella and hide if she isn't...well, dead by now?" I asked.

"Maybe the parlor we slept in last night, but she could be anywhere on the island."

"There is far too much ground to cover and far too little time, Simon. Osbert will have reached Alice by now and the outcome has every chance of going very, very badly."

The passageway in front of us was now jammed with indistinct, glowing shapes murmuring among themselves. The spirits that had fled when the Dark Man was there had now rejoined us.

"Maybe they can help," I told Simon.

"Worth a try. Go for it!"

Taking a deep breath, I called, "Please! We need your help. We are looking for Matilda and our dog. They are in danger, and the one you all fear will be back soon."

A long silence followed and then a shrill voice called back, "She is in the place of books. The dog did not go with her willingly, but is quiet now."

A shiver shot through me. She was old, and I remembered all too well Cinda's fate. "Come on!" I shouted to Simon over my shoulder as I took off at a run.

Still wobbly, he did his best to keep up with me as I retraced my steps to the Red Room then out the door and down the hall to the main staircase. We were running side by side when we reached the library where I flashed my light inside. Matilda was sitting on the floor by the window cradling Bella in her arms.

"She was tired and sleeps now," she murmured when we reached her. "We ran and ran until I thought of here where I have found comfort in the books within these walls. I learned from their pages much I didn't know of the world and its people. Been to places I would never see and..."

She broke off what she was saying as Bella woke up and wriggled free of her arms. Soft 'woofing' sounds bubbled to the surface, and her tail wagged furiously as she greeted each of us in turn.

Matilda shook her head. "She loves you both above all else. I should have known I could not keep her. Not for long. Where are the others? The one you call the Dark Man and Geoffrey Blackthorne?"

"That's a very good question," Simon replied as he rose to his feet. "A better one is: What do we do now?"

Behind us in the hall, I heard a mix of voices all pleading for a second chance. The spirits had followed us there. We couldn't let them down.

"Listen to them! We might still be able to save them if we hurry," I urged Simon.

To my surprise, he tipped up my chin then kissed me with infinite tenderness before he replied, "Then let's do it no matter what the cost."

"It may be our lives."

He smiled wryly. "We know about the Light, so it won't be our souls. Let's release them. All of them before the Dark Man comes back and tries to stop us."

"Come on, Matilda! We have to go," I told her as I pulled her to her feet. "Help us find the closest exit in this labyrinth."

"I would rather stay here where I feel safe," she whispered as she shook off my grasp. "You need to find your own way out."

Celia was among the glowing spirits that now spilled into the room. "Follow me," she told us over her shoulder as she cleared a path through the others and zoomed back the way we had come. A side passage took us to a room with a hidden door behind a garden mural. From there, we exited outside beneath the full moon that had just reached its zenith and blanketed the island in its silver light.

I looked back at the spirits who had followed us then at Celia who was as solid as I had ever seen her. "You all remember what is needed," I called to them. "Shed your fear of him and believe it will happen. Do it fast for he could find us again at any moment."

A ripple of voices rose then fell. Only the sound of the waves broke the intense silence and then someone shouted, "I see something! Up there below the north star!"

I saw it, too. Just a tiny speck of light moving our way at an incredible speed like a long tailed comet. Closer and closer it came as we all watched in awe. As it drew still nearer, it re-shaped into a cloud floored tunnel lit from the top by a brilliant white Light. A figure clothed in shimmering rainbow colors emerged from there and began to descend. As the tunnel hovered just overhead, I saw it was now a woman wearing a print housedress and carrying a baby in her arms.

"I see you down there, Horace! Time to come home," she called.

A spirit dressed in the tattered garb of a seaman shouted, "Maddy!" then sped skyward. As he gathered them both in his arms, more shimmering, iridescent figures passed through the Light, and began their descent. Crying, shouting, and laughing, many of those around us shot upward as they recognized their loved ones among them. John Long the pirate might have been with them, but there was no way to tell.

Tears streaming down her cheeks, Celia's eyes never left the tunnel and then she shouted, "Sebastian!" A young boy screamed "Mama" and headed her way at a run. They met half way up the tunnel where she dropped to her knees and swept him into her arms. I could feel their immense joy like a palpable thing as he took her hand and led her back up through the clouds towards the Light. She paused at the top then looked back at me, smiled and was gone.

I kept brushing away the tears that dribbled down my cheeks as more and more of the ghosts who had been trapped here by fear joined those waiting for them. One of them was Joe. Hesitant at first, he finally soared skyward then paused on the edge of the tunnel and looked below. I thought he was about to change his mind when I heard a woman call his name. It must have been his parents who took his hands and led him into the Light. I knew he would never be afraid or lonely again.

It was Simon who spotted Ms. Blackthorne. As imperious as ever...back ramrod straight...she was headed for the tunnel with a squawking Bart perched on her shoulder. An excited Bella had been watchful but silent till she saw him then uttered a long, eerie howl that sent goose bumps racing up my spine.

Simon drew me close. In the moonlight, I could see his own eyes were wet with tears, and I knew how deeply he was moved. He would be remembering, just as I was, the exodus at Greystone and all that followed. Now it was happening again. They were all finding their way home, and we had helped them.

Silently, we continued to watch. The last of the spirits were still soaring skyward when Geoffrey arrived.

"Where have you been?" I asked purely out of curiosity. Whatever hold he once had on me was gone.

"Secretly spying on Osbert and Alice," he replied with a wry grimace. "Their reunion was...well, surprising. The infamous terror of this island looked quite pitiful in his eagerness to see her. She was magnificent. Strong in a way I doubt she had ever risked being in life. He took her to where he had buried her. A stone cairn on the edge of the cliff where she could 'see the sunrise across the water'...his words. There was another grave next to it. It seems they had a daughter who had survived the birth and died on her nineteenth birthday. Took a fall from the cliff while exploring one of the higher caves. Alice wept and wailed like a banshee. He tried to console her in his clumsy monster way, but she wouldn't listen to what he had to say though she should have. It was most informative though I already knew that of which he spoke. I found the whole thing most disconcerting and left at that point. They could well be headed here now. Alice is convinced she will find her daughter in that Light up there despite him telling her otherwise."

"She'd better hurry!" I told him. "The tunnel is starting....."

I never finished what I'd been about to say as a glowing Alice sped out of the darkness followed by a giant of a man. He looked, well, almost human instead of the creature he had been before though no less dangerous.

"Where is my daughter?" Alice cried.

"Follow the others through that tunnel and into the Light. She'll be there. I'm sure of it," I told her hoping I was right with all my heart.

"No! I am not there," a voice spoke from the shadows, "I am here, Mother."

Simon and I whirled around in surprise as Matilda stepped forward. "I am inside this one they call by another name. My own is Birdie. He named me after the seabirds I love and after you, Mother. I have inhabited many of the living who came to this island since I died. Learned through them the things I had no time to learn...no place to learn them. I wish so much I had known you. Father wept for you a long time when he thought I couldn't hear. He told me what he knew of you. That you were beautiful as a fairytale princess and would have given anything to have lived long enough to hold me in your arms."

"Yes, anything and everything, but death took that chance from me. Please let me hold you now."

Bella howled as Simon and I watched the glowing spirit of a young girl emerge from Matilda's body that slumped to the ground. "I possessed her and played the role of 'Matilda the maid' though I wasn't always in control. Sometimes she was herself and wondering where the time went when her body belonged to me. She'll be confused...dazed for a bit I think...but will mend," Birdie reassured us as Alice gathered her close.

While they wept and murmured things I couldn't hear, we knelt next to Matilda who seemed to be in a deep sleep but unharmed. A whining Bella flopped down next to her and nudged her with her nose.

Birdie joined us there. "I only have a moment, but I want you to know I liked all of you and wanted you to stay here with me. I damaged the things that would take you away, but I did not cause your boat to sink. That was one called Joe who acted for my father who had his own reasons for keeping you here. He and I have been estranged for some time with good cause. He would lock me in the house when a boat was in peril. Told me it wasn't safe, and he would do what he could to save those wrecked on the rocks, but I crawled out the window and followed him one night. I will never forget what I saw...the blood...the screams...the death of the innocent. I came to fear him after that and never spoke to him again. Not in the short years left of my life or the many years that followed. He ceased to exist for me and with him it was the same."

She sighed then paused for a moment before she continued. "But enough of that. Let me confess that I made the circle of sugar and not salt. I could not risk being discovered if I failed to enter it, for there is evil in me I bury deep. A darkness that claims me from time to time. No doubt from my tainted blood. I might have killed the old woman though I'm not sure why other than I did not like her overmuch. It certainly wasn't because she had refused to obey my father. At the last moment, she had decided not to jump, and I *might* have pushed her over the edge though my memory of it is unclear. I am sorry for all the wrong I may have done and would go now into the Light with my mother. Go to a place of unconditional love where my sins will be forgiven."

Rising to her feet, she took Alice's hand. "Come, Mother. We must leave now before the tunnel disappears and our chance is gone."

The Dark Man had listened quietly as his daughter spoke, and I wondered what he was thinking. It seemed unlikely he would let them leave without trying to stop them, and I was right. "You are not going anywhere! You are staying here with me!" he roared.

Alice shook her head and floated upward taking Birdie with her. "We are not afraid of you. Not any more. Not ever again."

"Please! I beg of you. Do not leave me, Alice. I cannot bear the loneliness."

"Perhaps if you repented your atrocities you could join them," I suggested though I had an abundance of doubt. "Are you at all sorry?"

"I did what needed doing and quite enjoyed most of it," was his reply.

"There's your answer! He needs to stay here. A prisoner of this island forever," Alice told me as she and Birdie hovered just above us. "He has promised not to harm you, so you should be safe until the sun reaches its zenith. Farewell and thank you."

Hand in hand, they soared upward and entered the tunnel just before it withdrew and disappeared in the night sky.

An angry, bereft Dark Man morphed into a seething mass of red then shouted, "I have given my word to let you go come morning. Should your departure be delayed for any reason, I will tear all three of you to bits." The black fog he favored engulfed him, and he was gone. Only Geoffrey remained.

"I would really like nothing more than punching you in your aristocratic nose," Simon told him.

"Why don't you sprinkle more of that holy water on me? Other than providing a distasteful wetness, it was as useless as your fists would be. I quite enjoyed possessing you. In time, I would have been able to play the role of simple Simon to perfection as I have already told Serilda who had her doubts…unjustified as they were."

"Why didn't you leave with the others just now when you had the chance?" I asked. "You told me you were a rake but innocent of the crimes you'd been charged with."

Geoffrey looked up at the moon that was now headed for the horizon. It was a long moment before he answered. "As to your first query, I very much fear there in no one in your heaven waiting for me, nor is it a place I would favor. Too many righteous souls for my taste. As to your second statement, my father was the one who raped and murdered those women as he confessed to me one night over his cups. It was years later when the workmen were still here, so I had them add his death trap to my modifications. Afterwards, I waited and didn't spring it for a very, very long time. Savored the notion of it till one night...well, you saw the result."

"Why are you telling me this now?"

"Because I was there when you found his body and figured out who it was. The wall was thick, but I often listened on the other side to his pitiful cries and hopeless scratching. I had hated him enough to enjoy his suffering. Relished it. I confess all this now because I don't want you to think me guilty of patricide without just cause, which would make me, in truth, the monster you once thought me."

"You certainly had ample reason to despise him considering the hell he put you through, but why were you blamed for his crimes?"

"As you no doubt noticed from the family portraits, we looked much the same. It was he the witness saw running from the scene of the crime. He lured them to a rendezvous with a forged note supposedly from me. Notes found among their belongings after their death. He had watched me with those I had brought home through a peephole in the wall and desired them...stalked them...raped then killed them to ensure their silence. His hired men rescued me before the hangman's noose ended my life, and he brought me here because he felt remorse that I should die in his place, yet he blamed me for putting temptation in his path. Making him into a monster of lust and blood. He locked me away to punish me for his own crimes and, in his madness, thought it justified. This house is yet another testament to that madness. What sane person would have had it dragged over here and rebuilt at such enormous expense of time, labor and money? He put it down to his royal eccentricity and that he could 'damn well do as he pleased'. Told those few who would listen, that it was his private kingdom where he was the wielder of justice...the master of all. A trait perhaps inherited from my great grandfather who had similar delusions and proclivities on a much smaller scale. Father had been a powerful, important man in the society of our time that he shunned, and here he was nothing. This island became his prison as much as mine until I released him in my own way and time."

"You never told me how you died. How did you meet your end?" I found myself asking.

He smiled wryly then replied, "Father kept a large amount of money on hand to pay for the staff and supplies...repairs and such...that he regularly replenished from his account in the Bank of England. When he disappeared, his well of wealth went dry and the staff went unpaid. In lieu of their wages, they looted this place and left on the next supply boat. By then, I had fallen ill with a raging fever and had taken to my bed, or I would have gone with them. They abandoned me here to die, and so I did. In killing him, I had unwittingly sealed my own fate. End of story."

"So, you were the lump I landed on when you took me down there," I surmised with a grimace of distaste.

"Yes, that was all that was left of me. A pile of bones buried in satin. Ah, look! The maid sans 'Birdie' stirs to life...at least a bit. I knew about her, of course, but chose not to tell you. It was far more entertaining watching the three of you. I dared not seduce her lest I rouse her father's ire despite their mutual claims of detachment. You know all too well what a mistake that would have been, so I limited myself to playing with Matilda when she was herself and no other. Bye the bye, you will both stay here with me, but Simon will have to be eliminated. Ah! See how he glares at me! He would kill me if that was not an impossibility."

A coldly angry Simon had listened quietly to his tale. Now he thrust me behind him...where I didn't stay...then told him, "We're leaving together...all of us...and you won't stop us!"

Geoffrey laughed. "Ah, the drama of it all. The heroic posturing. And who will stop me from stopping you?" he drawled.

"We will," called a familiar voice from the shadows. It was Allison dressed in the green gown I had last seen her in ...the one I had worn to the Christmas Ball. A tail lashing Cinda was cradled in her arms. "And I am not alone. We are their family and together more powerful than you could ever be!"

I could see them then...a glowing red headed Millie and her Eric...a smiling couple who must be the parents I had never really known...and Henry with his Edith just as I remembered them.

Geoffrey's dark gaze swept them all. "It seems you have an army to protect you. Hardly sporting. So, I will take my leave for the time being." He sighed deeply then vanished. From the darkness, he whispered close to my ear, "You have awakened my passion and perhaps stirred my love though I am not sure what that emotion feels like having never known such in life or in death. This said, I fear I will be lonely without you. Don't leave me."

When I didn't reply, I sensed he had left just as Allison pulled me into a hug then told me, "Your strength amazes me. I have watched over you since you set foot on this island as I think you knew, but you always managed to survive even the worst of it without my help except for a nudge or two when necessary." She smiled then added, "You may not have needed our intervention just now, but we all wanted you to know we were here for you and will return should you need us again."

"And that includes you, boy," Henry told Simon, "Me and your grandma will be watchin' over you, too. Don't ever forget it."

"I don't think he's likely to, Henry, judging from that look on his face," a laughing Edith pointed out. "Always remember, Simon, we love you...you and Jodie...and that love is forever."

They began to fade as a desperate Bella tried to reach them. A tearful Henry gathered her in his arms. "I'll be coming for you, old girl, but not yet. Them two still need you." They vanished then and Bella's mournful howls shattered the silence that followed.

I thought about what Allison had just said. I wasn't nearly as strong as she believed. I had almost succumbed to Geoffrey's seduction and been way beyond terrified most of the time. My survival had been due to luck more than anything, or was it because I believed that she and Cinda would protect us? There had been so much I had wanted to say to her before she left, but then hadn't she always known what was in my heart? Right from the very first day when she had taken a rebellious teen under her protective, guiding wings, she understood me as no one else ever had.

I found myself smiling when a now fully awake Matilda broke into my thoughts. "What happened? Where am I?"

"You're safe and here with us. You were possessed by an entity named Birdie who is the daughter of the Dark Man. She has gone into the Light with her mother and won't be using you again."

"Is that what's been happenin' with me? I thought I were goin' barkin' mad and didn't want anyone to know. Least of all, the Mistress who would have sacked me for sure. I kept havin' these blank spells where I didn't remember squat. Would feel real queer like and then off I went. Sometimes it felt like there were two people inside me... peerin' out my eyes...usin' my hands, but I weren't the one in charge."

"You could have told us," I pointed out. "We would have found a way to help you."

"You were me friends. Treated me like one of you. Would you have done that if you thought I was crazy?"

"I can't even begin to imagine how terrifying that must have been for you, but it's over now, and Birdie's gone. We'll all be off the island soon," I told her then asked Simon who was hunkered down next to a whimpering Bella, "Do you really think the Dark Man will keep his word?"

"He loved Alice in his own way, so I hope he will," he replied then added, "I'm going back inside to check the NVR recorder and the camera feeds before we pack everything up."

A quiet Matilda followed us back to the kitchen where I headed to the bathroom in the scullery. I had just returned when I heard Simon shout, "It's all here...or so I think! Let me fast forward...yeah...right down to where you get snatched then the cameras crap out. Probably battery drain. This footage will blow their narrow, disbelieving minds and....."

He continued to ramble on, but I wasn't looking or listening. I was remembering what that footage had almost cost all of us and then another thought nudged me. Capturing the exodus was an intrusion on something private and beautiful. Something not meant to be held up to scrutiny...poked and prodded like a lab specimen.

"You said you would let me see the finished product and have the final say," I began to tell him.

"Why are you reminding me of that now?"

I sighed. There was no way he would agree to cutting out the grand finale. There was no way I could ask him to do it, so I simply said, "Never mind. Let's just finish packing up all that stuff and get out of here."

***

Matilda found the salt, and we spread it in a circle that overlooked the harbor. Wrapped in our blankets with Bella curled up between us, we all watched the gray light that brushed the horizon grow brighter...listened to the lulling sound of the eternal waves…the cry of the nesting seabirds as they woke to a new day.

"Where are you going from here, Matilda?" I asked her as drowsiness slowly overtook me.

"Got me a cousin in Bristol who I could stay with. Saved up me wages since there were nothing to spend them on. She paid me in cash, which is inside with my bags. There's enough to get me a ticket there and some to live on till I get me feet under me. What about you and Simon?"

"He and I aren't really married. We have separate lives, and I'm headed back home to mine. This ghost releasing thing was something that just sort of happened and won't be happening again."

Simon had listened silently to our exchange. I knew what he was thinking. My plans hadn't included him and then he said, "We have a lot to talk about, Jodie, but not now. I'll keep watch while the two of you get some sleep."

"Wake me when it's my turn," I managed to mumble then fell asleep moments later.

CHAPTER TEN

The rising sun had cast its rosy gold and lavender light over all that surrounded us when Simon pulled a sleeping me into his arms. "We're almost out of here. Need to bring all our bags and equipment out of the house as soon as it gets a bit brighter. I don't think any of us wants to go back in there any time soon."

"You were supposed to wake me for my watch, so you could get some sleep," I reminded him around a yawn.

239

"Didn't want to. You looked adorable, and I didn't have the heart. Matilda is still asleep. This possession thing is exhausting as I know firsthand. She needs time to rest and recover. How are you feeling this morning?"

"Just glad to be getting out of here soon. About that talk you want to have that I don't, I...."

He pressed his fingers against my lips and smiled. "Not now. Stay here while I go down and check out the dock...or what's left of it."

"I'm going with you, and I don't think Matilda should be left on her own. Just give me a moment and some place out of sight while you wake her up."

A short time later, we all took the trail to the dock with Bella well in the lead. Little remained of it, and I wondered how the supply boat would manage, so I voiced my concern.

"Captain Greenley will handle it once I give him a heads up," Simon murmured absently as he stared into the water where Edith's Gift had gone down.

I caught a glimpse of her deck way below the surface and knew how he must feel. Something beautiful...something that had once skimmed the water like a winged angel looked dead...drowned...forever lost except for the memories she had left behind. Slipping my arm around him, I murmured, "Henry understood. There was nothing you could have done to save her."

I had forgotten about Matilda until she added fiercely, "There was something I could have done! I should have fought her harder.

240

Not let her use me to do those horrid things. You could have sailed away and been safe."

"You couldn't have stopped her, Matilda," I told her with my most reassuring smile. "She was a powerful entity who admitted to a dark side she might not have been able to control if you had struggled harder."

"It's over, Matilda. Over and done with, and we have things to do," Simon told her as he swiped at his eyes with his sleeve then headed back up the dock.

I caught up with him and pulled him to a stop. "Matilda can't hear us now, so I'll ask you again. Do you think the Dark Man will keep his promise?"

"I wouldn't count on it...and then there's Geoffrey," he replied. "Right now he's probably sulking somewhere, but that could change. Let's get back up top and bring everything down to that flat spot over there. That way we'll be ready to get out of here as soon as the boat arrives."

So, we headed back up to the house where Simon snapped on Bella's leash and tied it to a dead shrub to keep her out from underfoot during the move. Reaching the kitchen, we all grabbed what we could carry or pull behind us and headed down to the designated spot.

We had returned for a second load when Simon suggested, "It feels so different in here now. Purged and clean. I'm willing to risk a quick trip down to the cave and see if I can't retrieve some of the equipment we left there."

241

"And I'm not even close to *willing*!" I shot back. "Let's just finish up here then wait for the boat."

It was then I noticed Matilda had slipped away, or had someone snatched her?

Panic seized me. "She would never have left on her own, Simon. One of them took her. I know he did!"

"Okay! Okay! Calm down!" he told me. "We'll find her."

"If she can be found!"

"Maybe she left on her own. Forgot something and went to get it."

I shook my head. "She would have told us first."

"Say I'm right. Where would she go?"

"She has lots of hiding places, but why would she do that?" I persisted. "She was safe with us...*sort of.* But if I had to choose, it would be the parlor where we stayed. Let's head there but keep calling her name."

Simon sighed. "You do know that's the surest way to attract the wrong kind of attention...to alert the others she's missing and vulnerable?"

"'Fraid so, but we need to risk it. It may be the only way we'll find her in this maze unless we fetch Bella."

"Matilda's scent will be everywhere. She won't know which trail to follow. She's better off where she is and out of harm's way."

Grabbing flashlights, Simon led the way down the dimly lit main hall, calling her name as we went. I was trying to remember the side route we had previously taken, when he thought he'd found it. The darkness became more intense as we hurried on. We had gone some distance when the floor took a downward slope and our lights swept the structural damage we had seen before. Simon's guess had taken us to the west wing.

"Feel that? The floor is shaking! We need to get out of here fast!" he shouted as he grabbed my hand and spun us around.

We had begun to retrace our steps at a flat out run when the slight tremor we felt increased in intensity...then increased a whole lot more. Creaks and groans reverberated around us as large, gaping cracks fingered their way across the floor then trailed up the walls and ceiling. Chunks of plaster rained down as we sprinted back the way we had come. Not far behind, we heard a horrific roar...a groan...the screech of ancient timbers being twisted and torn. It almost sounded like the death throes of a giant beast. A cloud of dust billowed around us as the house shuddered... then a profound, eerie silence followed.

Coughing...choking...we somehow found our way to the main hall through pure luck or divine guidance. Some minutes later, we reached the kitchen where we found Matilda making sandwiches as though nothing had happened. A well stuffed tapestry bag lay at her feet.

My fear for her safety turned to anger, and I shouted, "Where have you been?"

She dropped the knife she was holding and smiled uncertainly. "I forgot somethin' and went to fetch it. When I got back, you both were gone, so I thought you were down at the dock again. Decided to make us some breakfast while I waited for you to come back up for the rest of your stuff. Sorry if I put a fright in you. Didn't meant to, but it seemed safe enough, and you were busy and all."

It was Simon who told her, "What part of we all stick together didn't you understand? Didn't you hear what just happened? It sounded like the west wing collapsed."

She nodded. "That last storm must have gobbled up a big chunk of the cliff, and it fell right into the sea. Coffee's about ready."

I was feeling very unsettled by her strange calmness then put it down to shock after all she'd been through. She'd been possessed, and I couldn't begin to imagine what toll that must have taken.

We ate quickly then grabbed the remaining gear and hurried down the trail towards the spot where we had left the rest. Pausing for a moment, I looked behind me. From there, the house still looked intact...as though nothing out of the ordinary had happened. A sinister relic of an ancient time no longer inhabited by ghosts...well, almost 'no longer'. Where was Geoffrey, I wondered? Would he try to stop us from leaving? Then there was the Dark Man and his tenuous promise. He had ample time to think about that by now. Would he continue to honor it when he was royally pissed off at Alice, Birdie and the others for leaving him?

Adding what we carried to the stack above the dock, we went back to get Bella then returned to our circle of salt and watched the sun rise higher as seagulls drifted lazily in the clear blue sky above us. Time passed too quickly as we all kept an eye on our surroundings and looked for the boat. The morning was dwindling fast. When it ended, the Dark Man would come for us.

I saw Simon repeatedly checking his watch and knew he was thinking the same thing. "Judging from the sun... which is what he'll be going by, we have 30...maybe 45 minutes left before all hell breaks loose," he whispered to me.

"And no boat in sight," I whispered back.

"Yep. Let's...."

He never finished what he was about to say as an excited Matilda shouted, "I think I see it. Way out there on the left."

She was right. It was a boat and headed our way. We watched it come closer and closer threading its way through the narrow channel into the harbor scattering the gray seals warming themselves on the rocks and the seabirds that rose from their nests in a great cloud of fluttering wings.

We hurried down the trail to greet them. They were within hailing distance when Simon shouted, "Head port side! Our sunken sailboat is on this end, and you might get your props tangled in her lines."

"Obliged for the warnin', Simon!" Captain Greenley shouted back from the wheelhouse as he maneuvered the supply boat to the far side where his crew jumped down on the damaged dock and tied up to the pilings.

A few moments, later, he joined us. "Saw the west wing of that old mansion up there when we were comin' 'round the point. Most of it's fallen into the sea and the rest looks like it'll be joinin' it 'fore too long. Where's Ms. Blackthorne?"

"Didn't make it," Simon told him grimly. "We need to load up and leave...now!"

"I'm taken that to mean she's dead. Where's your gear?"

"Just up top. I'll show you. But first, let's board the women. They've had a rough time of it."

A teenager, who looked enough like the captain to be his grandson, helped us board then left with the rest of the crew to get our stuff...all but the tapestry bag Matilda had carried with her. It took only a short time though it seemed like forever as the minutes ticked past. While we waited, I could hear Captain Greenley questioning Simon about the events that had occurred.

Simon's answer was brief. "Look. The place is haunted. Ms. Blackthorne died, and we need to get out of here. The sooner the better."

The Captain scratched his beard and drew his pipe from his pocket. "Hold your horses, Son. We'll get there. Did the old lady have any kin?"

It was Matilda who stepped forward and supplied the answer. "Not a livin' soul. Told me she was the last of the Blackthornes, which was why she came here to end her days. Her ancestral home she called it. She was walkin' in her sleep and went off the cliff. I tried to save her, I did, but was too late."

"Well then, I'll report what happened and let the authorities sort it out," the Captain told her. "Could be the Coast Guard if they take an interest. This place is in international waters and outside their jurisdiction. Might mention I don't exactly git along with them boys for reasons best not shared."

"There's no time to worry about all that now. We need to get out of here!" I urged as I looked up at the sky. The sun was now almost directly overhead.

Five minutes later, the lines were tossed back on board, and the powerful twin engines roared to life. Slowly, we pulled away from the dock then out across the harbor. The three of us stood at the stern rail watching the island when a solitary figure appeared at the top of the cliff. At that distance, it was impossible to tell whether it was the Dark Man or Geoffrey.

"Whoever is up there can't hurt us now," Simon murmured as he wrapped his arm around my shoulders and drew me close. "I didn't want to worry you, but I was afraid one of them would attach himself to us. Thankfully, I was wrong." He hesitated then continued, "You didn't mention me in your future plans when Matilda asked about them. I want to go with you when this is over. I can work out of your guest room. Complete the documentary there while we share the rest of our lives. I know that didn't exactly work out before, but I think that could change if we both try hard enough. Make a few compromises."

Before I could reply, Matilda smiled slyly then said in a voice I scarcely recognized, "Now isn't that sweet? Making plans for a happy ever after. I have plans of my own that I've decided to share. Everything I've told you about me to date has been a lie. Pathetic little Birdie possessed me, but I was in control much of the time. I was listening when she revealed her so-called sins...the circle of sugar...the damage to your boat. She believed there was a darkness inside her...an evil that she despised. The darkness is within me, and I relish it."

She smiled again then continued, "After we make port, I'm headed to Boston to see Peter Williams, Attorney at Law and Executor of Ms. Blackthorne's very large estate. My last name is Black. The 'thorne' was dropped by my side of the family generations ago. The forgotten side. She hated all those she knew about. Called them money-grubbing parasites and was both happy and proud when she outlived them all. Wearing a bit of theatrical makeup and a wig, I worked at the law firm for a time and found out all I could about her. Knew she must have a large stash of cash and jewels on hand because she didn't trust the banks. Really didn't trust anyone...not even me her not-so-faithful slave. She was far cleverer than I gave her credit for, and it took me quite a while to find it, which is one of the reasons I stayed on so long. That and the fact she interested me in a strange kind of way. I also wanted a witness to her demise, so no blame would be attached to me before I could disappear and reinvent myself."

She paused for a moment then added, "Joe was useless and then she told me she had sent for you. You two made the perfect witnesses to her horrible 'accident'. I quite enjoyed the time spent with you both. So sympathetic. So kind. So totally clueless that you were being played. Now the game is over, and I am headed

248

back to the real world with all my goals almost accomplished. What I have in this bag will tide me over quite nicely till I get the rest. It will all be mine when I prove my identity, which will be simple enough. Now I think I will go down below and rest for a while. It's been a wild ride. I never dreamt when I set foot on that island I'd be inhabited by a ghost named Birdie of all things, but it was rather fun in an eerie kind of way. To be completely honest, I'm not really sure if she killed the old lady, or I finally did. Not that it matters. No one will ever know she was murdered, and you can't prove otherwise, Serilda. Toodles!"

We stared after her as she headed below deck. To say we were both stunned would be a colossal understatement. "She was right! We were completely clueless!" I finally managed to murmur, "And why did she call me Serilda? She couldn't have known Geoffrey called me that."

"I don't know. Maybe she or Birdie overheard it somehow. I really don't want to think Geoffrey has hitched a ride off the island in her."

I shuddered. "Nor do I though, of the two, I think I prefer him."

"Let's just say he was on the cliff back there. That Matilda was just jerking your chain with the Serilda thing and let it go at that."

I hid my abundant doubt as best I could and managed a weak smile. "Deal. I *am* disappointed in Bella. She seemed to like her."

"Yep. I thought dogs were supposed to be good judges of character, but then I thought we were. Might need to work on that before our next adventure."

"Next horrific, beyond crazy, major mistake I will never participate in ever again, is that what you meant?"

He smiled ruefully then yanked the end of my ponytail. "We have some great footage of what happened. The kind that will convince the skeptics that death is far from final."

"Right now, I just want to put this all behind us. Wipe it from my memory and get back to some kind of *normal*, which probably won't include you...at least for a while. You are a very disturbing man in so many ways."

"Mostly the good kind I hope?"

"Let's just look at what happened before I put it away. You kidnap me. Make me come to that island. Make me help you in all the disasters that followed and...."

He kissed me then. It might have been to silence me, but it felt like a whole lot of something else. It was a very long moment before I could think clearly. Damn it! I loved him, and most...though far from all... of the moments I spent with him were some of the happiest I had ever known.

My train of thought was abruptly derailed as he cupped my chin, looked deep into my eyes then asked, "What about Mr. and Mrs. North, Paranormal Investigators on our soon to be business card?"

It was a weak moment, and I had almost said 'yes' when sanity claimed me. "You haven't been listening to anything I said!"

"Nope. I learned everything I needed to know from that kiss. Just say 'yes'. You know you want to," he coaxed.

"What I want to do right now is push you over the rail which will end my dilemma," I told him. "Back on my home turf, I will consider the Mr. and Mrs. part but not the other. Now let's just get through whatever comes between here and then."

His smile was devastating. "I'll settle for that, but does that mean no hanky panky even though we're almost engaged?"

I hid my own smile as I reached down and petted Bella who had fallen asleep in the sun at our feet. "Maybe" had been on my lips, but silence seemed a better answer. It wouldn't hurt to keep him guessing.

***

The island had disappeared in the distance, and it felt like a weight had lifted from my shoulders till I thought of Matilda, and what she had said. It preyed on my mind constantly as we traveled between islands making deliveries. I often saw her chatting up the Captain and wondered to what end.

I soon found out when he pulled us aside just before we reached Banning. "Bin thinkin' on the situation. Radioed the Coast Guard and someone will meet us when we make port. The old lady didn't have any kin, but she might have left her estate to some charity. There needs to be some kind of rulin' she's dead 'fore her Last Will and Testament gets read. Now let me git back to it. Another storm brewin' from the looks of them clouds up there. Be mighty glad to get back to safe harbor."

I watched him head towards the wheelhouse then told Simon, "She wanted to make sure she didn't have to wait too long to inherit what must amount to a fortune. No seven year thing or whatever it is. Looks like we'll be dealing with the Coast Guard when we dock."

Simon pushed his glasses up and frowned thoughtfully. "Best to keep it simple. She didn't *actually* say she killed her and any talk of hauntings, possession and ghosts will make them think we are whack jobs."

"Which may not be too far off the mark all things considered."

"If that's true, our children should prove to be interesting," he replied with a grin.

"Let's just deal with one thing at a time. What do we tell them?"

"Our children?"

I punched him in the shoulder rather hard. "No! Get serious! The Coast Guard."

"That Ms. Blackthorne was walking in her sleep in the middle of a storm and went over the edge."

"And we just let her off the hook...a probable murderess? A ruthless killer?" I asked.

"Ruthless, yes. A 'killer' is something we can't prove based on what we saw."

"But the rest of it...her story?"

Simon shook his head. "She's clever enough to wriggle out of that. There was nothing criminal about what she said no matter how evil."

"Where's justice when you need it?"

"You're not the first person to ask that, and you sure won't be the last."

**

An hour later, we chugged into the harbor at Banning, and I remembered the first time we came there in Edith's Gift. From the somber look on his face, I knew Simon was thinking the same thing. Two officers from the Coast Guard boarded the boat almost as soon as we docked then went down below with the Captain and Matilda. A short time later, we were questioned separately then signed our statements.

"Make sure we have your phone numbers if questions arise at the inquest, but that should do it," we were told by the blonde, boyish looking officer. "It's not officially in our jurisdiction, but we'll send a boat out to investigate. If her body isn't found...if there's no sign of her when we search the island...the case is pretty much open and shut. Your testimony will clinch it. She'll be declared Dead in Abstentia. Not all that uncommon on the water."

A short time after that, Bella led the way down the gangplank to the dock. There was no sign of Matilda as Simon rounded up the help we would need to unload all our cases and bags then bring them up to the town's only hotel. We followed on foot. As we climbed the narrow cobblestone street under the darkening sky, Simon told me, "Old Captain Greenley was right. There's another storm coming. Another bad one from the look of it. We'll spend the night at this Hotel Poseidon then head out in the morning if we can find some form of transportation. Be prepared to smuggle Bella in if they have a no pets policy."

As it turned out, that wasn't necessary. A very large deposit made it happen, and we soon found ourselves in a small room decorated in a nautical theme. A large mural of Poseidon with his trident poised to strike loomed above the bed.

"We could have gotten separate rooms," I pointed out, "Since we aren't in any danger here."

He shook his head. "Nope. We'll share until all this is a long way behind us."

"And if I don't want to?" I had to ask. Simon was far too used to getting his own way.

"You don't mean that."

"Maybe I do," I told him over my shoulder as I headed to the window and looked down at the harbor where boats of all sizes were either headed in or already tying up at the dock. The gray, white-capped water was much rougher now, and sooty black clouds were sweeping in fast.

He joined me there and looked over my shoulder. "You might want to consider that Matilda will be staying here, too. There's no place else. After listening to her story, I think she is more than capable of silencing the 'witnesses' now that they have our statements."

A shiver rippled through me. "If it even *is* Matilda. What if she's possessed again by someone whose name I don't want to mention out loud since it might summon him?"

Simon sighed then smiled wryly. "Has anyone ever told you that you worry too much?"

"Has anyone ever told you that you don't worry enough?"

He sighed again. "Okay. Whatever. Let's take care of Bella then go grab something to eat before the weather gets worse. Everything will be all right."

It was the usual meaningless reassurance most men tended to offer when they didn't have a clue. Simon was particularly good at it, but I wanted more from him than that. Wanted something he couldn't give me. A concrete promise that the nightmare had ended.

We walked Bella and returned her to our room then headed to the cafe where we had eaten when we first arrived in Banning. I hardly tasted what I put in my mouth as I watched the door to see if Matilda would enter. Much to my relief, she didn't, and we made it back to our room without seeing her.

The storm unleashed its fury on the old hotel just after we had climbed under the covers with Bella snuggled in the middle. Shutters banged...the wind shrieked...and I thought I heard the waves slam into the dock though that was probably my overactive imagination since it was some distance away. Suddenly, the lights flickered and went out.

255

"Reminds me of our nights on Blackthorne Island," Simon murmured drowsily. "Go to sleep and forget I just said that."

Like that would happen, I thought, as I plumped up my pillow and leaned back against the headboard. Judging from his breathing and Bella's sporadic 'woof', both of them were asleep just a few minutes later. I was 'alone' in the darkness for all intents and purposes...or was I? Was it my imagination again, or did I hear someone or something scratching on our door? Slipping out of bed, I grabbed a flashlight and padded that way then pressed my ear against it.

All was quiet on the other side...a thick, heavy silence filled with possibilities and then I heard, "I see your light under the door and know it's you, Jodie," Matilda murmured. "If you value Simon's life, meet me in the alcove down at the end of the hall. We have things to talk about."

I was furious she had threatened Simon...furious that she would get away with what amounted to murder...furious that she would taunt me with the Serilda thing, so I stupidly unlocked the door and headed that way.

I found her sprawled across the window seat dressed in a black satin something or other that made her look completely different. My light reflected off her glittering eyes and revealed her smile. It was positively chilling. She was mad as a hatter, and already I was deeply regretting my rashness. Spinning around, I started to retrace my steps, when she rose swiftly and grabbed my arm.

256

"I won't hurt you unless you make me," she whispered hoarsely. "Or maybe I will. I find that I have a taste for it."

I shook free and backed out of her reach. "Get out of here and leave us alone, or I'll tell the Coast Guard the whole truth. Who you really are, and that Ms. Blackthorne's death was probably not an accident."

"*Probably* doesn't mean squat," she scoffed as she circled me slowly. "There's no proof I did anything but care for an old lady until she had a mishap and died. No one knows of our familial connection except you and Simon. You won't tell anyone because I won't let you."

"And how do you plan on accomplishing that?"

She laughed. "I am not alone, you know. Someone is with me who still wants you...though I don't see why. Someone who could quite easily kill Simon in his sleep. Care to guess who?"

An invisible hand brushed my cheek. "I could not let you leave me, Serilda, so I used that one to take me off the island. I heard all she told you. She is both calculating and truly evil. If I kill her for you and spare Simon, will you come with me? Let me have you...love you if only for this night?"

He materialized fully...his glowing figure dressed in a scarlet frock coat with a froth of lace at his chin and wrists. His hand reached out to stroke my hair, and I slapped it away.

"Not going to happen as I mentioned more than once!" I told him emphatically. "Look at her! You have the perfect mate right over there glaring at us. I do think she's jealous or maybe

257

furious...not that it matters. You can change her evil ways...tame her. You'll never tame me. Take her back to the island. When she dies, you can haunt it together."

"Don't listen to her!" she cut in sharply. "Do what you came here to do! Rid me of them both now that they've served their purpose. That's what you promised when I let you enter me."

"You are a witless little thing, aren't you? What will they think when one of your witnesses is missing and the other found dead?" Geoffrey murmured. "You clearly haven't thought it through. As to my promise, I have been known to tell a woman whatever suits me without being over bothered by scruples. In your case, I had no scruples whatsoever."

"I am going to live the life I was meant to have...the one I deserve...and nobody is going to stop me!" she told us fiercely as her eyes darted back and forth between us. "I won't go back there to starve...to die. It would be hell on earth!"

From somewhere, I dredged up a smile. "Maybe there's justice in that. Something you thought you had escaped."

"May I remind you both that I do have a say in this," Geoffrey broke in. "You fascinate and torment me, Serilda. Stir my passion and perhaps the other thing already mentioned."

"You mean love?"

"There is that possibility though I am unsure if that is what I feel."

"*Love* would mean putting my welfare above your own wants and needs. Can you do that?"

He frowned thoughtfully. "I don't know. I have never been forced to do so before."

I sighed then told him, "I can't return your feelings, but I will always remember your sacrifice if you take her and go back to the island."

It was his turn to sigh. "Will you remember my kiss?"

"Always."

He smiled wickedly. "I remember as well and find my lust is stronger than what passes for my love."

"Have you forgotten those who came to our rescue a short time ago? I can summon them again, and it will get messy. Take her and have a happy ever after...like that's even possible with the likes of her."

"You are the most obstinate woman I have ever met," he muttered as he made a grab for Matilda who had tried to slip away. "Perhaps another time. I have seen what this age has to offer. The strange metal contraptions on four wheels that speed about without horses...the people who mingle together without a sense of the proprieties...their garb that is scandalous in its brevity...the music that is nothing more than noise...an atrocity that offends the ears...."

"See, you won't fit in at all," I interjected before he could finish what might have been a very long list. "Quite the contrary. You would be considered a freak."

His second sigh was long and deep. "I greatly fear you may be right though 'freak' is a bit extreme. Freedom is not all I thought it would be unless the rest of the world is better?"

259

I shook my head. "Fraid not...it only gets worse. Take her and go."

"I won't! You can't!" Matilda spluttered as she struggled to break free from his grasp.

He sighed a third time then pulled her up against him and clapped his hand over her mouth. "I rather enjoyed my past flirtation with her though I could not consummate it when she was inhabited by the other. Even my island has its appeal in a bleak kind of way...the house comfortable in its familiarity. How do I get back?"

"It seems in your state you can travel from point to point at will. You saw Alice and those who came for me, but I'm not sure how you'll manage to take her with you."

To my surprise, he laughed. "I have another trick up my sleeve that might work now that we have solved the other issue. Tis a reverse possession sort of thing I have tried but once before. The outcome was far from pleasant, but I believe my second attempt will fare better."

A struggling Matilda somehow managed to push free then shouted, "That won't happen! I am not going anywhere with you!"

Geoffrey smiled seductively. "Come," he told her as he moved closer. "Come with me. I might enjoy you after all in lieu of Serilda who thinks she has seen the last of me."

"Don't you dare touch me!" she screamed as her eyes searched frantically for a way to get past him.

"She protests at the moment, but methinks she will soon change her screams of fear to those of passion," he murmured to me then told her, "We will need to change your name. Matilda no longer suits you."

She made a run for it but was easily caught. He shape shifted to a white mist that slowly engulfed her. Her screams became muffled then were silent as they vanished into the darkness.

All along the hall, I heard doors opening and then Simon's shout, "What's going on, Jodie? Where are you? Are you all right?"

Bella reached me first with Simon right on her heels. Pulling me into his arms, his voice was hoarse with emotion when he told me, "I woke up, and you were gone then someone screamed, and I thought it was you and.... You little idiot! You scared the crap outta me! What are you doing out here all by yourself?"

I don't know why I didn't tell him what had happened. Maybe I just didn't want to relive it all again, so I said, "Everything's fine. I couldn't sleep, so I broke the rules and went for a walk. Let's all get back to bed. Tomorrow is going to be a very busy day."

"But if it wasn't you screaming like an angry banshee, who was it?"

"No doubt some poor soul having a nightmare. It happens."

Those who had come out to investigate the disturbance returned to their rooms, and we did the same. I slept what was left of the night cradled in his arms. If he wondered why, he didn't ask, and I didn't tell him. Didn't want him to know that Geoffrey had discovered how easily it was to come and go at will...that he could decide to

261

return at any time. It was a deeply unsettling thought until it occurred to me that his passion could have been pure reflex. After all, it had been a long time since there'd been an available *living* woman on the island. He couldn't have Matilda, so that left me. Maybe I had nothing to worry about. There was hope in that thought, and I clung to it. Briefly, I wondered what would happen when they discovered Matilda was missing and hoped we'd be long gone by then. I was still mulling that over when sleep claimed me.

***

Thankfully, that sleep had been dreamless, or...if not...I didn't remember it when I woke up the next morning. After we walked and fed Bella, we grabbed breakfast at the cafe where we found a notice pinned to a bulletin board by the front door. It was a For Sale by Owner ad that read: *Used VW van for sale. Got a lot of miles and years on her, but runs good.* The price was cheap, and Simon called the number posted. Thankfully, the address was in walking distance. An hour later, we drove back to the hotel to collect all our cases, bags, and Bella.

"We don't have a plate on this thing, which means we might get pulled over a few times on the way back," Simon told me with a smile as he slammed the side doors shut and patted them affectionately. "Used to have one of these in my college days. Named her Sally."

"Why Sally?" I had to ask.

"She just seemed like a Sally. Let's go."

262

Bella slept most of the way on the trip that followed. Beyond half listening to Simon and absently answering his questions, I was silent...lost in my thoughts. He had offered to relocate, but 'we' hadn't even survived his short-term stay. There would be compromises to make...lots of them. We were such different people, would love be enough? Would that love survive in his world? A world that filled me with dread and horror despite the glorious moments when the spirits of the dead were reconnected to their own lost loves? I had told him I would never go with him again, but how could I watch him head off to some haunting knowing all too well he may never return? I couldn't ask him to choose between his passion and me. I loved him too much for that.

As the miles sped past, Simon grew quiet, too. When the turn off to Melbrooke came up, he pulled off the road and parked. It was a long moment before he said, "You can grab a plane there and head back to your loft alone, or we'll drive there together. I know what you said earlier...about your idea of 'normal' not including me for a while, so there's no pressure. This has to be what you truly want. No kidnapping this time. Your choice."

I was torn...really needed that pressure, or I was very much afraid of my answer and then out it popped. "I think maybe we need some time to think about all that happened and about us. I know this sounds very familiar. That we've been down this road before, but I think it would be best if you focus on your documentary without me there. I had had some reservations, but that's changed. Make your point. Show the world of disbelievers what happens after we die. That's important work, and you don't need me to distract you. I......"

My voice trailed off, and he sighed. "I get it. Like you said, we've been down this road before which ends nowhere. Okay, if that's what you want, that's what you'll get. Let's find that airport. The sooner the better."

After he dropped me off and sped away, I don't remember much of my trip home. Most of the way, I felt like I was operating on autopilot. I wondered if that was the last I would ever see of him. He had loved me since Greystone, and I had loved him. It had taken a long time for me to admit it because it made me vulnerable again in the worst kind of way. Vulnerable to a devastating hurt. People changed as life pulled at them. They grew apart. Wanted different things which was already a problem for us. Would our love survive that? My churning tangle of thoughts had brought me back to square one.

EPILOGUE

Simon's documentary rocked the world of paranormal research. Many disbelievers tried to disprove it. None of them could. Someone had once said that true love would never have a happy ending. That with the death of their loved one, the other would be left behind to experience an aching loneliness that went soul deep. Simon and I had come to learn otherwise. That love was eternal, and his film proved it beyond doubt.

He had sent me a formal invitation to the premiere with no personal note attached, but I hadn't attended. When I checked the Internet afterwards, I saw photos of him with Wendy the beautiful Eurasian woman who had been his team member until the nightmarish events at Greystone. Had she become more than that since I had gone my own way to sort things out? If he truly wanted me there, he would have called me...sent that personal note. He was still pissed at me. Nothing had changed except that I really, really missed him and now it all could well be a moot point if what I had seen meant what I feared.

The aloneness I had once enjoyed became...well, lonely, so I threw myself into my work. I was helping others, and it felt right...good...but empty. Simon wasn't there to listen when I was bursting with news...soothe me when I was upset...or hold me when my body ached with need. Simon was gone.

In the back of my mind, something else worried me and persisted despite my best efforts to shake it off. What if someone...some *innocent someone* out sailing one day found their way to Blackthorne Island? There had been no mention of the name or location in Simon's documentary, but that didn't mean others couldn't find it merely by chance unaware of what was waiting for them there. The tiny twinge of guilt I felt about my part in Matilda's fate came and went. She had been more than willing to see Simon dead and me sharing the life she was now leading. She would seize any chance she had to escape and then there were the others I didn't want to think about, so I tried not to without much success.

A month passed then two then three. It was a rainy Saturday, and I was busy pouring over a proposal for a bakery Judy Adams had sent me when there was a knock on the door. Hating to be disturbed at that moment, I headed there fully prepared to brush off whoever it was. A thoroughly drenched Simon and Bella were standing in the hall.

Completely stunned, I stood there for all of a moment then grabbed his hand and yanked him inside where I flung myself into his arms knocking us both to the floor. His glasses went flying one way. The rose he'd been carrying another as an excited, tail wagging Bella shook herself dry over both of us.

Leaning over him as tears ran down my face, I cried, "What's with you and Wendy... who's gorgeous and exotic... and why did you let me go when all you had to do is this...and this...and this?" Each 'and this' was a kiss until he rolled me over...smiled down at me...then kissed me long and passionately firing up all those bits of me that had ached for his touch a very long time.

"And here I thought you wouldn't want to see me," he murmured as he added a kiss to the tip of my nose. "Wendy was in town and wanted to come and, yes, she is all you said plus married and pregnant, and you are...."

"Sometimes a mess and a klutz?" I cut in before he could finish.

"And what part of that doesn't spell adorable in my book as I may have told you a zillion times? You know I love you just as you are from the top of your red head to your crooked left pinky toe."

266

"It's not crooked!" I protested reflexively. "It's a rebel toe that leans a bit."

"Well, we both know where it gets that from."

"Which means what exactly?"

He grinned and murmured, "My black will always be your white."

"Not always. Sometimes I can settle for gray."

"I've let you go your own way to sort things out when I wanted to be here with you every single day. What's it going to be?"

"It won't be easy. It may be impossible or worse than impossible. I've been thinking."

"Oh, oh! Here we go again."

"This has been worrying me for some time."

"More than the Wendy thing?" he teased.

I sighed. "This is serious, Simon. What if someone finds the island...someone innocent...even looters. They will be waiting for them and...."

He pressed his fingertips against my lips and smiled. "They'll be waiting a long time. I sent Captain Greenley some of the footage we shot there, so he wouldn't be tempted to loot the place, which I wouldn't put past him, then paid him a very large sum to blow up the harbor entrance."

"How do you know he didn't pocket the money and do nothing?"

"He sent me proof. If you care to see the photos, they're on my phone."

I shivered. "No thanks. What about future ships and boats wrecked on those rocks? No one can rescue them if the harbor entrance is gone."

"Thought of that, too. Talked to a few guys I know with deep pockets who were concerned about the same thing though it took awhile to convince them. They paid the enormous cost of setting up high visibility marine navigation buoys around the entire island that should warn off all boats. Anything else on your mind?"

"Nope. That should do it for now."

He laughed then kissed me again. I wasn't at all sure where any of it was headed, but at the moment...and perhaps forever...I just didn't give a damn. Simon and I were meant to be together and somehow we would make it work, or so I hoped with all my heart. Thankfully, as I had already told him, the word 'obey' had been removed from the marriage vows years ago since that would never happen if we ever decided to take the plunge.

--The End--

This book is dedicated to my Captain Jim who is my best friend and love of my life.

Printed in Great Britain
by Amazon

19000146R00153